LAUREL'S BRIGHT IDEA

BILLIONAIRE BABY CLUB

NEW YORK TIMES AND *USA TODAY* BESTSELLING AUTHOR

JASINDA WILDER

LAUREL'S BRIGHT IDEA

BILLIONAIRE BABY CLUB

.

CHAPTER ONE

I STOOD IN FRONT OF THE MIRROR IN THE POWDER ROOM OF Seven and Autumn's house, fidgeting with my dress. I couldn't get the cups to stay in place, and my boobs kept trying to escape, a condition I called wandering nipple.

Or, peek-a-boob.

Either way, not a good look for a backyard wedding for one of my best friends.

I mean, the dress was killer. Givenchy, custom tailored for me. Off-the-shoulder, cut to emphasize my hourglass figure, which, of late, was becoming more focused on the lower portion than I'd like. By which I mean, my ass was taking over. I wasn't, like, pear-shaped quite yet, but I used to have a true hourglass figure, with proportions Marilyn Monroe would've been jealous of.

No matter—I could just emphasize my cleavage with some nice supportive bras and no one would be the wiser, until they saw me naked.

Which, lately, has been a sadly lacking part of my life.

I'd never admit to it, even to my best friends, but I was…gasp…in a dry spell.

The worst part was, I wasn't even *trying*.

Since I discovered boys at thirteen, I only had to give a male a look and they were mine for as long as I wanted to toy with them.

It was no different now. If anything, I had the look down to an art form. Pickup lines were for amateurs—I could pick up some fun for the night with a single *look*.

Of them, at me. If I gave them The Look, they'd be under my spell by the time we got to my Aston Martin DB6.

Yes, I drove a vintage sports car.

It's very hot of me.

But lately, I just hadn't been interested in the same-old-same-old cast of loser wannabes and vapid playboys.

I wanted a *man*.

I knew the girls had posted an ad, and I'd gotten a few bites, but simple cursory sleuthing had precluded me from going out with any of them. Maybe I wasn't giving them a fair shake, but shit, none of them interested me.

I was lonely.

I was sad.

I was bitter.

But I had a reputation as an icy sex goddess to

maintain, and I couldn't let my friends down, so I put on The Face, the bright smile and the glittery look to my eyes, which were a pale blue that was nearly white.

My hair was perfect, coiled into tendrils of naturally platinum ringlets around my face, the top tied back, the rest loose.

The dress hugged my curves, supported my boobs—when they weren't wandering out—and made my hips look like straight-up man-killers.

Which, TBH, they were.

See, the thing about this dry spell was, my heart and mind weren't playing along with my body—which was every bit as borderline nymphomaniacal as ever.

It was my soul that was on a dry spell. My body wasn't with that plan, and was doing everything it could to remind me that I hadn't had sex in months.

And even my vibrators had been off duty for a couple weeks.

It was getting positively dusty down in my nether regions.

But, time to suck it up. Be a good girl for Autumn's wedding.

Her wedding to the man I'd jilled off to every night and every morning for the past several years.

Not that that was connected in any way to my dry spell. No, no…

Not at all.

Unrelated.

Totally unrelated.

Finally, with one last tug to make sure my boobs were firmly seated in the cups, I headed out.

And I saw God.

Or, a god, at least. Little "G."

But if he didn't deserve the capital "G," I don't know who would.

Tall, dark, and handsome, just the way I liked them. Only, this one took the cliche to sinful, devilish new heights. Six-six, if he was an inch, with naturally dark, swarthy, caramel skin tanned darker yet by the California sun. Long black hair in tight spirals hanging down loose around his back and shoulders. A short, neat beard framed a hard, rugged jawline. A silver hoop adorned the center of his lower lip. More earrings on his ears than I had, all of them heavy silver. Tattoos all over, colorful, masterful, of birds and tigers and guns and knives and angels and pinup girls and hands of cards and guitars and amps and I didn't know what all.

He wore a leather vest, open, over a bare torso.

And *fuck me*, I'd never seen any man in real life as shredded as he was.

Eight razor-sharp abs, a V-cut peeking up out of his faded, ripped black jeans. Long lean hard arms with rippling cords of muscle—guitarist forearms, fingers glinting with rings.

Heavy black boots, shitkickers.

A rock star.

THE rock star.

Titus Bright.

The baddest bad boy in music. Front man for a long-lived hard rock band notorious for taking the rock star lifestyle to its wildest extremes. And then, when that band broke up following the sudden overdose death of the drummer, he'd done an about-face and started a new project, Bright Star, which did ballads and touching acoustic pieces with delicate melodies and haunting lyrics. Bright Star could rock out, but they were not a metal band of the same vein Titus's previous band had been. Bright Star defied genre. They'd featured rappers, flamenco guitarists, cellists, accordionists, opera singers, gospel choirs, banjos…anything and everything, and every single song was a platinum hit.

Titus Bright was the mastermind behind it all, the musical genius who also happened to be the single hottest and most eligible bachelor on the planet, now that Seven St. John was marrying my best friend, Autumn Scott.

And he was *here*, in Seven's backyard, setting up a rack of guitars.

He saw me floating, stunned and hypnotized, across the yard, and he paused. Froze, really. Slowly set the guitar down into the rack without looking away from me.

I'd *never* been looked at like that in my entire life.

Like *prey*.

Like something to eat, a helpless little bunny caught out alone in a field.

He was the wolf, prowling along the tree line.

His eyes were a tan so pale they were almost yellow, lupine.

He shoved his hands in his back pockets and met me in the middle of the yard, eyes narrowed, jaw flexing.

"God*damn*." His voice was hoarse, raspy, guttural. "You're even more fuckin' stunning than I'd imagined you would be, Laurel McGillis."

I blinked, swallowed, tried to breathe. "You…you know who I am?"

He shuffled closer. Towered over me, his presence imposing, powerful, primal. "Yeah, I do. I know you. Not as well as I'm going to, though."

"I see," I said, trying for the icy demeanor that had never yet failed me. Until now. "You're sure of that, are you?"

He reached up with one hand, twisted a ringlet of my hair around his finger, brought it to his nose and inhaled. "Yes," he murmured. "I am."

"Awful confident of you, Mr. Bright."

His eyes ravaged me. "You're mine, Laurel. You may not know it yet, but you will, soon enough."

I gulped, an audible gulp. "You can't say that to me," I whispered.

"But I just did." He smirked. "What are you gonna do about it?"

I had not a single clue.

For the first time in my life, I felt as if I was at the mercy of a man, rather than the other way around.

This would either be the most fun I'd ever have, or…

It would utterly change me. Forever.

I turned on my heel and click-clacked across the lawn, away from Titus Bright. I ducked into the first doorway I came to—the laundry room.

"Laur?" Kat's voice.

I peeked out, saw my friend. Reached out, snagged her arm and tugged her to me. She squealed in surprise.

"Laurel? What are you doing in the laundry room?"

"This is bad, Kat," I whispered under my breath. "Really, really bad."

She laughed, and wasn't even quiet about it. "Why are you whispering? We are literally the only ones in the house."

"Titus Bright is out there."

"So?"

"So…he knew my *name*. He *said things* to me."

"Again, so what?"

"It's *Titus Bright,* dammit. You don't understand."

Kat pulled me out of the laundry room and toward the staircase to the spare bedroom where Autumn was getting ready. She glanced over at me as we paused outside the closed door of the bedroom. "You met Titus Bright. He's hot. He knows your name. So the hell what? He probably saw The Ad. He wants you. Great." An eye roll; she pulled her phone out of her clutch, tapped and scrolled a moment, and then showed me her phone.

On it? The Ad. A photo of me—a selfie, as a matter of fact. In my bathroom, at home.

God, this photo? Really? I'd just gotten back from vacation in the Caribbean, where I'd spent a lot of time tanning on the beach, and the photo in question was a private one, meant to show off to my girlfriends how tan I was. I was naked, in the selfie. My body was twisted to the side from the waist down, showing my thigh and buttock in profile, thereby blocking any view of my hoo-ha, but it was clear I was naked as a jaybird. My arm was barred across my tits, left hand clutching my right boob, forearm over my right, upper torso twisted around to face three-quarters to front. Long platinum blond hair loose, curly and kinky from having been in a braid all day. No makeup. Granted, it was a damn good shot of me, showed off my bangin' ass and thighs, my toned waist, and my boobage was spilling over my wrist and hands to rather dramatic effect. Under the photo was the now-standard caption, which had now adorned The Ad beneath photos of both Lizzy and then Autumn before me: *Beautiful, successful single woman in search of a wealthy, handsome man to help her get pregnant the old-fashioned way. Financial validation a must. Serious inquiries only. DM for more info.*

"It's Titus Bright," I repeated.

"You're overthinking it, babe," Kat said. "I've heard

stories about that man that'll make your toes curl. I'm
sure you have too. I mean, shit, there's a whole sub-Reddit
about Titus Bright urban legends and sex stories. You
wanna get on that cock for a quickie after the wedding,
I'm sure no one will be surprised. If you don't, we'd
be a little surprised, but you do you. You've been kinda
weird lately, so not taking advantage of the attention
of a sinfully sexy rock star worth, last I checked, five
hundred million, who also happens to have looked at
you, in your own words, like something to eat…well,
that would be weird."

"I don't care how much he's worth. Honestly, I tend
to avoid rich guys. This whole billionaire thing is you
guys. I've been there, done that." I sniffed. "Rich guys
are lazy. They think because their bank account has a few
extra zeroes that I'm gonna suddenly just start spontaneously orgasming and they aren't gonna have to put in
the work to get me there."

Kat laughed. "Honey, I have a hard time believing it's
difficult to give you an O. A stiff breeze will get you off."

I snorted. "And what gives you that impression,
Katja? When was the last time you were in the room
while I had an orgasm?"

"Ew. I was teasing, Laur, you don't have to be gross
about it."

"So now my orgasms are gross to you?"

Kat frowned at me. "You're picking a fight, and I'm
not here for it. My point is, have sex with him, don't have

sex with him, it's your call. But don't make it into this whole big thing."

"You're the one who mere moments ago was all like *ohh, he's so rich, he's so famous, there's a whole swath of the internet dedicated to his sexual prowess.*"

"All of which can be considered reasons both for and against you having anything further to do with him. And you're the one who just said wealth isn't interesting to you."

"Kat, Laurel, are you going to stand out there arguing all morning, or are you going to get your asses in here and help me with my hair?" Autumn called, from the other side of the door. "It's not going to braid itself, you know."

We exchanged looks and went in. Zoe was doing Autumn's makeup, and Teddy was steaming her dress. Autumn sat in a tall chair, wearing a strapless white bra that was more sheer lace than anything else and provided rather little by way of support, and a thong that was similarly sheer and white. She looked stunning, sensual, and I was seeing more of her than I maybe needed to. Not that I was prudish about it—we were all comfortable with each other's nudity, especially Lizzy, Kat, and me, having been friends since college and having shared rooms with each other on numerous occasions.

"You look sexy AF, Autumn," I said. "That lingerie does amazing things for you."

She smiled at me. "Thanks, Laur. Seven picked it out."

I arched an eyebrow. "He did, huh? And has he seen it on you?"

She smirked, rolled a shoulder. "I mean, he was in the changing room with me, so yes. But not yet today."

Zoe had the tip of her tongue sticking out as she ran lip liner over her older sister's lips. "I guess it's one of their things, lingerie shopping together."

"He likes picking out my underwear," Autumn said. "And it's fun. He picks stuff I'd *never* pick for myself, but I figure that's the point of fancy panties, right? It's not for me, it's for him."

I flicked a finger at her. "Clearly. That bra looks great, but it's not really doing much by way of support."

Zoe sat back, twirling the lip liner pencil between her fingers, and then tapped at the underside of her sister's boob. "She doesn't need much support with these cute lil mosquito bites."

Autumn stuck her tongue out at Zoe. "Hello, Pot? This is Kettle, come in Pot, over." She pointed at Zoe. "You're not rocking anything more than I am, princess. Less, if anything."

"Maybe. But mine are *perkier*." A flouncing shrug. "Because I'm *younger*."

Autumn faked a glare. "You're age- *and* boob-shaming me, your beloved elder sister, your only family, on my *wedding* day?"

Zoe burst into laughter, and fell against her sister, hugging her. "You know I'm teasing, Autumn. I'm just jealous because I'd never have the courage to wear lingerie like that. I'm too much of a scaredy-cat."

Autumn pushed her away, patting her cheek. "Someday, you'll grow up and find a man of your own, and you'll understand."

Zoe snorted, setting aside the lip liner and reaching for a contouring pad. "One can only hope. I'm beginning to think otherwise, though."

"Your date with the hot mechanic didn't go well?" Autumn asked.

I moved behind Autumn and began dragging a brush through her long copper locks. "Do tell, Zoe. Did he replace your spark plugs?"

"Or did he fix your carburetor?" Kat said, snickering.

"Maybe he changed your oil," Teddy suggested.

Zoe snorted, focusing on her sister as she answered. "He was awful. I was *so* bored. I barely made it to dessert, honestly. All he wanted to talk about was *cars*. Like, listen, I like a sexy car as much as the next gal, but buddy, in no way, shape, or form do I give one single shit about the sixty-eight Chevelle you're restoring. He talked for literally an *hour* straight about how he bored out the cylinders to get all this extra horsepower. I legit told him I wasn't all that interested and could we talk about something else, and he was like, yeah, sure, and started in on—I shit you not—the *upholstery* he was planning on using."

"Ohmygod," Teddy said, putting the steam wand away and leaning against the wall near Autumn. "I had a date a lot like that a few weeks ago. This guy I met on Tinder. Yes, I'm still using Tinder. He was hot, I swiped, we DM'd, he made good conversation, had a good pickup line, so we met. In person, he was nowhere near as hot as his bio made him seem, and he literally only wanted to talk about airplanes. He's a pilot, I guess, which is great. But *god*—airplanes. For two hours."

Autumn wanted her hair done in braids that wrapped around her head, and Kat and I were by far the best braiders of the group, so we'd been tapped to do her hair. Of course, Autumn could have paid for a glam squad herself, and you know Seven offered, but Autumn insisted it was us. And, I had to admit, this was more fun. There was champagne, for one thing.

The worst date stories continued as Kat and I worked on the braids.

"Your turn, Laurel," Lizzy said; Lizzy's job was to help Autumn into her dress once hair and makeup were done. She'd been sitting off to one side, out of the way of the hair and makeup, sipping champagne. "Worst date. Go."

I sighed. She knew this story already, but the other girls didn't. "My first year working with Lizzy, it was just her and me, as Kat hadn't hired on yet. We would trade which of us got the good listings, right, so we both had a chance at the bigger commissions. It was my turn for the good listing, and when it came in, it was this plum of a place in Laguna Beach. Top floor condo, two units that had been combined. The biggest listing we'd had, and I was freaking out. I was there every day, fiddling with the staging, updating the photos, just obsessing. I discovered there was a drip leak under one sink, and I just freaked the fuck out. Called every plumber I knew, but they were all weeks out, and I had a showing that day. I mean, the first showing I'd scheduled on this massive listing, and I had a leak. No one could come look at it. So I was sitting in my car in the parking lot, yanking my hair out trying to figure out what the hell I was going to do. And I saw this guy carrying a toolbox to a truck. He was big, he was sexy, and he had tools. Problem solved, right? I had a feeling it was just a loose fitting or something, but what the hell do I know? So I do my best flounce over to him where he was messing with the tools in the back of his truck."

Lizzy started snorting.

"Shush, you." I tied the braid off and started on another. "I asked him if he could fix something for me. 'I have a plumbing problem I was hoping you could help me with,' is verbatim what I said. I hadn't meant it as a come-on, but hell, he was cute, maybe I could get the leak fixed *and* have him check my plumbing, right?" I sighed. Continued. "He fixed the leak in about ten seconds, and said, 'now, about the plumbing issue.' It's on like Donkey Kong, right? Oh, it was on. I had an hour still before the showing, so I got him to do me up against the wall in the bathroom. Plumbing issue fixed. He laid some serious pipe, you might say. Good, right? He asks me out afterward."

"*After* he screwed you?" Kat asked.

"Yep. He was still tucking himself back into his pants, which, let's just say took a while. There was a *lot* to tuck." I sighed wistfully, remembering. "God, he was hung. Anyway, I agreed, because I was still in that post-orgasmic la-la-land, and I wasn't thinking. So he says, 'I'll pick you up tomorrow night at eight.' Great. I'm ready by seven fifty-five. Because maybe we could get a quickie in before dinner *and* get it on after the date."

Lizzy was trying hard to not laugh, now.

"Money doesn't impress me. Show up in the sexiest car on the planet, I'll be like, great. Nice car. Now let's see your package."

Kat snorted. "You have a one-track mind."

"Yes, yes I do." I waved at her. "Now shush. We're getting to the good part. He showed up ten minutes late, in his work van. Not his personal truck, oh no. That was a nice truck. Newer, kind of plain but nice. I'm fine with that. I'm not gonna judge you based on what you drive. I judge you based on how good the dick is."

"Ohmy*god*, Laurel," Teddy cackled. "You're horrible!"

"How is that horrible? I'm not making any excuses. I let them know ahead of time that it's not going to be a situation where we walk off into the sunset together. We're going to have a little date for the sake of appearances, we're going back to his place, and we're going to fuck. And if the dick is good, I'll give you one more ride on the pony. If not, bye-bye. And listen, I'm not picky. I don't care what you drive, how much you make, whether you're built like The Rock or Seth Rogen. My criteria is, do you interest me *at all*? If you're funny, great. If you're built like a superhero, great. You just need one thing to catch my attention, and I'll give you a shot."

"What you're saying is, you have no standards whatsoever," Kat said, eyeing me sideways, "and that you'll fuck anything with a dick and a pulse."

"A dick, a pulse, and something interesting."

"And the plumber in this endless story of yours," Autumn said. "What did he have?"

"Well, to be honest, he was picked for his looks. I *am* most easily swayed by looks. And he had the looks." I waved. "Anyway. All that to say, I'm really, really not judgmental about what I'm picked up in. I've gone out with guys who picked me up in their grandmother's ninety-six Buick LeSabre. I'm okay with that. But the work van? The plumber's van? Red flag. But he had a good excuse—a last-minute call to some sort of exploded pipe." I sighed, remembering. "I tried. I really did. I got in, climbed over the mountain of McDonald's bags and liters of Mountain. Dew. Red flag number two, because ew. But then as we were driving, I kept smelling something. And it was *not* a good smell."

"Oh no," Zoe said, laughing, covering her mouth. "That's not good when he's a plumber who just had an emergency."

"Turns out, the emergency had been a burst sewage pipe." I closed my eyes, because the smell was something you don't forget. "He'd gotten pretty messy, and he'd put the soiled coveralls or whatever in a plastic bag in the back of his van. But that bag was *not* equal to the task of containing the stench. And, even worse, *he* himself still stank. Like raw sewage, to be exact."

"Why didn't he call or text and say he needed a few extra minutes to shower and change?" Teddy asked. "Like, did that not cross his mind?"

"I guess not," I asked. "I asked him exactly that question, and his response was, well, 'I was already in the area. I figured we'd go back to my place and I'd shower and change.'"

Zoe snorted. "Ooh, sexy. Didn't you *want* to take a shower with a man who smelled like raw sewage?"

"Right?" I asked, cackling. "Isn't that every girl's fantasy?"

"And I'm guessing Mr. Plumber didn't get a second ride on the penny pony," Kat asked.

I shook my head. "He did not. I got out at a red light and walked home."

"You got out a stop light and walked home?" Teddy asked. "That seems kinda harsh, even considering."

I stared her down. "You weren't in that van with that smell. You ever smell something that stinks so bad you can taste it? Like, in the back of your throat? It was like that. Literally nauseating."

Teddy made a face. "Wow. I guess it's more understandable. Did he not notice the smell?"

I shrugged. "I dunno. I guess not. I mean, maybe he was used to it? I really don't know. But that's my worst date ever story."

"That's pretty bad," Autumn said. "But I have a better topic of discussion, seeing as I'm about to get married. *Best* dates."

"Well if that's what we're talking about," Zoe said, "then you and Lizzy are excluded, because the rest of us will just get jealous."

Lizzy snorted. "How is that our fault? You guys are the ones who keep putting up The Ad."

Kat eyed me, because she and I both knew Titus's interest was almost assuredly due to The Ad. But the unspoken rule surrounding this whole weird game we were playing was that we never openly discussed it as a group.

"I'm not saying anything is your fault," Zoe said. "I'm just saying for those of us who *haven't* been swept off our feet by Prince Charming, hearing about your ooey-gooey rich and chewy dates of ultimate romanticism is just torture. Especially since I in particular seem to attract the douchiest of douches." A sigh. "Such as hella sexy mechanics with arms the size of my head, a chest you could break rocks on, and an ass like two cannonballs in a denim sack. And the IQ of a potato. Which is not a dig against mechanics, just that one in particular."

"Being unable to talk about anything except cars doesn't make him a douche," Teddy said, ever the one to try to find the good side of someone. "It just makes him…of narrow-minded interests."

"How about I share my best date?" Kat said. "There isn't one. The end."

Teddy gently backhanded Kat's arm. "Ohh stop. You have to have had at least one date in your life that was good."

Kat laughed. "Yeah, yeah. Fine. There *was* the one time I went out with this high-powered attorney type. His name was Damien, and he was one of those bizarrely intelligent types, like he graduated high school at sixteen, and had passed the bar by twenty-two. Like, as weird as it sounds, he was just one of those people who's just literally on this earth for one specific thing, and for him it was law. He was…" A sigh, almost wistful. "You can't make fun of me, okay? But he was *dreamy*. Just over six feet, with nice broad shoulders. He wore the *hell* out of an Armani suit, I'm telling you. Blond hair that was just perfectly not quite dirty blond, not platinum. Blue eyes, like almost Elijah Wood level blue. For our date, he had stubble. We went out on Saturday, so he hadn't shaved since Friday morning, and it was just…fucking yummy, you know?"

Teddy sighed. "Two-day stubble is the best. I love how scratchy it is on my thighs." A surprised blink. "I mean, face."

Kat snorted. "You meant what you said, girl, don't take that back. You have the innocent act down to an art, but we all know it's an act."

"Didn't you tell us as much yourself, once? That day at Kat's friend's bar, for my birthday, wasn't it?" Lizzy asked. "You were like, I like sex as much as anyone else. Something like that."

Teddy bit her lip, laughing. "Fine! Whatever. I never claimed to be *innocent*. I'm just not a dirty slut like the rest of you."

"I'm a proper married woman, thank you very much," Lizzy said.

"And I'm about to be a proper married woman," Autumn added.

"Hey, I'm clean," I said, laughing, "There's nothing dirty about me. I take plenty of showers."

Zoe and Kat exchanged looks. "I guess that makes us the dirty sluts, huh?" Kat said.

"You, maybe," Zoe said, faking an arch tone. "I'm neither dirty nor a slut."

Kat and I had Autumn's many braids now wrapped in a complicated crown around her head, bobby-pinned to within an inch of its life. We finally both sat down with fresh glasses of champagne while Autumn stood up and examined her reflection in the mirror.

"So, Kat," Autumn said, tilting and turning her head this way and that. "What happened with Mister Lawyer Man?"

Kat shrugged. "Oh, it was just a great date. He took me to a rooftop restaurant in San Diego, and we went for this long walk on the beach, and drank wine on his penthouse suite balcony."

Zoe frowned at Kat. "Sounds magical. Then what?"

"Then we screwed, and that was also magical, so I panicked and took an Uber home."

"From San Diego?" Teddy asked. "That's like, two and a half hours."

"Well, I *said* I panicked. He was too nice. He was smooth, charming, considerate. He had his own money, a really nice condo, a really nice car. He paid for dinner like it was just how things were supposed to be, without being weird about it, you know. Like I've been on dates where the guy makes a big deal out of it, loudly asking for the check and making a big dramatic show of slapping down an Amex Black or some shit, like I'm supposed to go 'ooh, big pimpin' over here, I'm really horny now.'" She rolled her eyes. "Damien was none of that. Even sex was nice. He thought of me, he made sure I felt good, and he was smooth about making sure we were clear there were no expectations without being a dick."

Zoe nodded. "I'd have panicked. Sounds like a setup.

Like, where's the red room with the whips and chains? Where's the secret basement cellar where he keeps victims?"

Teddy groaned. "You guys are *so* cynical, ohmygod. Not every guy who is nice and considerate is going to turn out to be a complete dickbag, or much less yet, flat-out evil."

"My hair and makeup are so great, you guys," Autumn said. "Thank you so much. For real. I'm so glad to have you guys here with me for this."

Lizzy pointed at her. "No, no, no, *no*. Do *not* start that bullshit, Autumn Scott. You *just* finished your makeup, and you don't even have your dress on yet. No waterworks, missy. We are *not* crying until you've said 'I do,' you hear me, young lady?"

Autumn tilted her head back and hissed, blinking. "No crying, no crying, no crying." She glanced at Kat. "Someday, you have to take a flyer on one of these guys, babe. Because someday, the guy will turn out to be the real deal. My proof of that is currently stuffing his fine ass into a five-thousand-dollar hand-sewn suit."

"Mine is downstairs trying like hell to hide his inner nerd around Titus Bright and Seven's boxing buddies." Lizzy glanced at me. "And I happen to have it from a reliable source that Titus Bright *likes* you."

"Not likely," I said, working at sounding even-keeled and cool and casual, even as my giblets shivered at the very sound of his name. "I didn't know Titus Bright did private events." Hey, I even sounded casual.

Kat wasn't fooled. She just smirked at me.

Lizzy had Autumn's dress off the hanger and was unbuttoning the ninety-five hundred million tiny little buttons running down the back so Autumn could step into the gown, which, apparently had been custom-made for Autumn by a designer Seven had met at one of the many galas he'd attended.

"Titus Bright *doesn't* do private events," Autumn said. "He barely does events, period. You don't book or hire Titus, he doesn't do stadiums, or concerts. He's actually very elusive and almost impossible to get ahold of, according to Seven."

"So…how is he here?" I asked. "I went to a Bright Bones concert back in the day with one of Mom's pool boy toys. It was crazy fun. They could seriously rock, man."

Everyone stared at me.

"I have *so* many questions about that statement," Lizzy said. *"You*…went to a Bright Bones show? With one of your mother's pool boy side pieces? And you liked it? Bright Bones was, like, heavy metal."

I huffed. "When will you guys stop being so shocked at this stuff? Yes, I went with Javier. He was Mom's newest pool boy, which meant she hadn't gotten to him yet. He didn't know the rules or anything yet, so he didn't know any better than to go out with me."

"Wait, rules?" Teddy asked.

"Yes, rules. Once Mom found out I was dipping into her fund of hot boys before she got to them, she put the kibosh on it. Made sure all new pool boys knew I was off-limits. I mean, I was seventeen at the time, so I should have been off-limits anyway, but hey, I didn't *look* seventeen, and most of them were twenty or under anyway." I waved a hand. "Point is, Javier was hot. Columbian, had this sexy as all *fuck* accent, he was ripped, and he was super nice. I honestly don't think he had any clue what he'd hired into, with my mom. He didn't last long anyway—I think he quit when he realized fucking Mom was part of the gig. Which, good for him, right? And as for Bright Bones, yes, I liked it. They were technically heavy metal, but not every second of every song was like *rah-rah-rah*—" here she did an imitation of a metal singer angrily shout-singing, "and angry guitars and all that. It was…artistic. There was anger to it, sure, and it was heavy, but when he actually *sang*? Oh man, his voice was like…rough, but beautiful."

Shit. I'd just given myself away.

"Yes, fine, I did also have a minor crush on Titus Bright at the time," I said, defensive. "But who didn't? He was the brand-new big thing. He was everywhere, opening for Metallica and Sevendust and Deftones and every major name in hard rock. He was on magazines and MTV and all that."

Lizzy just laughed, shaking her head. "I would never

in a million years be able to picture you at a heavy metal show."

Kat snickered, and then burst out laughing and had to put her champagne flute aside to bend over and let the laughter out. "Oh my god, you guys, she's nuts for this guy!"

"Katja Evan Spears!" I shot to my feet, sloshing champagne over onto my fingers. "I told you to keep it between us."

She was breathless with laughter. "I'm sorry, I'm sorry, I'm sorry, but this is too good to keep to myself, honey."

All eyes were on Kat.

"Spill already, Kat," Autumn said, as Lizzy began fastening the buttons, now that Autumn had managed to wedge her long, lithe body into the tiny little white wedding gown. "What happened?"

"I met Titus outside, okay?" I cut in before Kat could turn it into something it wasn't. "He made some crude, offensive, sexist remarks, and I'm going to avoid him during the wedding."

Kat's eyes twinkled, literally twinkled, as she slowed her breathing. "You are such a shitty liar, Laurel Evita McGillis."

Teddy was watching the exchange. "Wait, wait, wait. Kat, your middle name is Evan?"

"Evan, like Evans but no S," Kat answered. "Yes. My dad had been sure I was going to be a boy, and if

I had been, my name would have been Evan. He was devastated when I was a girl, the asshole, so my mom coddled his baby little ego by saddling me with Evan as a middle name."

Teddy snorted a laugh. "And you, Laurel, your middle name is Evita?"

I rolled my eyes. "Yes, it is. After the musical, obviously, and as far as I know, there's no funny, pithy little story about it, except that they chose the name for me well before it had the mega popularity and well before the movie was ever made."

Teddy eyed me. "I feel like you're lying about what happened with Titus."

Kat pointed at me with her half-empty flute. "He told her, and I quote—according to this one here—'you're mine, Laurel. You may not know it yet, but you will soon enough.'"

Teddy pretended to swoon. "Oh my *gawd*, that's hot."

"I'm not a steak or a sports car to be owned," I snapped. "I belong to no one, least of all some scruffy, self-absorbed, egotistical jackass rock star. No matter how fucking delicious he is."

Kat shrugged, grinning at Teddy. "See?"

Lizzy was finished with the buttons by now, and Autumn was twisting in the full-length mirror.

"I look hot," Autumn said. "I'm not sure Seven is going to make it until tomorrow night."

"I still think the whole thing is fucking strange and unnatural," Zoe said.

Autumn and Seven had decided that, instead of a typical wedding week where bride and groom have separate bachelor/bachelorette parties and then a honeymoon, there would be a wedding and then instead of a reception, the after-party would be one big party that ended with Autumn and us partying here, and Seven and the boys somewhere else. And then the following day, Autumn and Seven would rejoin each other and head out on a honeymoon, which for them meant two full months in a secluded beachside estate somewhere in the Caribbean that Seven had leased.

The idea being, neither was interested in a typical bachelor/bachelorette party. The lead up to the wedding was stressful enough without adding that in, so why not just have one big party, hang out with friends in the backyard, and then Seven, a married man, has one last night to cut loose with his friends before heading off with his new bride. It's not like anyone actually ever had sex on their wedding night anyway—you're always too tired from the spectacle of the wedding. Not to mention, they'd been living together for months at this point, so the wedding night sex thing wasn't the same deal it used to be when that tradition was started, so there didn't seem much point in following a tradition that was useless to them both.

"Can we go back to Laurel and her weirdly defensive

freak-out about Titus Bright?" Kat said. "I mean, Autumn babe, you look incredible. Seven is going to have a chubby the whole wedding and if you two disappear for a minute afterward, no one is going to be at all surprised."

Autumn turned to check out her backside, smoothing the dress over her hip. "Oh, it'd take *way* more than a minute. But, a little secret, we've actually not had sex at all this week, just to make it that much hotter when we do get that time alone. Which will be on the beach in the Caribbean, and not a moment sooner." She eyed me. "And I'm more interested in Laurel's little situation myself."

"This is Autumn's day," I said. "There's nothing to talk about. It's a nonissue. If he thinks he's going to own me, like rope me into some Dom-Sub Fifty Shades nonsense, he can think again. Unless he wants to be the sub, in which case I might be persuaded to at least hear him out. But that's not how he sounded, and I've already done the rock star bit anyway. Not all it's cracked up to be."

Well shit. If I'd wanted attention off me and my little issue with Titus Bright, this was a dumb way to go about it.

Lizzy snorted. "Well *now* you have to tell us. Which rock star did you bang?"

"Jamison Flare," I sighed. "From Sun Storm."

Teddy's head shot up and her eyes met mine. "How on earth did you manage that? The only musician more reclusive than Jamison Flare is that guy with three names from Tool."

"It was accidental. Meeting him, I mean, not the sex. The sex was intentional, obviously. Remember a couple years ago—three years? Maybe four, it's hard to remember—when I took those five days in Maui? We met in the hotel bar. He had the penthouse, and I had the next best suite under his. We basically spent every night that whole week together. We'd do whatever separately during the day, but once we were back at the hotel for the night, I'd go up and we'd drink champagne and screw. And it was a lot of fun. He was really, really hot, and had a really great dick, but...he wasn't that great in bed, and talking to him was like talking to a brick wall. He was just shitty, terrible, and absolutely abysmal at making conversation. Like, he was a caveman. Grunt once for yes, grunt twice for no, and sex was even worse. He'd just hump and pump until he came and then roll over and grab his phone and ignore me. The fame and the dick weren't worth it. It was still better than no sex, and it's fun to be able to brag that I banged Jamison Flare, but...two out of ten, would not recommend."

Kat made a shrugging gesture with her champagne flute. "But then, that's just Jamison Flare, that's not every musician, every rock star."

I sighed. "Yeah, but what you're missing is that he treated me like I was interchangeable with every other groupie, like I'd chased him backstage and begged him to fuck me. That's not what happened, and I never acted like I was fucking him because of who he was. Yet to him, I was just another nameless, faceless set of tits and ass." I waved a hand, dismissing the topic. "Regardless, it's not about whether or not Titus Bright is a rock star, it's about how he assumed he would own me."

"He didn't say 'own,' though, did he?" Teddy asked. "He said you'd belong to him. That's not the same as owning."

"Belonging to him implies the reverse is also true," Lizzy said. "That he equally belongs to you."

I groaned. "Why are you guys pushing this? If I'm not interested in Titus Bright, what is that to any of you?"

Teddy came over and sat on my lap, put an arm over my shoulders. "Because, dumpling, you're saying no before you've given him a chance."

Autumn came over, stood in front of me, pressed her palms to my cheeks, bent forward and kissed my forehead. "My advice? Give it a shot. See what's he about. If you discover you don't like what he's about, you can nope out. And none of us will blame you for that if you do. But if you stay away just because you had a bad experience with someone else who isn't him and for all you know is nothing like him, then we kinda will hold that against you. I feel like there are lessons to be learned from Lizzy's and my experience. Risk nothing, gain nothing. Risk a lot, gain a lot."

I sighed, more of a groan than anything. "And what if I risk and it doesn't work out?"

"You get hurt, and we're there to pick up the pieces," Teddy said. "It's what friends are for."

"Just like that?" I asked.

Teddy shrugged. "Sure. I'm not saying it'd be easy, but yeah, just like that."

I wasn't so sure. It seemed far easier and far safer to just stay on the other side of the yard from Titus Bright.

CHAPTER TWO

S EVEN ST. JOHN STOOD ALONE IN FRONT OF THE WHITE, RED rose-wreathed archway, clad in a fitted tuxedo. The girls and I were seated in the front row, with Seven's father, his agent, his manager, and half a dozen of his friends—two world-champion boxers, a certain A-list actor whose name was known by every household in the world, just about, Frederick Lyons the restaurateur, and a handsome, well-dressed black man who Autumn had said was a famous NFL running back, and a massive man with short curly black hair and dark brown skin, who Autumn had said was a Maori from New Zealand and a professional rugby player. Gorgeous, that one. But I, to my eternal damnation, had eyes only for the man on the stool, with a beautiful acoustic guitar, off to one side, playing an acoustic, instrumental version of "Kiss Me" by Ed Sheeran.

Autumn was positively radiant, striding toward him. Since we five girls plus Braun were Autumn's only family, and since Seven's guest list was similarly small, there was no block of chairs, no center aisle, just one row—so Autumn walked up to Seven from the side.

Autumn glided, slow and smooth, approaching Seven with a glowing smile on her face, clutching a bouquet of wildflowers. The minister was a short, svelte black woman, her hair a dozen thick dreads braided through with colorful beads and wrapped with silver and gold wire, bound back with a brightly colored beaded band, wearing a white gown that was designed to reflect her African heritage. She held a folder in her hands, and smiled beatifically as Autumn halted in front of Seven. Lizzy rose and took the flowers from her, then sat back down while Autumn and Seven joined hands.

"Hi, everyone," the minister said. "Today is a glorious, beautiful day." It was, indeed—sunny and warm, but not too hot. "We're here to bear witness as true love unites two souls, Autumn Scott and Seven St. John. I'm not going to ask if anyone objects, because if anyone did, you wouldn't be here, would you? No, there can be no objection to this union. It's love, made plain as day. I mean, come on, just look at them. Have you ever seen a man look at a woman the way this guy is looking at her? I haven't, and I've done a lot of weddings. That's love." She held her folder in one hand and placed the other over Seven and Autumn's joined hands. "As their hands are joined, so now are their souls, and their very lives. This is a ceremony—it's a declaration, from them, to you and the world, that they're committing to each other. A marriage, on the face of it, is not anything more than a legal procedure. But, when two like-minded souls decide to unite in holy matrimony, like Seven and Autumn, it becomes something far, far more—it's a braiding of hearts. No longer will there be the heart of Autumn and the heart of Seven, but one heart, one soul, comprised of two halves. That's what we're doing here. *They* give this ceremony meaning. As long as their hearts are one, this marriage will stand strong and define the course of their life. And I say *life*, singular, rather than *lives* plural, on purpose. Theirs is now one life. You all are witnesses, as I declare them husband and wife."

She looked at Seven. "Your vows?"

Seven nodded, took a deep breath. Let it out. "Autumn, I…I wrote these elaborate vows, using all the best words I know. I memorized them. They were damn near poetry. But damn if I didn't forget every word of them the moment I saw you, just now. So I guess I'll try my best to recapture what I was going to say, but I'll just…freestyle it." He sighed again, nervous, emotional. "You changed me, babe. There was nothing for me in this life except getting through day to day. And then I met you. You're the softness these hard hands crave. You're the sweetness this rough heart requires." He let go of her hand with one of his and pounded his chest with his fist, then rejoined her hands. "You're the wonder that makes each day better, the light that shines out of the sun itself every morning. You're the love that tells my heart it's okay to feel again. You're the trust that tells my mind it's okay to be vulnerable…I'd say again, but it'd be more accurate to say for the first time ever. Autumn, you're the future that makes this life worth living. I never thought I'd be a husband, and more than that, I never thought I'd *want* to be a husband." He squeezed her hands, let out a soft breath. "But I am your husband. So my vow is that I'll fight with every ounce of myself to be the best husband I can be, as hard as I fought every time I stepped into the ring. I'll fight for you, and I'll fight for us. I'll love you till the sun goes cold, not just till death do us part, but past that, in whatever it is that's on the other side of living. Rich, poor, sick, healthy, hard times and good times, I'm yours through it all. That's my vow."

Autumn sniffed, smiled. "You're a hard act to follow, Seven, but here goes." She gazed up at him for a moment, then let out a shuddery breath. "You said I changed you—you stole the words out of my mouth. You absolutely altered the very fabric of who I am. I wasn't sure I believed in love until you. I know I didn't. I'd never seen it, after all." She broke off and gazed at Lizzy, with Braun beside her. "Until you two, at least." Back to Seven. "They made it seem possible. You proved that it's possible for *me*. And that's what I never believed I'd ever have. But here you are, marrying me, loving me—*choosing* me. So that's what I promise, Seven: to love you. To choose you, again and again, even when you piss me off as only you can. I promise to love you so hard that you'll never want to spend a single night apart from me."

"Already did that part, babe," Seven interjected, laughing.

"Hey now, I didn't interrupt you," she joked. "I promise to prove to you that love is real and that our love is forever, no matter what." She squeezed his hands, and stepped even closer to him, eyes shimmering. "I promise to wife you so hard, you don't even know."

He laughed, we all did at that.

She wasn't done, though. "I have one other promise to make." She inhaled shakily, and when she spoke, her voice was tremulous. "I promise, Seven St. John, to be the best mother I can be to the life that's growing inside me."

Silence, then, as we all took in what she was saying.

"Wait, you…" He stared down at her. "For real?"

She nodded, took his hands and placed them over her womb. "I found out this morning."

He dropped to one knee and pressed his forehead to her belly, and his shoulders shook. "Best day ever just got better. It's like a two-for-one special." He pressed a soft kiss to her belly. "Thank you, Autumn. Thank you for this. For you." Another kiss to her belly. "And for you."

She pulled him to his feet, and glanced at the minister. "Are we married yet?"

The minister laughed. "Yeah, I think we best get on with it, shouldn't we?" She plucked something from the pages of her folder—a length of pale blue silk. "It came to my attention that no one had brought anything borrowed or blue to this wedding, so I brought this. This piece of silk is older than the state of California. It was first used to bind the hands of my many-times great-grandparents almost two hundred years ago. They fled slavery in South Carolina together, and built a new life out here, by pluck and by courage and by love." She wrapped the pale, frayed length of silk around Seven and Autumn's joined hands. "It has been wrapped around the hands of my forebears in every marriage in every generation since. There's so much love in the fabric of this silk, I think you can just about feel it coming off of it in waves. In all the generations of marriage for which this silk has been used to bind hands, there has not been one divorce. Not one. Marriages in my family last, on average, a minimum of forty years. This very silk was wrapped around my hands and my husband's as we were married thirty years ago, just yesterday in fact. Before I wed you, I place upon you the blessing of long life and lifelong love, pressed into your hands as they are joined by the symbol of this handfasting."

There was murmuring among us in the crowd—that was something truly special, and we all knew it.

"As this piece of silk binds your hands together, so it also binds your lives, and your hearts. With that in mind, do you, Seven, take with a willing heart and mind this woman, Autumn Scott, to be your wife, for all time and through all things?"

"I do." His voice broke, and he tried again. "I do."

"And you, Autumn, do you take with a willing heart and mind this man, Seven St. John, to be your husband for all time and through all things?"

"I do."

"Then by the power vested in me by God and by the State of California, I pronounce you husband and wife, wife and husband, now and forever." She withdrew the silk, held it in her hands. "Amen, and let it be. You are now wed, before God and these good people. Kiss each other and seal the deal!"

Seven kissed the ever-loving shit out of her. Gathered her in his arms and bent her backward, kissing her with gusto and with passion, until we all began to whistle and clap and laugh.

It went on until it was nearly uncomfortable, and then he lifted her to her feet and then they turned and faced us.

"Who's ready to get their party on?" Seven said. "We're married, ya'll!"

❧

Titus traded his acoustic guitar for an electric one, a keyboard, and a microphone, all fed through a loop pedal. With the keyboard, he lay down a complicated series of synthesized beats, which he layered and looped into something like a dance club beat, and then swung his electric guitar around and picked a haunting, delicate melody which he put on loop. Returning to the keyboard, he then layered an ascending riff on the piano, repeated and looped. Back to the guitar, then, angling to the microphone and strumming a slow, chugging rock riff.

Played that for a moment, and then sidled up the mic and began a low, wordless note, a gravelly hum that smoothed as his voice went louder and higher, sliding up the register of his remarkable range until he was singing an aria, and I was amazed again, as I'd been when I saw him with Bright Bones, that he could so seamlessly go from growly and deep to almost smooth and melodic and operatic.

The lyrics, when he began actually singing, spoke of moonlight love and sunrise kisses, a chorus repeated with variations on that theme.

Seven and Autumn danced, their first dance together moments after saying "I do," and then after they'd spun together a few minutes, they gestured to us and we all danced, as Titus's song transitioned to a faster, happier bop, a fun little number that was, if you listened to the lyrics closely, kind of dirty.

Autumn and Seven's backyard was large, their house sitting on a full acre with a small front yard and a lot of space between the houses on each side and a long rectangle behind leading to the ocean, and their private beach, accessible via a wooden stairway leading down from the bluff to the sand. The entire back of their house opened, accordion doors sliding apart from the middle, with wide flagstones paving a large area behind the house, featuring a built-in outdoor kitchen, a hand-built pergola, a fire pit with amphitheater-style stone bench seating, with a huge swath of silky grass leading the dune grass bluff. There was a white cloth-draped bar with a bartender and several long tables with catered food, courtesy of Fredrick Lyons, all set up on the flagstone-paved areas.

We all danced barefoot in the grass—that was, as a matter of fact, part of the invitation: dancing after the ceremony, barefoot in the grass. So there was a pile of shoes in the grass, with Titus Bright off to the side with his electric guitar now, playing it solo, no backing music, just his guitar and his rough beautiful voice singing "your eyes in the car light, your skin in the starlight, let me out of this limelight, tangle up in these sheets all night."

Was it me or was he looking at me as I danced with Maaka, the big Maori? Was he watching me as he played? Were his pale, tan, almost yellow eyes following me, as I swayed with Maaka?

Was it jealousy in those eyes?

I'm no expert on men, but it looked like it, to me.

I danced with Lon, one of Seven's boxer friends, next. He was a welterweight, only an inch taller than my five-seven, but densely muscled and even dancing with me he moved like a panther, his inky black skin gleaming in the light as the sun would gleam off the coat of a panther. His smile was bright white, his eyes deep brown and friendly, and his voice as he made polite conversation with me was smooth and leonine. He danced with several inches of space between us, his hand polite and proper on my waist—he had a serious girlfriend, he informed me, who couldn't make the wedding due to a work commitment.

Maaka had been interested, I could tell. He'd danced closer, and his smile had been hopeful, his conversation leading to personal questions. But then I'd caught an exchange of looks between him and Titus, and suddenly, Maaka had vanished, and I saw him now making conversation with Seven as they stood off to one side, sipping at drinks and laughing.

The evening wore on, and Titus kept playing, and we kept dancing and drinking and eating. It was a small, intimate party, only a dozen or so people and all of them the closest friends of Autumn and Seven, and it was all the more fun and lovely for that. There were no awkward conversations, no stilted moments with strangers. Granted, most of Seven's friends were strangers, but they were all polite, easy to talk to, handsome, funny, and interesting.

None of them openly hit on me. None of them informed me I was theirs.

Titus played for almost two hours, and even though I was wary and suspicious, I could allow myself to be amazed—he played a dizzying array of instruments—if it had strings, he could play it, and then some. He had a ukulele, a twelve-string acoustic, a big bass, a mandolin, a violin, an electric cello, and even a didgeridoo, plus the keyboard, several electric guitars, and two acoustic guitars. And he played them all beautifully, with skill and talent, using his loop pedal to layer them until it sounded like he had a full band with him.

Finally, he set all the instruments aside, and stood empty-handed in front of the mic. We all stopped, faced him.

"Seven, my man. We've been friends for almost twenty years. I remember the day we met like it was yesterday. It was this big tournament, you were this young guy, hungry and kinda crazy, and everyone was talking about you. You'd just KO'd Marius Milley in the second round, and you looked so amped up that you coulda fought another four rounds without breaking a sweat. I was there because they wanted Bright Bones to play between matches, right there in the ring, so we had this ghetto-ass mobile setup, a shitty amp, a shitty electronic drum kit that Tommy fuckin' hated with a passion. It was just him and me. We played our set after you kicked Milley's ass, and then there you were, in your boxing robe, hands taped, pacing around like a caged wolf, waiting for your next match. You were just the fuckin' *coolest*, man. I knew then, the moment we talked for the first time, that I just *had* to be your friend. And here we are, eighteen, almost nineteen years later, and I'm playing your fuckin' wedding, man." He accepted a pint of beer from Maaka, and held it up. "Here's to Seven, and to his beautiful bride Autumn, and to the start of their lives together. Congratulations, you two. I'm happy for you, more than I can say. You guys, and that little seed of a life you've got going, you're gonna be so fuckin' happy. I can tell." He gestured at the minister, who had been invited to stay and celebrate. "Reverend LeShae, that was some beautiful shi—stuff you said. The ribbon, the handfasting? Just beautiful. And with that, folks, I'm done for the night. I'm gonna get myself a beer or ten, and some food. Seven, Autumn, congratulations. Seven, brother, I'm happy for you, I'm proud of you, and I love you, man. Peace, ya'll."

There was applause, whistles, and cheering and then Titus connected a cord to a laptop and turned on a playlist from his sound system, and he wandered away toward the bartender, and I lost sight of him as he was surrounded by Autumn, Seven, Frederick, and couple other friends of Seven's.

After Titus had started his speech, I'd lost my conversation partner, Seven's agent, Jonathon, so I went in search of my friends.

Lizzy was deep in conversation with Braun and Lon, Teddy and Kat were dancing with the other boxer friend of Seven's, Vincent, and Zoe was standing at the bar.

She was alone.

Autumn and her husband were now swaying alone off near the arch and looking more in love than ever.

I watched them, feeling a twinge of jealousy.

Or, more than a twinge. A big, fat, vicious bolt of it, lancing into my gut.

I wanted that.

Deep down, where the feeling was vague and ephemeral and slippery, under the surface of years-long suppression, I wanted it.

To dance like that with someone, to be looked at like that by a man.

"Laurel McGillis."

I jumped a foot in the air, shrieking, spilling most of the glass of chardonnay I been sipping for the past hour. I whirled, and there was Titus, hands in his back pockets.

"Titus Bright," I said, ignoring the thump of my heart.

He didn't say anything else. Just looked at me, eyes searching mine. His eyes didn't waver from mine, didn't lazily slither down my body, didn't fasten on my cleavage. Just seared into mine, boiling with a thousand thoughts and emotions I couldn't decipher and which he didn't elucidate.

I huffed. "Well, as fascinating as this conversation has been…"

His hand caught my arm, gentle but firm—his hands were gargantuan, with long fingers and a wide palm. His hand wrapped easily around my bicep, held on. "Dance with me."

I stared at his hand, then up at him. "Let go."

His grin was dark, wolfish. He let go of my arm,

but his hand instead slid around my waist and his other neatly twisted my empty wineglass from my fingers and tossed it off into the grass, then clasped hands with me. We were dancing, then, swaying to a Jason Derulo song.

He was *so* tall. Even if I'd been wearing my heels with their four-inch stiletto spikes, he would still tower over me, which meant barefoot in the grass, my face was chest height. I wondered at our joined hands: mine seemed so tiny nestled within his, so pale, so delicate. I could feel the guitarist's calluses on his fingertips.

He swayed with me in his arms, stared down at me. "You're beautiful, Laurel." His speaking voice sounded like the contented purr of a lion.

I hated the way I was instinctually inclined to preen, to feel *seen*. "Thank you, Titus."

He stepped back and held my hand, and the years of ballroom dancing lessons I'd been forced to take at the private European academy had me moving automatically into a spin, left me pressed back to his hard lean front.

"You dance amazingly well," he murmured.

"A solid decade of ballroom classes every single day will do that," I said.

"Really? Every day for ten years?"

"I went to a boarding school in Switzerland. You had a certain number of elective classes, and the options were ballroom, gym class which meant, like, soccer and whatever, and choir. There were others, too, but the only one that appealed to me was dancing, and I just stuck with it." I smirked up at him. "What's your excuse for being able to dance?"

He laughed. "Boredom."

I frowned in confusion. "Boredom?"

He nodded. "Yup. Long story, so the short version is that I spent what the media called my vanished years in Brazil, in Rio. I was playing in this shitty fuckin' local band who had no fuckin' clue who I was, and I liked it that way. But I could just never sleep. It was two solid years of insomnia, so to just fill the time with literally anything except more drugs and alcohol, I did all sorts of crazy shit. Like ballroom classes. I can do a hell of a samba, let me tell you."

"I'm sorry, but I can't see you doing the samba."

He stopped moving, stared down at me. "No? How about the rumba? That shit is downright *sexual*."

I shook my head, snorting. "There's a big difference between being able to sway around in a lazy four-step, and being able to properly samba."

"And you don't think I can?"

"No, I don't."

He stepped closer, so our bodies were less than an inch apart. "Care to wager?"

I rolled my eyes. "Sure. Put on a song we can samba to, and if you fail to impress me with your magical samba skills, you have to leave me alone."

"And when I prove you wrong, you sexy little doubter, you go on a date with me."

"Deal."

I had no doubt he could samba. But samba *well*? What he didn't know was that I still danced regularly. It was my second favorite way to work up a sweat, the first being sex, obviously. I had a ballroom group I danced with down in the valley every Monday night, and these were not casual dancers, these were semi-pro, the kind who brought their own special dancing shoes. And they always fought over who got to be my partner.

Impressing me wasn't easy.

He tapped me on the nose. "It's a wager, then. Stay here."

He went over to his laptop, spent a moment finding and cueing up a song, and then swaggered back to me. He had my shoes in one hand.

"Can't samba barefoot," he said.

"No, I guess not." I slid my feet into the shoes, and then gestured at the paved area. "Grass, or flagstones?"

"Up to you."

"Grass, then. Less of a risk of tripping on the cracks."

He slid his vest off, folded it, tossed it aside on a nearby chair, and then tugged a braided leather cord from his hip pocket, used it to tie his hair back. The pop song that had been playing ended, and the distinctive Latin rhythm of a samba started.

I felt the eyes, knew everyone was watching.

Shit, this had been a mistake. Big, big mistake.

He was gorgeous. Fucking perfect, is what he was. Every line and curve and angle and plane of his body was hewn as if from marble by the hand of da Vinci himself. Bare-chested, wearing those ripped, faded black jeans tucked into knee-high biker boots with buckles and straps running up the front, the top several buckles left undone, hair bound back to emphasize his sharp cheekbones and deep-set tawny eyes and chiseled jawline…

Fuck me.

It was hard to breathe, to swallow, being this close to him.

The music was in full swing, now, and he held out his hand to me, waiting.

My downfall was the rhythm. I couldn't not dance. My feet took over, put me into motion. Immediately, within the first few movements, I knew I'd lost the wager.

Titus could *dance*.

He led me, effortlessly.

His posture was perfect, his turnouts crisp and precise. His rhythm was flawless. What was more, he was *enjoying* it. He knew the dance well enough that he didn't have to think about the movements, he could just focus on me.

Fuck it.

I threw myself into the moment, abandoned my intent to dislike him and let myself be led through the samba. His hands were everywhere, his body, his eyes.

His smile was broad, contagious, and cocky. He knew he'd won, and he'd known he would.

As we danced, I saw the whole wedding party in a crescent around us, clapping to the beat, watching us move together in complete harmony, as if we'd danced the samba together a million times.

Finally, the song ended, and we were both out of breath, panting and sweating, and there was cheering and whistles.

"Laurel!" Lizzy was laughing as she came over to me. "When the hell did you learn to dance like that?"

Titus snorted. "You keep your ballroom skills a secret from your best friend?"

"Hush you, it's none of your business," I said, then faced Lizzy. "I've always danced. I still do, every Monday, with a club down in the Valley."

Lizzy gestured at Titus. "So, I'm with him on this. You keep these incredible dancing skills a secret from me? I've known you for damn near fifteen years, and I don't know you're a master ballroom dancer?"

"It's not a secret," I protested. "It's just something I do. It's fun, I enjoy it, and it keeps me in shape."

The whole group of girls was around me, then.

"Aren't you the one who said you don't get sweaty and out of breath unless there's a dick involved?" Kat asked.

"You also said your only form of exercise was

walking around while squeezing your butt cheeks," Teddy added.

Titus was watching this exchange with a grin. He said nothing, though, just bit down on laughter and listened.

I huffed. Tried to ignore him. "Sex is still my number one exercise. I do walk almost every night, and I do squeeze my ass cheeks while I walk. I just *also* happen to belong to a ballroom club. It's not a big deal."

"It is, though, kinda," Zoe said. "I feel like there's a lot about you that we don't know, and that we don't know we don't know."

"Except now," Autumn said, "we're starting to figure out how much we don't know that we don't know."

I blinked. "Wait, what?"

"You have a lot of secrets," Kat said. "That's our point."

I waved them off. "Not a secret."

"We've been your best friends since college. We're all just about forty," Lizzy said. "At this point, anything we don't know about each other pretty much counts as a secret."

"What, you guys are legit upset about this?" I asked. "It's ballroom dancing, not a secret divorce."

Teddy cleared her throat. "Um, I suppose now might be a good time to come clean on the secret divorce front." We all pivoted to focus on Teddy; she lifted her shoulders and grinned sheepishly. "I was actually married to Thomas."

We all just blinked.

I frowned at her. "Thomas, your ex-boyfriend, who hit you, whom Lizzy's Magnum P.I. buddy beat up? That Thomas? You were *married* to him?"

She nodded. "I was. For six months. And that wasn't actually the first time he'd hit me—but it was the last. After Lizzy's friend worked him over, I had a client of mine who was a lawyer draw up divorce papers, and I got a sheriff friend to serve them. And then that same private investigator friend of Lizzy's intimidated him into signing them without contest. And then *another* friend, this one a judge, got the divorce pushed through in record time." She sighed. "I called in pretty much every favor I had saved up."

"And you didn't tell us?" Kat asked. "We're so fighting."

"I was embarrassed," she said. "And scared. And confused. Thomas had me so mixed up. Unless you've been in a situation like that, you don't know what it's like. How easy it is to...to get mixed up, in your head, thinking it really is your fault. And then trying to get out of it, to get away from him without dragging you guys into it?"

Lizzy hugged her. "We're your friends. It's our job to get dragged into things like that."

Autumn was on the other side of Teddy.

"Honey-bunny. We would have gone to war with that asshole for you. You should've told us."

Titus had his arms crossed over his chest. "You guys are something else."

"Titus!" Seven's voice boomed from across the yard. "Come do a shot with us, dancin' man!"

Titus waved at us, and strode—swaggered, really—across the yard, catching his vest off the chair and shrugged it back on, joining the circle of guys around the bar, his long sculpted arms slinging across the shoulders of Seven and Lon as he leaned between them.

Lizzy watched me watching him, smirking. "You like him."

I ripped my gaze off of him. "Do not."

Kat socked my shoulder. "Do too. You guys look *good* together."

"Yeah you do," Zoe said, eyeing him appreciatively. "I mean, I know you've got dibs, but that man is sex on a stick."

"He's a dick on a stick, is what he is," I snapped.

"Good kind of dick or bad kind of dick?" Kat asked.

I groaned. "The bad kind, Katja. *Ob*vi."

"Why?" Kat asked, her expression a mix between a confused frown and an amused grin. "Because he has the utter, unmitigated gall to be an incredible musician, a great dancer, sexier than socks on a rooster, *and* likes you? The asshole. How dare he?"

I shook my head. "You guys suck."

"No, but I bet you will before the night is out," Kat said, wiggling her eyebrows. "Him, that is."

Autumn held up a hand. "Actually, if you're going to do any sucking or any other sexy time activities, you'd better do it soon, because our party bus to the hotel is going to be here soon."

"There's no hanky-panky happening tonight," I said. "Zip, zero, zilch, nada."

"Maybe not tonight," a leonine voice said, behind and above me. "But you *do* owe me a date."

I turned slowly to look up at him. "You played me."

He smirked. "How? I *told* you I was good at the samba. You're the one who didn't believe me."

I huffed. "Fine. One date. Let it never be said I don't honor my wagers." I glared up at him. "What's the date, big fella? Sex party in your fancy penthouse condo?"

He just laughed. "You think you know, but you don't know." His gaze heated. "The one thing you'd better learn now, Laurel McGillis, is that nothing you think you know about me is going to be accurate. Being able to samba is only the first and smallest of the ways I'm going to surprise you."

I rolled my eyes. "Okay, sure, whatever. Just name the time and place."

"Titus!" Seven's voice again. "The limo is here, buddy. Time to get lit the fuck up!"

Titus grinned down at me. "You'll find out. It'll be what you least expect, and when."

I sighed, annoyed. "And I hate surprises. So this will be fun for one of us."

He stepped into me, hips to hips, chest to chest, his hot tawny eyes on mine. "You'll have the best time ever, Laurel."

His big callused hand went to my cheek, thumb brushing my cheekbone, while the other wrapped with possessive, casual familiarity low around my waist. As if I really was his. As if we were an item, a couple, a *thing*.

"Every single fuckin' second we spend together will be a second you *never* forget." He bent down, nose slanting across mine, and his lips slid over mine in a teasing whisper of an almost-kiss. "I promise."

And then he was gone.

And I was dizzy, my lips still tingling where his had not exactly touched, my hips tingling with leftover electricity where his hands had been.

"Goddammit," I hissed, watching him swagger around the side of the yard to where the wrought iron gate opened to the front yard and driveway, breaking into an easy trot as Seven leaned on the horn of the party bus. "I am *so* fucked."

Kat wrapped an arm around me. "Not yet you're not. But something tells me the moment he gets you alone, you will be. A lot, and hard, and well."

"Once upon a time, that would have sounded great," I whispered, "now, I'm not so sure. I'm not so sure my heart would survive that intact."

"What do you have to lose, Laur?" Kat asked.

"Everything," I breathed; realizing I was still touching my lips, I jerked my hand away.

"Oh, well that explains it," Kat said, her tone dripping with snark.

Autumn and Lizzy both laughed, coming alongside me and putting their arms around me.

"Actually, it does," Lizzy said.

Autumn kissed my temple. "My advice, babe? Just go with it. Fighting is useless."

Teddy joined on one side, and Zoe the other, so the whole group of us were in a line abreast, arms around each other's shoulders.

I pushed away from the group hug. "Can we just go get drunk, please?"

Lizzy just laughed and hooked her hand around my elbow. "I understand, Laurel, trust me I do."

"Yeah, but it worked out for you," I said. "That stuff never works out for me."

She just laughed. "Yeah, well, it never worked out for me either, until it did."

"You wanted it to."

"And you don't?"

Yes, I did, deeply, desperately, down in the lightless depths of my secret soul.

"Nope," I said. "Not at all."

Lizzy just cackled. "You're a shitty liar."

"Goddammit, I am not!" I protested. "You're the second person today to say that. I'm a terrific liar."

Lizzy just laughed and herded me onto the party bus, with the rest of the group trooping on behind us. Kat had a bottle of Patrón in one hand, a bowl of lime wedges in the other, and behind her, Zoe had a stack of red Solo cups, and behind *her*, Teddy was carrying a case of lime LaCroix and a case of hard seltzer.

"Oh, shit," I breathed. "We're getting turnt *up*."

Kat uncorked the bottle of tequila, propped one foot up on the nearest seat, and slugged from the bottle. "Yes, my love, we certainly are. This wedding marks two down, four to go," she said, her voice hoarse from the liquor, and then shoved a lime wedge in her mouth; she handed the bottle to me. "And you're next, Boo," she said to me.

"The fuck I am," I muttered, and pulled on the bottle.

For tonight, at least, I could ignore, forget, and pretend.

If only through the blessed, despicable means of a lot of alcohol.

I'm a grown-ass woman—you'd think I'd know better by now. But no. Tonight, we party, tomorrow, I regret.

CHAPTER THREE

I LOCKED UP THE CONDO I'D JUST FINISHED SHOWING, SENT A text to Kat to meet me for lunch, and headed down to my car. I hadn't sold it, but the clients I'd shown it to were considering it, along with one other option, a little two-bedroom ranch in San Diego, which I, for obvious and selfish reasons, was advising against.

I mean, my reasoning was sound—they were a young couple with a child, and they'd need more than two bedrooms, and the condo they'd just seen had an extra bedroom for fifty grand less than the house—no yard, granted, but their little nugget was four months old and didn't need a yard yet, and there was a nice park within walking distance. Save the cash for a bigger house in a few years. That was my advice. It was good advice too, it just had the additional bonus meaning I'd get a nice little commission out of the deal.

I left the condo parking structure, mentally trying

to figure out what else I could do to entice these people to spring for this unit.

My phone rang, an unknown number, but an LA area code. I put in my wireless earbuds as I waited at a red light and answered it. "Hello, this is Laurel."

"Laurel, hi," a smooth, older female voice said. "My name is Alaina and I represent the interests of Troubadour Enterprises. My client is interested in looking at a couple properties you have listed for sale in the Malibu area. Can I schedule an afternoon of your time?"

"Who did you say you represent?" I asked.

"Troubadour Enterprises," she answered.

"I'm assuming your client wishes to remain anonymous, then."

"For the moment, yes. In the interest of privacy, as I'm sure you understand."

"Certainly," I answered. "Send over your NDA and I'll look it over, sign it, send it back, and then we can get your client on my schedule. I'm booked for this week, but I could probably carve out a few hours next week."

Complete bullshit—I did have several showings this week, but I wasn't so booked I couldn't make time for more. But if you make it seem like you're booked solid, it puts a little pressure on the buyer to commit sooner.

"My client only has time this Saturday, eleven a.m. I should add, my client is a cash buyer, with the ability to write a check on the spot, should they see a property which strikes their interest."

I mentally high-fived myself. "Hmmm, hold on, let me look at my schedule." I had it memorized, obviously, and knew I had the morning open—I muted the call for a good thirty seconds, then popped back on. "I can do Saturday at eleven. Does your client have a particular property or properties in mind?"

"Yes, indeed. I email you with a list, in order of priority."

"Very good."

"The NDA should arrive in your inbox soon, I just sent it over. It's standard language, but my client has and will enforce it, being a very, very private person."

"Understood. Discretion is an utmost priority for me personally, and for all of us at Six Chicks Real Estate."

"That's the word on the street, which is why my client chose you."

"Well, I'm honored to be chosen, and if none of the properties on your client's list work, I can promise I'll find something that does. Thank you, and thank you to your client for the opportunity to earn your business."

We ended the call, and I finished the drive back to the office. I printed out the nondisclosure agreement, read it—it was indeed standard language, meant to make sure I didn't sell to tabloids or anyone else any details of the client or the showing or anything at all. I signed it, and sent it back; NDAs were standard fare in the luxury market, especially in this area, as we'd all shown and sold homes to high-profile clients and we'd all had to sign our share of NDAs.

There was nothing in any of the emails to give away who "Troubadour Enterprises" was, and my admittedly mediocre internet sleuthing skills turned up nothing.

Well, I'd find out who it was on Saturday. Probably some aging record executive with money to burn and a bald spot. Whatever—his, or her, money would spend the same, right?

Saturday, ten-fifty in the morning, and I was pulling up to the first property on the list. I'd been emailed this morning that the client themself—that was the word used: "themself" would meet me there and we'd see the rest together. I figured I'd be a few minutes early, turn on some lights, maybe set up a Keurig. I always kept one in my trunk, along with an assortment of pods, bottles of filtered water, and nondairy creamer.

When I pulled up into the driveway, though, there was already a car parked on the left side. The car intrigued me—it wasn't the car of a moneybags, cash-flasher industry exec; it was a classic pickup, big, red, burly and beefy, with oversize knobby tires, and not a single piece of chrome. Masculine and macho, without being the kind of truck that screamed: "I HAVE A TINY PENIS."

I parked my Aston Martin DB6, itself an understated piece, sexy and cool without being flashy, beside it. As I exited the car, bending in to retrieve my purse from the passenger seat, I felt something ripple over me.

I straightened slowly, noticing for the first time the figure kicked back in the rocking chair that was part of the staging—the house featured a huge, deep-covered porch that had just begged for a pair of antiqued rocking chairs.

Frayed cutoff khaki shorts, the frayed ends hanging below his knee. Slouchy, untied combat boots, faded and battered from years of wear. A black Rolling Stones shirt, the classic '75 tour concert logo with the sticking-out tongue, sleeves cut off. Amber bead bracelet, a hemp bracelet, and a thick leather strap with a chunky watch face on it adorned one wrist, a profusion of rubber bracelets on the other, as well as more bead bracelets, of the kind you'd get at one of those crystals and reiki healing stores on the other wrist. A backward ball cap, black, fitted.

Loose black ringlets under the cap, touching his sharp hard bare shoulders.

Mirrored aviators hid his eyes, but I felt them on me as I ascended the steps.

Every inch of him screamed rock star. He just drew the eye, absorbed attention. I'd have eyes only for him even if he wasn't the only other person on the porch with me.

Titus Bright.

"Troubadour Enterprises, huh?" I said, leaning against the railing in front of him.

He just grinned. "It's my corporate front. Easier to do business with that as my DBA than using my real name. People see my name on an email or something, and they see dollar signs. You see the business name and talk to my gal Alaina? I get proper business treatment."

"Makes sense." I gestured at the house, a five-million-dollar, five bedroom, five and a half bathroom, six thousand square foot property designed for entertaining. "And this is, what? All a ruse to get me alone?"

He stood up, unfolding in a single lithe movement to his full six feet, six-inch height. "Maybe. Or maybe I'm actually interested in seeing it. It's a gorgeous home. Imported African teak hardwood floors, Carrara marble counters throughout?"

So he'd actually looked at the listing. Interesting.

I'd play. Why not?

"Okay, well, let's see it, then." I punched the code into the lockbox on the front door, withdrew the key, unlocked the front door. He immediately took the storm door from me, reached around me, and twisted open the main door. "Thanks."

Inside, the foyer was bathed in natural light from the rosette window over the front door, and you could see into the kitchen and through to the backyard view of the Pacific. He wandered past me, pulling his sunglasses off and setting them upside down on the brim of his backward cap.

"Nice," he said. "Pretty sweet kitchen."

I watched him as he trailed fingertips over the counter, toyed with the gas range grate, opened the sub-zero fridge, closed it again. "My question is whether you really need six thousand square feet and five bedrooms, though."

"Does it matter what I need? If I like it, and I want it, and I can pay cash, who gives a fuck if it's too much house for lil ol' me?" He shoved open the door to the back deck, which was the true *piece de resistance*, being a massive outdoor living area with built-in seating, a full kitchen, an infinity pool with a glass bottom that cut into the actual interior of the walkout basement, so the pool water would reflect and refract the sunlight and cast rainbows on the whole basement. It was a cool effect, actually.

"No, I guess it doesn't. But I have to let the sellers know when they have a showing, and these people are super motivated to sell, so if you're just using this as a way to get to me, then I kind of resent the manipulation. I take my career seriously, Titus."

He closed the door and went past me again, ignoring me as he moved for the stairs to the second floor. Of course, I followed him. Upstairs, he peeked into the four bedrooms before heading into the master suite, which occupied a full third of the upper floor. It was fully staged, with a king bed and sitting area.

Titus wandered through the bathroom, his and hers walk-in closet, checked out the view from the balcony, and then came back into the bedroom and sat heavily onto the bed.

"I am looking," he said. "Just not for me."

Leaning against the doorframe, I tilted my head. "Oh? Meaning?"

"Troubadour Enterprises employs twenty-four people. I have a whole recording arm, distribution, booking, merch, all that. Alaina is my PA, and she's indispensable, but my real top dog is Jeremy Mullins. He just turned thirty, he's got a beautiful young wife and four little kids already, and she's about to pop with their fifth."

My eyes widened. "Busy couple, huh?"

He nodded. "Yup. I pay them well, maybe a little too well, but they've been holding off on buying a house suited to fit their needs. Jeremy grew up dirt-ass poor and he's a hell of a cheapskate, and his wife isn't much better. I don't think they'll ever go look for houses they can actually afford, so I'm looking for them. Jeremy started as a guitar tech for Bright Bones, and when I do a set that needs an actual band, Jeremy is in it. But he's a wizard with logistics, and he can talk anyone into anything. And he's just a really cool guy."

"So you're looking at houses for Jeremy and his wife and their four, almost five, kids."

"Yeah. Last couple years, he's really gone over and above for me, working a shitload of hours, scrambling to get my last-minute flash concerts up, and I figure I should do something to say thanks."

"A house is a pretty nice thanks."

He grinned. "What can I say? I'm a nice guy."

I gestured at the room. "So, is this it?"

He shrugged. "Maybe. Their kids are young—the oldest is, like, seven, and their youngest is just barely two. I'm not sure an unfenced infinity pool is going to fly with Mrs. Mullins."

"Obviously I don't have kids, but my clients with younger kids usually don't end up going for the places with pools like this. Too much risk, I guess."

"Right, that's what I'm thinking."

"So, on to the next one?"

He nodded. "In a minute."

"And in the meantime, what? Is there another feature in the house you'd like to see?"

"Sort of." He stood up, his movements leisurely, languid. "Come here. It's something I wanna show you."

I pushed off the doorframe, following him into the walk-in closet. The "hers" closet featured a boutique-quality full-length mirror, the three-panel kind so you could see yourself from every conceivable angle.

He stood in front of the mirror, glanced at me as I entered the closet. Gestured for me to come closer, to where he was standing.

My heart thumped.

Play it cool, Laurel.

"It's a mirror," I said. "You see these kinds of mirrors mainly in the kinds of stores that sell wedding dresses. It's so you can see—"

"I know what it's for," he murmured, cutting me off.

He was behind me, somehow. Towering over me. His hands slid down the curtain of my platinum blond hair, which hung loose over my shoulders. Not quite touching my hair, but close enough I could feel his touch, *almost*.

"Just wanted to see you in it."

"Titus…"

He ducked behind me, and I watched in the reflection as he pressed his nose to the side of my neck. "You smell so fuckin' good."

"Custom perfume," I whispered, "mainly jasmine and vanilla."

He straightened. Gathered my hair in his hand, pulling it through his fingers so it lay behind my shoulders, down my back. I was wearing a white, tight-fitting, knee-length dress, knee-high tan leather boots, a matching belt under my breasts, and a jean jacket with the sleeves pushed up to my elbows. Turquoise bangles on my wrists and a matching necklace.

He just stared at the reflection of me. "So fuckin' gorgeous, Laurel."

"We should go if we're going to see the next house."

He wrapped his arms around my middle, his hands

palming my stomach, his hips pressed against my back-side. "We have plenty of time."

I swallowed. I felt him, his hard body, the heat of him behind me…his erection a thick ridge.

"Titus."

"Laurel." He drew his fingertips lightly up my body, over the belt buckle, over the swell of my breasts and against the exposed dip of my cleavage, up my throat. To my chin. He pressed my chin up, and I was looking up at him, into his deep tawny eyes.

"Remember at the wedding, when I didn't kiss you?" he whispered, his voice a rough, dark buzz.

"Uh-huh." I was falling into his eyes, falling upward, somehow, drawn into the roiling heat of them, into the expressive wilds of them. I felt incoherent. Intoxicated.

"Not gonna miss this time. Just giving you fair warning."

"Okay."

And there it was, that mouth that could sing such beauty, that could growl and scream with such tortured anger, it was slicing across my lips, fusing to my mouth. His lips were firm, warm, strong. His kiss was slow, ex-ploratory. I tasted him, tasted coffee, and just *him*. He didn't relent, but continued to deepen the kiss, to slither his tongue into my mouth, to demand my desire.

And desire I had, in spades, to show him.

His body behind me was hard and taut, and his hand played at my waist, toyed with the buckle of my belt. His kiss created desire in me, his body elicited need out of me, brought it raging to life within me. Not that it was hard to do under even the worst of circumstances, and these were far from the worst of circumstances.

I felt his fingers move, and my belt dropped to the floor.

His tongue tasted my teeth and my tongue, and I was dizzy with his kiss, and then my jacket was falling to the floor at my feet. What drug was in his kiss? It had to be a drug, to so completely fluster me, to drown me, to eradicate my senses and my wits.

All I knew was Titus. His mouth on mine, his tongue against mine, his body blasting heat, his hands busy here, there, everywhere.

My dress was stretchy, molded to my body. Titus's hands stole over my curves, from hip up to waist, to bust, then back down. His kiss continued, a relentless onslaught, and I knew I'd never been kissed quite like this, and I wondered in the faint fuzzy back of my head if he kissed all his conquests like he was kissing me.

He caught at my shoulders. At the neckline. Pulled, stretched, and the material of my dress skimmed lower, and the white cups of my bra peeked out, and then my breasts, still contained in the bra, bounced out from under the tight prison of the fabric, and then the dress was stuck on my hips. Not for long. He now broke the kiss, only to press his lips to my neck, to my shoulder. He was so tall he had to bend to reach my shoulder, which put his hands at waist height. Let him tug the dress down further, past the bell of my hips. God, I was really going to let Titus Bright strip my dress off, right here in this client's home? In front of this three-way mirror?

Yes, yes I was.

His kiss was hot on my skin, and his fingers were busy and clever and I hadn't come at all in weeks, and I needed pleasure, and surely if he could like this, if he could distract me with his mouth and tease my clothes off so skillfully I barely noticed, he would make me feel good.

And fuck, I just wanted him. Even drunk on his kisses, I knew that much was undeniable. Just physically, I was hot for him. My thighs were clenched and my sex was drenched, and he was just getting started.

Oh god, oh god.

I wanted this.

Right here, like this. It would be so fucking hot.

It would get him out of my system. Get me over him.

I let him kiss my shoulder blades, let him peel the stretchy white dress down over my hips until it fell around my feet, leaving me clad in nothing but bra and panties.

White as well.

But more lace than silk, because I liked feeling sexy, and it was fun to put on hot underwear for no reason at all.

He broke away from kissing my back and shoulders,

stood upright. "You're a fucking goddess, Laurel. Look at you."

I managed a cocky smirk. "I saw myself in the mirror this morning when I got dressed."

He stood behind me, fingers at my spine. "Not like this, you didn't."

Pinched at my bra closure.

I arched away from his touch. "Ah-ah-ah." I met his eyes in the mirror. "You want that off?" I jutted my chin at his reflection. "Shirt off, bub. This is a two-way street."

He crossed his arms at his hips and peeled the shirt off. "Anything else? Or are we going tit for tat?"

I reached behind me and found the button of his shorts. "I can manage from there, I think." I freed the button, tugged down the zipper, and the loose shorts dropped around his feet; he kicked them aside.

He let me fumble at his thighs, his waist, until I found the ridge of his erection.

Holy.

Mother.

Of all.

Fucks.

Titus Bright was a legend in the rock and roll world. There were urban legends about his backstage antics— multiple groupies at one time, pointing at girls in the front row and bringing them backstage. Inviting whole groups on his tour bus. Urban legends as well about his sexual prowess, his size, his stamina. There were photos of him, but of sketchy provenance, and grainy to boot. In LA, you'd meet someone whose friend had slept with him, and *she* would claim that his cock was just absolutely monstrous, and wouldn't you know, he could fuck all night and never get tired.

It all seemed too ridiculous to be true. It had to be made up.

The moment I pressed my palm over his underwear-imprisoned member, I knew the stories of his size, if nothing else, were not only true, but possibly undersold the truth of him.

"Jesus," I whispered, grasping at him, angling my hands behind me, fingertips down and flat against his belly, scraping down his thighs to push his underwear off.

"Don't worry, darlin'. I'll take care of you." He slid a strap off my shoulder, kissing over the skin just behind the slide of the strap. "Real, *real* good care."

He chuckled. "Sweet thing, all you'll feel is good. Promise." He slid the other strap off, and then paused at the closure of my bra. "But first…I gotta get my hands on these babies."

He pinched, loosed, and flung the garment forward and off. My breasts swayed free, bare, and I felt his cock, now partially bared against my backside, throbbing. "Fucking hell, Laurel. I've seen a fuckin' shitload of tits in my life, but never…Jesus god, woman…I've never seen any as perfect as these." He gingerly, reverently cupped his hands under my heavy breasts. "Are they real?"

I laughed. "Do they feel real?"

He rolled a nipple in his fingers; I watched, biting my lip as the zing of pleasure buzzed through me at his touch. "You know what I mean."

"Yes," I whispered. "All natural. I've had plastic surgery, but not to those."

"Someday, we'll play a game where I guess what you had done. But not right now." He moved around in front of me, knelt. Gazed up at me. "Right now, I have other things in mind."

The three-way mirror reflected him from three angles, and all I could see was him worshipping at the altar of my sex. His hands braced my hips, and he let out a harsh breath. As if he was attempting to drag out the moment of exposing my sex, but couldn't hold out any longer.

His fingers hooked into the waistband of my underwear, which was every bit as sheer as my bra, so the white lace left very little to the imagination, revealing hints of my nether lips, teasing glimpses of the pink seam, the waxed plump lines pressing against the lace, which stuck damp to my skin, as desire seeped out of me.

I half expected him to rip the lace apart, and I'd have been pissed off if he had—this was one of my favorite sets, being that rare undergarment unicorn of comfortable *and* sexy.

Instead, he was gentle, almost delicate. Barely touching my skin as he slowly drew the lace down, stretching it over my hips and then dragging it down my thighs and to my feet. He cradled an ankle, lifted my foot, the other, and then plucked the panties away. I was naked, then, in a stranger's home, a client's home. Naked in front of a mirror that showed me from three angles, straight on and one side as well as the other.

Titus's hands glided up my calves, caressed behind my knees. His eyes were fixed on mine, staring up at me from between the mounds of my breasts which swayed with my breathing. He sat back on his heels and let his gaze rake over me, now that I was fully nude.

"Good and holy *goddamn*, Laurel," he breathed, and I couldn't possibly mistake the awe in his voice. "You are too fucking perfect to be real."

I laughed. "Liar. I appreciate the compliment, Titus, but I know for a fact you slept with Eliza Memphis, for one thing, and there's no way I'm prettier than her."

Eliza Memphis was one of the most sought-after women on the planet, who'd been featured in center-folds of every magazine there was, and who'd starred in several very famous adult films before transitioning to mainstream acting, albeit still largely in roles which required little or no clothing; her body was also famously all-natural, and commonly referred to as the gold standard of female sexuality.

Titus's eyes narrowed. "There's one thing I do not *ever* fucking do, and that's compare. Another thing I never

ever fucking do is talk about anyone else I may have spent time with. You just did both."

I frowned. "Um, sorry?"

His smile returned, hot and eager. "Just don't do it again or I might have to punish you."

I arched an eyebrow. "Not into that, sorry. Pretending that something I want you to do is a punishment is just stupid."

"Who said you'd enjoy it?"

"If it's something I won't enjoy, why would I allow it?"

"Because you want me." He stood up, naked, glorious, all hard muscle and masculine planes; he was not erect, but rather hung partially engorged, thick and long, but swaying and pointing downward. "You know I can make you feel good."

"But you want me as much as you claim I want you. You're going to deny yourself what you want…" I swiped a finger over my seam, ending at my clit, circling it once, gently, for his benefit, "this…just to punish me?"

He shrugged. "I have the discipline to do so, yes. I'd rather not, so maybe when I compliment you—and genuinely mean it, I should point out—just say thanks, and believe me, instead of playing coy bullshit games." He closed in to tower over me, staring down at me, an arrogant smirk on his lips. "So, Laurel McGillis. Let's try this again."

I stood confident in my skin, desire making me bold. "Okay. Go for it."

"Nope, you ruined my mojo." He crossed his arms over his chest. "I don't even remember what I was doing."

I laughed. "What's the matter, Titus? Drugs ruined your memory?"

He gave a derisive laugh. "Yeah, pretty much. I snorted away my short-term memory before I got sober. You're gonna have to nurse me along so I don't forget what I was doing."

After Tommy's death, he'd gotten sober and the only publicity he ever did was in support of sober living; his struggle had been with drugs, not alcohol, so he still drank, which caused a lot of talk in the various sobriety communities, but his point was that sobriety wasn't necessarily an all or nothing prospect, but rather was personal and specific. He'd never had trouble stopping the drinking, whereas he'd only been able to cut off his cocaine usage after finding Tommy dead. He was famously open about his struggle and had recently gone so far as to be featured on a comedy roast, where his sobriety had been open for cheap potshots, with him laughing as loudly and genuinely as anyone else, and giving as good as he got.

My point being, joking about it wasn't going to offend him.

"This is a weird hookup," I said. "Stopping to talk before we've even gotten started."

He shrugged. "Your own fault, babe. I'd be tongue

deep in that pussy by now if you hadn't said some dumb-ass shit."

"So you *do* remember what you were about to do," I said, smirking. "Caught you."

He shrugged. "Hard to remember what I forgot."

I laughed. "That makes no sense." I reached for him. "Well, if you're not going to get this show on the road, I will."

I'd sworn off rock stars, after the incident with Jamison Flare. But…this was *Titus Bright*. And so far, his reputation was proving to be well-earned. Understated, if anything. The things he'd said…the way he'd looked at me. Touched me…I was willing to see this little tryst through, if only for the chance at an orgasm or two on the tongue of a man I'd…errr…daydreamed about, more than once.

He just grinned, lifted his chin even as his eyes flicked down to watch my hand clasp around his cock. "Be my guest."

I turned him so I could watch us in profile in the straight-on mirror, so I could watch our reflection as I caressed his length. I felt him thicken in my hand, gently stroking him in slow, arrhythmic movements. I watched as he engorged in my hand, straightening to point away from his torso and then gradually lifting, tilting upward, upward, until he was standing vertical, straight against his belly, the tip of him just beneath his navel.

"There," I said, letting go of him. "Now you're ready to play."

He brushed a thumb over my lips. "See, I was kinda hoping for something a little more than that."

"Oh?" I couldn't help but touch him; it was just such a beautiful, perfect cock, such heavy taut balls, such soft skin sheathing iron hardness. "And what would that be?"

His thumb tugged my lower lip down, and I played along, let him press his thumb over my lower teeth, slowly and gently but deliberately prying my mouth open. "This sassy mouth. I want to see if it feels as sweet wrapped around my cock as it tastes when I kiss it."

"I see." I caressed his sac, playing with the heavy delicate skin and the globes within. "I might need some incentive to do that, though. I don't much care for the taste of penis, you see. It has to be worth my while."

"You haven't tasted mine," he said. "I think you'll like it." His thumb ran over my chin, and then his fingertips trailed down my breastbone, pausing to feather over my right nipple, tweaking it; I gasped involuntarily—I wasn't about to say so, but my nipples were highly, intensely sensitive and one of my most erogenous zones. "How about I give you a little preview of how I'll make it worth your while? Just so you know I'm…generous. That I'm devoted to making sure you have as much fun as I do, you might say."

I let go of his erection and caught at his shoulders.

Pulled down. "Enough talk. Get down there and put your mouth where your money is."

He laughed and let me push him to his knees in front of me once again. Instead of diving right in, though, he traced a finger over my seam. I trembled, wondering how he could know I liked to be built up to orgasm, that I responded to light, slow touches better than rough, fast ones. How could he know? He shouldn't. But he did.

He just slid that one finger down my seam, back up. Leaned in, pressed a slow hot breathing kiss to the keyhole at the top of my sex. His tongue flickered against me, there. Briefly, so lightly it was almost nothing at all. Then away, and his finger brushed down again, this time teasing in, just slightly, delving between the lips up to the first knuckle.

"So soft," he breathed. "So wet."

"You make me wet," I murmured, the words tumbling unbidden from me. "So fucking wet."

He slid that one finger in, gathering upward and withdrawing slicked in my essence. He licked it, eyes closing on a groan as he stuck his finger into his mouth and slurped it clean.

"Fuck the games," he growled, eyes wrenching open and fixing on me, suddenly fierce and wild. "If you taste like that, I'll eat you out until you beg me to stop."

I laughed breathlessly. "Never gonna happen, but go ahead and try, champ."

"Challenge accepted," he muttered. "Better find something to hold on to."

His tongue slithered against me, and I realized he was indeed done playing around. He'd been teasing me, testing me before. And now he was ready to devour me in earnest.

And holy fuck, did he devour me.

He was hungry for me, mad with it. Skilled, as well. He knew his way around my pleasure as if he'd been given blueprints to my orgasm. He gripped my hips and held me in place, slathering his tongue against me, and within a few swipes had me shaking, had me gasping.

Then, as I began to whimper from the ecstasy of his tongue against my clit, he wrapped a hand around my ass and pulled me against him, and his other hand dove up between my thighs and he pressed a finger into my opening, curled inside me, drew out. Then two fingers, up and in and curling. Withdrawing.

I gasped at the intrusion, and so he did it again.

Three fingers, then, and that was the most I could accept, and those three fingers curled in and pulled away, toward himself, against the upper inner wall of my sex. Stroked me there, slowly, as his mouth worked at my lips and my throbbing, thickening clitoris.

I had my hands in his hair, tangled in his tight curls, pulling him against me, shamelessly urging him on. I didn't have to beg him to keep going—I knew he wouldn't stop until I'd found my release.

He chased my orgasm relentlessly, as if it was his only purpose in life.

He got me there in record time, and I rose to the brink, hips flexing against his mouth and riding his stabbing, curling fingers.

"Oh *fuck*—Titus, god, yes!" I gasped, shrill and shaking.

He just continued his assault, three long thick strong clever fingers cleaving my sex open and massaging within me and slicing in and out in fast rhythm, his tongue circling me, head swiveling to add speed and force.

I came, spasming hard, crying out, hips rocking forward against his mouth, my whole body shaking, back arched and head thrown backward, a scream ripping out of me.

I expected him to stop, then.

To stand up and push me to my knees and take his reward.

I'd have gladly, willingly done so.

He slowed his movements until I relaxed the tense, taut flex of my hips and stood with tremulous knees in front of him, sagging, gasping. His mouth, his lips, his beard were smeared with me, and his grin was self-satisfied. I thought that was it.

But he'd taken my words as a challenge, and clearly Titus Bright didn't back down from a challenge.

He stared at me, watched me with that cocky grin on his face, and when I'd caught my breath, he began again. Slowly. Just his mouth. And when I began to rise up into nascent climax again, he added a finger, then two, then three…

I lost track of everything, after that.

How long he knelt between my thighs.

How many times he made me come.

Who I was.

Where I was.

All I knew was his mouth and his fingers, his tongue and his lips and his touch, skillfully, masterfully bringing me to climax and over the edge with screaming abandon, keeping me there until I couldn't breathe to even scream before letting me topple down the other side…only to start over again, each time with less of a chance to recover between. Until I was shaking helplessly, until my cries of orgasm became desperate weeping shattered sobs.

Until the thought of coming yet again nearly ached, nearly hurt.

And, indeed, I did beg him to stop, finally.

"Titus," I gasped, fingers knotted in his hair. "Stop, fuck, *stop,* I can't take anymore. I can't—I can't—I can't breathe. Fuck, Titus, fuck. Stop." I stared down at him, and my eyes were hazy, blurred—he'd made me come so hard, so many times I was literally crying helplessly. "You win, okay? Jesus, you…you fucking win."

He backed away—rolled to sit on his feet. I swayed, balance evaporated in the boiling heat of countless wrenching orgasms. He reached up, caught me. "Hold on to me," he murmured, guiding my hands to his head, his shoulders.

I held on.

I couldn't breathe, still, couldn't think, could barely manage to keep my legs under me. I watched with befuddled, mind-numbed confusion, in a drunken stupor, as he reached for his shorts and dug a hand in a pocket, came out with something.

He grabbed my hand and supported me as he stood up. Moved behind me.

I heard foil ripping.

Felt his hand moving, sheathing himself. Part of me knew what he was doing, but the rest of me was just... shattered into incoherence, into stupefied dizzy shaking wonder, numb with ecstasy, drunk on bliss, high on the wild sexual release of an intensity I hadn't known was even physically possible.

"Eyes open, Laurel," he commanded, his voice a rough buzzing in my ear. "Watch us."

My eyes flew open at his words, and I watched in one of the angled mirrors as he bent at the knees. I felt him at my entrance, felt his fingers finding my opening, felt him guide himself within me. Despite our height difference, we lined up perfectly. Somehow. Impossibly. The angles and alignments shouldn't work in our favor, but they did. He straightened, and filled me, and I was lifted up onto my toes and stretched apart with him and ached with him and had to fight for balance, had to reach back and cling to his neck as he surged upward.

I saw us, in the mirror. Saw his cock slide into me, watched it disappear inside me, watched his hips smash against my ass, flattening it. His hands clawed at my belly and scratched at my diaphragm, and then he was clutching my tits and squeezing, roughly, fiercely, a growl escaping his lips.

"Fuck, Laurel," he snarled. "So fucking tight. So wet."

"God, you're fucking huge," I gasped. "So fucking big."

He remained seated fully within me, not moving yet. "You good?"

I couldn't do anything but stare at us, straight-on mirror reflecting my tanned skin the color of sunlight and cream, my big heavy breasts clutched his hands, my pink nipples peeking between his fingers, my body tilted forward, thighs pressed together to create a tight V, our joining shadowed. The other mirrors showed us joined, showed him buried into me, hips to ass.

"So good," I whispered. "I'm good. It's good."

He withdrew slowly. "Not hurting you?"

I watched in one angled mirror as his cock slid out of me, glistening and thick and dark. "Fucking perfect," I growled, groaned. "Keep going."

He paused in the instant before he would have fallen out of me, and then drove in. "Laurel…"

"Titus?"

He groaned, and leaned forward against me. I had to step forward, bent forward and braced my palms against the mirror. "You're good? You can take it? Tell me you can take it."

I arched my spine and drove my ass backward. "I can take it, Titus. I want it."

He let out a rough groan of need. "You want it? You want *this*?" On the emphasized word, he plunged into me.

I screamed, so sensitive from the abundance of stimulation, the overwhelmed explosion of orgasms he'd given me turning me into a puddle of need. "Yes, yes, fucking *yes*," I groaned, whimpered, whispered, "that, please, all of that. More of that. Give it to me. Fuck me."

He pulled me upright, clutching at my breasts and dragging me roughly against him, his chest pasted to my back, his erection buried deep. I reached behind me and caught at his ass, and then he groaned. "You feel so good, Laurel. I don't want to stop. But I can't wait. I can't stop it. I have to…" He withdrew, slowly, and pushed in. "I have to."

"I want it," I breathed. "Need it."

I did. I was just speaking the truth. A million orgasms on his skilled tongue would never satisfy my need to come around him like this, to come with him inside me. That was what I needed. The orgasms on his tongue and fingers had only primed me for this, had only shown me my need for this, for him.

His knees bent, and he stood up, thrust in. I screamed.

He dipped again, and lifted up. Thrust in. I screamed again.

Each thrust split me apart, made me ache, made me clench around him and shake, made my sex quake for more. And each time, he gave me more. Slow, hard, and deliberate.

I felt it stealing over me, felt a climax smashing open inside me, but this one was *more*, and I needed him to complete it.

"Titus…" I clawed at his buttocks as he drove up into me. "I need to come again."

"So come," he snarled.

"I can't." I dipped to meet his upward thrust, sinking on him as he lifted, feeling him pierce deep. "You have to. You come, so I can."

He growled, and dipped again, and this time he began a rhythm. Fucked in, and now he didn't stop, didn't slow, wasn't deliberate or rough or anything but taking his need in me.

"Fucking hell, Laurel," he gasped, "what are you doing to me? Who the fuck are you? How can you feel this good?"

Harder, rougher. Holding me upright, preventing me from toppling forward with his big rough callused palms on my breasts, clutching and gripping and squeezing, pinching and rolling my nipples until I was breathless from the excessive stimulation, making me ache, making me shatter.

I touched myself.

I needed more.

He watched, and I watched—both of us watched as we moved together, as I touched myself to bring my orgasm to life, as he chased his own release inside me.

Harder, and harder.

God, the man's rhythm was perfect. With each thrust, I swear he got bigger, fit more tightly within me. Each thrust touched me perfectly, set off another series of dynamite explosions, made me quake and ache with exploding need, with drowning bliss, and it was all him, all Titus.

There'd never been anything like this.

Fuck, it was so good.

He was so good.

So fucking good.

Too good. But I'd worry about that later.

First, I wanted his orgasm. I wanted to feel him come, feel him let go.

He was driving up into me, now, hard and fast, pounding with rough crazed primal thrusts, taking me with every ounce of animal dominance. Harder, harder, and with each slapping union, I screamed and cried and begged for more, sank down and pushed back against him, urging him to take all of me, to take more of me.

And he did.

Again, and again, until the clap of joining bodies was loud between us, but not louder than his grunting utterances of my name, and mine of his.

I knew, in the back of my head, that this was crazy. Sex this epic shouldn't exist.

Yet it was happening, and to me, and with him, and this man behind me was bringing me to *another* orgasm, or the same one extended, and now finally he began to shake, began to gasp and rasp hoarse, began to slam his thrusts with shaky force rather than timed, rhythmed purpose.

And then, finally, fucking finally, I felt him give in, felt him let go.

"FUCK!" he roared. "Fuck...*Laurel*..."

He came, and he came, and his groans were mad, soft, wild, primal. He clutched at my breast with one hand and my throat with the other, gently holding my throat and tilting my head up and as he came apart behind me, inside me, he kissed me, as if to seal in the fraught insanity of this with intimacy I knew neither of us was okay with.

I kissed him back even though the aching beauty of this moment was breaking something vital inside me, even though the kiss terrified me. I kissed him through it because I couldn't do anything except kiss him.

He kissed me as he came, and he was as broken and breathless as I was, even though he trembled all around me with something more than the vigor and tremble of release. He shook with the intensity of us.

He throbbed within me and slammed deep one last time, and I felt him pulse, push deeper, or try to, since there was no deeper for him to go. Gripping my hips, now, he bent me away and I leaned forward for him and braced my palms against the cold mirror glass and his fingers dug hard into the flesh of my hips and ass and he drove into me with utter abandon, roughly jerking me backward into his ragged, slamming, fucking thrusts.

At long, long last, he ceased coming, and pulled away from me.

I ached with the absence of him.

My breasts bore the dark bruises of his fingerprints, as did my hips.

He stood behind me, chest rising and falling heavily. His tawny lion eyes drilled into mine, in the reflection. My nude reflection was that of a sex-sated nymph, sweat shining on my forehead and upper lip, dotting droplets dripping down my breasts, which lifted and swayed with my gasps.

His hair was tangled and messy. Mine was no better. Silence.

What to say, then?

"You're a fucking goddess," he muttered.

And then he turned and walked away, and a moment later I heard the bathroom door close.

CHAPTER FOUR

I SPENT A GOOD MINUTE OR SO GATHERING MYSELF, SCRAPING together what remained of my wits. I had to turn away from my reflection as I gathered my clothing off the floor, because to see myself naked in that mirror again would be to see him behind me, to feel that whole episode all over again, and that just simply wouldn't do.

I stepped into my panties, fastened my bra at my belly and spun it around to enclose my breasts within the lacy cups, shrugged the straps on, adjusted the sit of them, and donned the rest of my clothing in record time. By the time I heard the master bathroom door open, I had my purse hanging from my elbow, my now hopelessly tangled hair bound back in a tight bun, and my sunglasses on.

There were handprints on the mirror, but there was nothing I could do about that now.

I headed downstairs, ignoring the twinge between

my thighs. Gathered the folder with the disclosures and marketing material I'd deposited there on the way in.

I heard Titus on the stairs, and endeavored to feel, or at least appear, cool as a cucumber, calm and collected and unaffected—when I felt precisely the opposite.

He had his hat on forward this time, aviators hiding his eyes.

"So." I sounded normal. Yay me. "I have two more properties you requested to see. Based on what you told me earlier, I think one of them would suit Jeremy's family best—it has a pool, but it's fenced and gated in a big backyard, at the end of a nice quiet cul-de-sac."

He nodded. "Sounds good."

"Okay then." I gestured at the door. "I just need to lock up, and then you can follow me."

We were both old hands at this game, pretending everything was totally normal when we'd obviously just fucked each other senseless. No talking about it, no referencing. It wouldn't happen again. It was a quick fuck and a good one, nothing more and nothing less.

He preceded me out of the house, and I locked it and returned the key to the box. Titus was in his truck, the big old engine rattling and rumbling. He was watching me, though. I could feel his gaze on me even though his eyes and thus his expression were hidden behind the mirrored lenses.

I climbed into my car, started it, backed out, and headed for the next property. On the way, I called Teddy, earbuds so I could talk hands-free; she'd texted the group earlier in the day that she would be in the office for a few hours if anyone needed anything; she was the closest we had to an office assistant, mainly because she was always so willing to do that kind of work, even though she was a fully licensed realtor who sold just as much as any of us.

"Hiya, pal," she said, by way of greeting. "How was the showing?"

What to say, what to say?

"Um." I sighed. I couldn't lie to Teddy, for some reason. I could avoid the truth, though. "Unexpected."

I heard the grin in her voice. "It was *him!*"

"You knew?"

She laughed, then. "No, but you just confirmed it. What happened?"

"Goddammit, Teddy," I laugh-groaned. "Are you psychic or something?"

"No, just highly intuitive. And you sound…weird. Off. Which meant something happened."

"He fucked the absolute shit out of me. I'm going to be walking funny for a week."

She broke into hysterical laughter. "I need details!"

I was, unaccountably, annoyed at her exuberance. "The details are, I need a cleaning crew to go over that house again. Specifically, there are…um…handprints on the mirror in the master bedroom closet."

She was conspicuously silent. "Laurel McGillis."

"Theodora Pike?"

"Up against a mirror?"

"I'm still shook, Ted," I said. "*Shook*, I tell you."

"That's a good thing, right?"

"I mean, sure. But that's it, I got to fuck *the* Titus Bright, and it was every bit as good as the stories would have you believe, and that's that. Over, done, buh-bye. He's out of my system."

Teddy just laughed. "Okay, Laurel. Whatever you say."

"You don't believe me?"

"I believe you think so, but my matchmaker intuition says that's not it for you and *the* Titus Bright. You can pretend all you want, and I'm not gonna say another word about it after this, unless you come to me. But mark my words, Laur, you haven't seen the last of him."

"Well, I'm about to show him the McCormick property, so yeah."

"Not what I mean, and you know it."

"I'm not fucking him again. Once was it."

"Okay."

"Stop being so agreeable!"

She just laughed. "Does epic sex always make you this cranky?"

"No," I snapped. "I don't know why I'm angry."

"Because you're denying your true feelings."

"No, because it shouldn't be possible to come *that* hard, *that* many times and still function as a human. And no man should be *that* beautiful, *that* talented, *and* have a dick that fucking perfect. *And*—" my voice was shrill, by this point, "*AND* be so good at sex I literally forgot my own name for a moment when it was over. It shouldn't be possible for one man to have all that. And it makes me angry."

Teddy's laughter drowned out my voice at that point. "Oh, darling. You are *so* screwed."

"Shut up."

"Is it just the mirror that needs cleaning? Or do we need a full detailing?"

"Just the mirror. And maybe make sure there's no other evidence. I sort of left in a hurry. I don't think there's anything, but hell, I'm still trying to get my shit together."

"That good?"

"Have you ever forgotten who you were afterward, Teddy?"

"No," she sighed. "But I dream of sex that good."

"It's not good. It's scary." I checked traffic as I made a left turn through a green light, and then continued. "It reminds me of that time I smoked what I thought was a normal joint. It turned out to be laced with heroin and it was the worst trip of my life because it was scary fucking intense. After that, I never touched drugs again because that shit scared me so bad. This, Theodora, what Titus Bright just did to me, is like that."

She was quiet then, no longer laughing. "Except he isn't hard drugs that can kill you."

"Wrong," I whispered. "He is exactly hard drugs. And I'm staying the hell away from him, after today."

"Ohhhh, Laurel," Teddy sighed. "What are we going to do with you?"

"Exactly what you said you'd do—not bring this up again."

"Fine, consider me mum on the subject."

A pause.

"There were no feelings, Teddy."

"I didn't say there were."

"I could hear you *not* saying it."

"You don't have to convince *me*, Laurel." She sighed another tinkling laugh. "I'll get someone over there."

"Thanks, Teddy."

"No problem. I have a showing in a bit, so if you need anything else from the office, tell me now, because I have a date after the showing."

"Oh you do, do you?"

She just huffed. "Tinder. My hopes are very firmly not up. If nothing else, it's something to do on a Saturday evening besides sit at home alone eating Ben and Jerry's and watching nature documentaries."

"Well, if your date goes bust, call me. We can add wine and call it a party."

"Sure, sure."

"I'm serious. I'll hang out with you. Ice cream, wine, and nature documentaries sound like a good time to me."

"Okay, I might just take you up on that. Assuming my date goes bust."

"So should I hope you don't call me? Because that would mean instead of your date going bust, your date busted…a nut, inside you."

Teddy screeched in shock, and then burst into cackles. "Ohmyfucking*god*, Laurel McGillis! Are you a grown woman or a teenage boy? God, that's gross."

"Just keeping it real, Theodora Pike."

"There will be no nut-busting."

"Then what's the point of Tinder dates?"

"I haven't gotten that far with anyone on the first date in years," she said, her tone breezy. "It takes a hell of a lot to get me that far out of my own head. Tinder dates, for me, are for actually finding someone I *like*. So I can have a *relationship*."

"God, you're weird," I said, but I laughed as I said it.

"Yeah, *I'm* the weird one of the group." A pause. "Oh, hang on, Lizzy is on the other line. Let me let you go. I'll get the cleaners to that house this afternoon."

"Bye, Ted," I sing-songed.

"Bye, Laur!"

I left the earbuds in, in case another call came in; the rest of the drive to the next house was occupied by my own internal attempts to corral the voice inside my head that was telling me something extraordinarily unusual had happened.

❧

"Six bedrooms, seven and a half bathrooms," I said, leading Titus through the upper floor hallway. "Lots of natural light, open plan kitchen, dining room, and den, plus a formal room and another den downstairs in the full walkout basement. Fenced-in pool, as I said. Big butler's pantry, huge closets in every room, every bedroom is en suite, plus a full bathroom in the basement and a half bath off the kitchen. Newer construction, top-of-the-line appliances, of course."

Titus was quiet, peeking into every room, every bathroom. Eying the ceilings, the crown molding, the thick carpet upstairs, the hardwoods downstairs and the marble floor in the kitchen. He was nodding here and there, but wasn't saying much.

I refused to break first, so I carried on like this was any old showing with just another client. "I know the sellers are motivated to get some movement. Their price is a little high, which is why it's been for sale for over a hundred days, at this point. Come in with a cash offer, I think you could get this for twenty percent under asking."

We were back in the kitchen by now, on opposite sides of the island, which was a mint green in contrast with the white cabinets.

Titus nodded. Glanced out the backyard, his aviators still in place, hat brim pulled low, what I could see of his expression inscrutable. "It's good. Jeremy and Bex will love this."

"Okay, then." I smiled, a fake, bright, professional smile. "I'll get the paperwork drawn up and we can put in an offer. You want to come in at…" I prompted, waiting. He didn't bite, so I finished it with my personal recommendation. "Two-point-zero-eight?"

He plucked at his beard along his chin. "Nah." He reached into his back pocket. "What are they asking? Two-six-four?"

I nodded. "Yeah, two-six-four, five hundred."

He had a checkbook in his hands, and a pen. He filled in the amount line and box and signed it. Tore it off, and set it on the counter where I could see it. "Make it out to whoever the hell it gets made out to. Send over whatever I have to sign to Alaina, just get me keys by the end of next week."

"Titus, that's not—"

He grinned. "Throw money at the problem, and it goes away. They've been renting a place and their lease is up next week. I don't want them to have to sign another lease, and they're too fuckin' cheap to buy a place like this. They're savers, you know? Cash-only life. Which is great. But they need a good home, and I like doing shit like this. It makes me happy to see people I like happy. So." He slid the check to me. "Full asking, in cash. If getting the deal done means greasing some palms or whatever, fine. Tell me how much and to who."

"It takes weeks to close, Titus. There's waiting periods. Inspections."

"The fuck I need an inspection for? Is the house sound?"

"Well, yes, of course, but—"

"I got the cash. No bank involved. None of the fancy mumbo jumbo bullshit." He tapped the check. "It's a purchase. I pay money, I get the house. The only complication is I want it in their name."

He rounded the island, moving with pantherish grace and rock star swagger. Breezed up to me, up against me. Lips nuzzled my cheek, briefly, ghostly. "Make it happen, Laurel."

And then he was gone. Just like that.

Motherfucker.

CHAPTER FIVE

I RESISTED THE URGE, BARELY, TO CHUCK MY PHONE AGAINST the wall. It was Wednesday, and I was still working on making Titus's absurd demand happen. The existence of a check for $2,640,500 definitely helped, but the real estate apparatus did not like being hurried, even by that much cash. He'd signed the inspection waiver, but the bank which held the seller's mortgage was being obstinate about dotting i's and crossing t's. But, I think just I'd managed to brazenly bully and intimidate the banker-nerd-in-chief into understanding that my client was determined to own this home as quickly as possible, and then sign it immediately over to someone else as a tax-free gift. It was complicated. It was hard. It required a lot of talking, wheedling, and convincing, and I'd had half a dozen showings in the meantime, and another closing meeting with clients and underwriters.

An hour after clinching that phone call, I had confirmation that the deal could go through as Titus had requested. I just needed him to meet me for some in-person signatures. Only…I didn't have his number.

So, I called Alaina.

"Hello, Ms. McGillis," she said, her voice smooth and cultured. "Do you have good news for me?"

"I do. It's all set. I have a big stack of paperwork for Titus to sign. I just need to talk him through a few things."

"He's out of town."

"He's the one who wanted this done by the end of the week," I said, exasperated. "Can I have his phone number?"

"Mr. Bright doesn't own a phone."

I coughed in surprise. "He doesn't? Not at all? Not even, like, a secret one only you have the number to?"

"Nope." A laugh. "He's in Chicago for a pop-up—he should be back Friday. Send me the details, and I'll make sure he's there."

"He really doesn't own a cell phone?"

"He really doesn't."

"Not at all?"

Alaina laughed. "It's an alien concept, it seems like, isn't it? But really really—Titus Bright does not have a personal phone and never has."

"Wow. Strange." I sighed. "Well, okay. The deal is ready to go as soon as he's available to sign this dictionary-sized pile of papers."

"Like I said, that should be Friday. Could be sooner,

could be after. You just never know. He's not exactly a predictable person."

"Wait…you said he's doing a pop-up in Chicago? What's that mean?"

"Oh, well, it's how Titus operates. He doesn't do stadiums or any of the usual venues. You don't book Titus. You don't buy tickets. He plans these impromptu shows, what he calls pop-ups, or flash concerts. He just shows up with his gear, picks a spot, sets up, plays a set, and leaves. He has Jeremy post it on Titus's social media—which, I should add, Titus doesn't even have access to, nor ever sees, he just leaves it in Jeremy's hands. So, an hour before the pop-up, Jeremy posts the details, and bam, impromptu concert. He has shirts printed with the date and location and a custom graphic, all done by Jeremy. There's QR codes handed out at the pop-up itself, which lets the audience access the livestream of the show, which becomes a downloadable, shareable video file once the livestream is over."

"And he doesn't charge for this?"

"Not a penny. It's all free."

"So how does he make money?"

Alaina laughed. "I mean, the details are private, for which you'd have to ask him yourself, but he owns the masters for Bright Bones's entire library, all the rights, everything, and he has his own label, so distribution and all that is him—well, Jeremy."

"I'm beginning to see why Titus is buying Jeremy a two-point-six-million-dollar house."

"Exactly. There's also the fact that on top of the pop-up tours he does, Titus records as Bright Star and publishes that work for sale, and he's selling very, very well."

"So does he get his various featured artist friends at these pop-ups?"

"Oh, sure. All the time. This show in Chicago is one of those. Kanye and...god, I forget her name. An R-and-B bassist, a woman. Tiger something? Something Tiger? I don't know. He was very excited about it. I don't handle those details, though, that's Jeremy. I handle Titus's personal affairs."

"I see. Sounds like Titus is very progressive."

She laughed. "Well, it is, but it's also that the whole touring and playing stadiums business reminds him of Tommy, and that's just too hard. Those two were like brothers, closer than brothers, and Titus is still very broken up from his passing." She huffed. "Why on *earth* am I telling *you* all this? I shouldn't have said any of that."

I wondered myself. "It's okay, Alaina. I won't repeat any of it to a soul. I won't even tell him you told me."

"Thank you for covering my indiscretion." She laughed. "I can't for the life of me figure out what possessed me to say those things—I'm normally much more tight-lipped about Titus's affairs. It's my job, after all. You just seem...I don't know—"

"Call it realtor-client privilege," I cut in, "I'd never discuss a client's affairs with anyone. We're good."

Friday, 8:55a.m.: the meeting to sign all the closing documents was scheduled for nine. I hadn't heard a word from Alaina or Titus. I was sitting in my car, sipping a triple venti caramel macchiato, munching on a chocolate biscotti that was the entirety of my breakfast. Which possibly, maybe, potentially, *could* be a contributing factor in my ever-increasing trend toward bottom heaviness. I mean, I know I should switch to, like, almond milk or some shit, and cut the caramel, and have real food for breakfast instead of what is, essentially, a dessert. But who has time for that? And besides, big asses are in, right? Can I get an amen? Because mine is going to have its own area code, soon.

I finished the biscotti, checked my makeup and adjusted a few strands of hair, and then said fuck it and added a layer of deep, violently red lipstick of a shade which I personally referred to as "Lady of the Night Scarlet," and while I knew in the pit of my stomach why—by which I mean *who*—I was putting the extra red lipstick on for, I refused to let the forefront of my mind know.

I was keeping secrets from myself, and we were fine with that.

Tilting the rearview mirror down, I checked my

cleavage: bangin'. Most supportive pushup Wonderbra, lifting and separating and displaying my all-natural 32DDDs to maximum effect, within the confines of a custom-made white button-down—an expensive as hell shirt but worth it so I could wear a button-down without the dreaded boob gap, which was otherwise impossible for someone as busty as me. The rest of my ensemble had been—if I was being honest with myself, which I was assuredly not—chosen with equal care to emphasize my curves: a pleated, crimson leather mini skirt, and my tallest black Louboutin stilettos, because even though I frequently bemoaned the expansion of my derriere, it *did* look pretty damn hot with the lift-and-tighten effect of four-inch heels and a killer skirt.

Hair done in loose spirals, makeup on point. Nails freshly French manicured. Rocking my favorite purse, my vintage black crocodile Birkin.

#Winning.

It was all in the name of looking my best professionally, of course.

It had nothing to do with anyone else.

Nope, nope, nope.

8:58. Time to go in. No one else in the lot except the ladies who worked here and me. Whom, shit, I hadn't forewarned that they were about to host a document signing with one of the most famous and infamous humans on the planet. Have to do that before he gets here.

Notably absent, a particular classic truck—I'd done

some research and discovered his truck was a 1948 Dodge Power Wagon. Sexy as hell, is what it was. I wanted a ride in it.

I wanted to drive it.

I wanted to be drilled senseless in the bed, under the stars, somewhere up in the Sierras.

Oops, I forgot, I wasn't allowed to think those things. I'd gotten my ride on the Titus-mobile, and there was one ride per customer. Done, done, on to the next one, done, done—as Dave Grohl once sang.

Inside, I greeted Linda, the receptionist, and then called a brief meeting of the rest of the girls in the office, preparing them for the man they were about to meet, and insisting they keep their heads and not ask for autographs or photos.

Moments after finishing the talk with them, I heard the distinct growl of an old straight-six engine, and saw the massive red pickup park beside my car. The driver's side door swung open, and a remarkably shitty black flip-flop extended to the ground, followed by the rest of Titus.

Fuck, he was gorgeous.

Today's don't-give-a-fuck rock star outfit: real, actual, unironically worn, baggy-as-hell black cargo shorts held up by a chrome-spike studded belt, a black, ribbed, wife-beater style tank top, a black slouchy beanie pushed back on his head to reveal a few inches of hairline with the rest of his hair tucked up into the hat, and of course his mirrored aviators. Lip ring glinting in the sun, a different set of beaded earrings running up the shell of his ear, heavy silver rings on his fingers, spike-studded black cuff on his left wrist and a heavy silver watch hanging loose around his right wrist.

Effortless perfection, rough, hard, ripped, and glorious with cheekbones you could cut glass with. The god of all rock stars.

Sigh.

Once was enough, and holy hell that once was epic. But it was over, done with, not to be repeated.

I heard several sighs behind me. I turned, noted the drooling expressions on the faces of every woman in the entire office.

I let out a sharp breath. "Okay, ladies. Let's wipe the drool away and be professionals."

There were laughs, but everyone straightened their backs, lifted their chins. I also knew I wasn't the only one who may or may not have adjusted my top in the wrong direction—to be *lower*, rather than higher.

The passenger door opened, and another figure descended—tall but shorter than Titus, black, with a shaved head, neatly trimmed goatee, and thick-framed black glasses, wearing a tie-less suit with a casual air that said he wore a suit every day, maybe even on Saturday.

Must be Jeremy Mullins, the recipient of the house Titus was about to buy.

They entered together, Titus holding the door for

Jeremy. Titus spotted me immediately and beelined for me.

A dozen questions fluttered through me all at once: did we hug? Kiss? Shake hands? Pretend we didn't know each other? Was I capable of looking him in the eyes without having to resist the urge to shove my hand down his pants and see what popped up? Could I do this signing without every other thought in my being a sharp, vivid memory of the things he'd done to me in front of that mirror?

Titus answered most of the questions for me, by virtue of sidling up to me, leaving an inch or two of space between us even as he leaned against me with one arm casually circling my waist, drawing me in for a casually familiar side hug. His lips brushed my cheek.

"Jeremy thinks he's here to look over contracts for me," he whispered into my ear. "Don't spoil the surprise." Louder, then, as he let go and stood away from me. "You look fine as hell this morning, Laurel."

"Thank you, Mr. Bright," I said, keeping my smile professional, meaning overly wide and totally fake. "You look…casual."

"Was I supposed to dress up?" he asked, snorting a laugh. "I've been trying to get this nerd here to wear jeans to work for years, but his ridiculous ass insists on dressing like a *professional*, whatever the fuck that means."

Jeremy didn't laugh, but remained impassive. His arms stretched the sleeves of his suit, and his chest stretched his shirt—he looked as much bodyguard as assistant. "If you want to be taken seriously, you have to dress the part," he said, in a voice the bottom of a well, his tone educated, proper, and articulate.

Titus shrugged. "People take me plenty seriously, and I dress like someone let an angry fifteen-year-old girl loose in Hot Topic."

I snorted at that, because it was true.

Jeremy just rolled his eyes humorlessly at Titus—I caught a hint of amusement in his expression though; I got the feeling he enjoyed playing the part of the strait-laced businessman to Titus's uninhibited rock star libertine. "They take you seriously because every single and every album you've ever released has gone platinum."

Titus shrugged. "Maybe, whatever. Suit yourself, bro." He rolled a hand. "Let's get this shitshow on the road, shall we? Show me what I got to sign."

I led the way into the conference room and showed Titus the stack of papers at the head of the table. He slumped into the rolling chair and picked up the pen, twirling it between his fingers.

He glanced up at me. "All this? For a fuckin' house? I'm not even taking out a mortgage. What the hell do I have to sign all this for?"

I sat in the chair kitty-corner to his. "There are waivers, disclosures, agreements, insurance. All sorts of stuff—I'll explain everything as you sign." I frowned at him. "You act like you've never bought a house before."

He laughed. "Because I haven't."

I stared. "You've never bought a house?"

"Nope."

"Condo, townhouse, nothing?"

"No, ma'am. I have never owned a property of any kind in my life."

I boggled at him. "You're worth, like, three hundred million. You've *never* owned a home?"

"Eight hundred, actually," Jeremy said. "His net worth doubled when his former label went under and he got his masters back."

Titus clicked the pen a couple times. "Which was all you. They were cheating me, and had been for years. You figured it out, went public with it, and they went under. *And* you negotiated the masters instead of a cash settlement."

"It's my job," Jeremy said. "Anyway. Show me the paperwork before you sign it." He eyed me. "No offense meant to you, of course, but it's my job as his lawyer to check everything he signs."

"I thought you were his manager?" I said.

Titus grinned. "He wears a lot of hats. Yale law degree, Harvard business degree, plus the street smarts of a guy who grew up in the hood."

Jeremy just shook his head. "It's more that you're too trusting."

"If someone's gonna try and cheat me or take advantage of me, they probably need it more than I do. I'm

not worried about it. I just like to make you feel useful."
Titus examined the first page, reading slowly. "Maybe it's
me being dyslexic, but this shit is mumbo jumbo to me.
Jeremy, paraphrase."

I tapped the page with my own pen. "Allow me. This
is a document stating you're accepting the house as-is,
meaning if there's any future issues, you can't try and
sue the former owners."

After that, it was a relatively quick and painless
process, as I explained each document to Titus, Jeremy
examined it, and Titus signed.

I still had a few pages left, the portion of the process
which signed ownership over to Jeremy. He may have
claimed otherwise, but when Titus flipped through the
remaining pages, he clearly knew what he was looking at.

He eyed me. "Yo, I'm getting bored, here. Can we
finish this at the house? I wanna see it. Jeremy, this place
is killer, you're gonna love it."

Smooth, Titus, very smooth.

Jeremy shrugged. "You're my ride, so I'll go wherever you're going." A grin. "But I admit I'm curious as
to what kind of a house could entice you to finally buy
it. I thought you'd die in that trailer of yours."

I frowned. "Trailer?"

Jeremy laughed. "Don't let the term 'trailer' mislead
you. It's a full-size semi. The tractor part of it has a full
set of living quarters for the driver. The actual trailer
part is twice as high as a normal semi box, and includes

a gym, a sauna, a bathroom bigger than the one I've got, a bedroom, obviously, a full recording studio, and a parking spot for his truck. It's his full-time residence. Until now, that is."

"Oh sure, asshole, just give away *all* my secrets," Titus joked. "Anyway. Laurel, pack up the rest of those papers and meet us there with the keys. Yeah?"

I nodded, gathering them up, marking the page we left off on with a yellow sticky note, and sliding them into a folder. "Sure thing. I'll head over and unlock everything."

Titus grinned at me. "You're the best, Laurel. Thanks for putting this together so fast."

Jeremy shook his head. "Still not sure what the rush was."

Titus ignored that. Checked his watch. "What are Bex and the kids up to, Jer?"

Jeremy shrugged. "At home, probably. Breakfast, cleaning their rooms, watching TV. Why?"

"Well, the house has a pool. I thought maybe the kids would like to go for an inaugural swim."

Jeremy made a face. "Huh. I mean, shit, sure they would. But brother, you gotta know once those kids get into that pool, you won't ever get them out. I mean, ever. And I won't ever hear the end of it." His voice took on a fake, high-pitched whining tone. "'Daddy, can we go to Uncle Titus's? I wanna swim.'" An eye roll. "They're monsters, man. Half fish, I swear to god. Just so you're aware what you're opening yourself up to."

Titus just grinned. "They're always welcome at Uncle Titus's." He made a shooing motion at Jeremy. "Get your wife on the phone, man. Have her meet us there."

I suppressed my laughter. He was so devious. Not a hint of anything other than friendliness. Jeremy slid his phone from an inside pocket of his suit coat, dialed a number, and walked over to the far side of the conference room, had a brief, murmured conversation. I shot a quick grin at Titus, who just winked at me.

Jeremy returned to the table, shoving his phone into his suit coat again. "Well, they're getting their suits on and heading over. I hope you know what you're doing, man."

Titus clapped his hands onto his thighs and stood up. "Let's go, then."

I glanced at Linda on the way out. "I guess I'll bring the paperwork back over later."

She just grinned dazedly at Titus as he swaggered out. "Okay."

I snapped my fingers at her. "Pull your tongue in, Linda."

She shook her head. "Sorry, what? I was daydreaming."

I laughed. "Trust me, I get it. I said, he wants to

finish signing at the house, so I'll bring the papers back over after."

"Oh, sure." She gave one last longing look after Titus as he climbed up into his truck. "I was just telling my husband the other day that Titus is the only celebrity on my hall pass list. I love my husband, but if Titus Bright propositioned me, I'm not sure I could say no."

I just laughed. "You would say no. You love Bert too much."

She shook her head. "I don't know. Titus Bright is Titus Bright. And there's no one like Titus Bright."

Honey, you have no fucking clue, I didn't say. She just might kill me out of pure jealousy if I told her I'd had sex with the man she was jokingly half in lust with. I waved goodbye at her as I headed for my car.

Not long later, we were pulling into the driveway, Titus's big truck first, my little Aston Martin second, and a white Chrysler Pacifica a minute or two later. Titus climbed out, gesturing at my car. "Sweet little ride. I wouldn't have pegged you for a classic's kind of girl. I pictured you driving, like, a pink jeep like Barbie or some shit. A Range Rover, at the very least."

I rolled my eyes. "I loathe pink. I may look like Barbie, but I'm not." I closed my door and headed for the front door. "I actually used to drive a Range Rover. It was big and black and powerful. I hated parking it, hated driving it, never used the back seat, rarely used the cargo space, and paid way too much for it. So I sold it and bought this."

"Hot girl, hot car." Titus's eyes raked over me—even hidden behind his sunglasses, I could feel his eyes on my body.

"Quit harassing the realtor," Jeremy said.

"I'm not harassing," Titus retorted. "I'm complimenting."

At that moment, the doors of the minivan all opened at once, and children spilled out, yelling, laughing excitedly, chattering in overlapping cacophony, followed by a short, curvy, beautiful, and very pregnant Hispanic woman, who was scolding the kids in a fast and complicated mixture of Spanish and English, snapping orders and corralling them with remarkable efficiency. There were only four kids, but the noise level and energy level made it feel like there was double that number.

Three girls, one boy. The boy was oldest, looked to be nine or so, with the girls at around seven, five, and three. Jeremy headed over and scooped up the youngest, and in the process transformed from serious businessman to an adoring, affectionate father.

"Hey, Monkey!" he said, kissing the girl until she squealed and batted at him.

"Too many kisses, Daddy!" She grabbed his face in both hands and did her dead level best to stop him. "We goin' swimmin', Daddy!"

"I know," Jeremy answered, setting her down and

pointing at Titus, who was watching with a curiously, carefully blank expression. "We're gonna say thanks to Uncle Titus, right?"

Titus unfroze, a smile blooming on his face as he knelt to get face-to-face with the youngest girl. "Well, you can't very well say thanks when you haven't even seen the pool yet, right? Come on, ya'll. Laurel, you got the keys?"

"Sure do!" I was suddenly the focus of several pairs of eyes. "Who wants to go swimming?"

The middle girl, five or six at my best guess, came up to me. "Are you a princess?"

I snorted. "Would it make me cooler if I said yes?"

"Not if it isn't true," she answered, not a hint of humor on her face.

"Well, I wouldn't lie to you, so…no. But, I did go to school with an actual princess. Her name is so long I can't even pronounce half of it."

"You knew a real live princess?" This was the oldest girl—the boy, who my estimate was revising upward to be more like eleven or twelve, just watched without expression. "That is so cool! What was she like?"

I smirked. "The truth is, she was kinda snooty. But her sister, the duchess, was pretty cool. She and I used to steal…uh, I mean, *buy*—candy together after school."

My slip had been caught; the middle girl frowned at me. "You *stole* candy?"

I sighed. "I did. And it was very wrong of me. But

the part that's so funny about it is the duchess's family had so much money they could have bought the whole town the store was in. And here's their youngest daughter stealing two buck's worth of candy." I led the procession up to the porch, and the front door. "Enough about me. I need to know your names."

Jeremy's wife was ambling up the stairs, carrying a giant bag full of pool toys. "My boy here, his name is Emmanuel. If you can get him to say two words together, he'd say to call him Manny." She pointed at each of the girls in turn. "Kenzie is next, and miss honesty here is Luisa, and my little princess is Violet." She huffed, wiping at her forehead. "I'm Bex."

"Laurel McGillis. Nice to meet you, Bex, Emmanuel, Kenzie, Luisa, and Violet." I pushed the door open and held the storm door, gesturing inside. "After you. Take a look around."

Titus was last through the door, pausing beside me. "You ready for this? Jeremy's gonna shit himself, and I'm guessing Bex is gonna cry like a baby." He was eager, excited—vibrating with energy.

"You're really having fun, aren't you?"

He nodded. "Yup. Giving people crazy gifts is my favorite thing." He winked at me. "Besides the obvious, that is."

"Really? I mean about the gifts, not the obvious."

He shrugged. "Sure. It's my own personal therapy. My dad was a real dick to me, all growing up. Like, he'd alternate between kicking my ribs in and acting like I wasn't there. A few years ago, I bought him a condo down in Mexico for him to live in full time. Bonus for me is, now he's thousands of miles away from me. My mom wasn't much better, so I bought the entire business franchise she worked for and gave it to her. My brother? Same deal. He used to beat me up and give me wedgies and all that shit, make fun of me for being into playing guitar and violin and shit, so when his life took a shit, I paid for his divorce, settled his legal bills, and sent him to the Bahamas for a month." He waved a hand as we moved into the kitchen and watched Bex overseeing the kids as they fought over who got the unicorn float and who had to settle for the donut one, while Jeremy was tasked with blowing them up the old-fashioned way. Titus was still grinning. "Best one was my old producer. He was the mastermind behind the whole scam to cheat me out of millions of dollars. He'd made sure he pocketed it all. Well, when the whole fiasco came to light, he lost everything. His wife left him, he had to pay me back in full, I got the masters back, his whole label went under, he was fuckin' ruined. Only reason he avoided jail time was because I asked the judge for leniency. Once the dust settled, he was dead-ass broke, and I mean like he was damn near homeless."

I watched him, surprised at this. "So what'd you do?"

"Hired him as a roadie. He sets up equipment, cleans

up after the show is done, all that. I bought him a car and paid for an apartment for three years out."

"He cheated you out of *millions* of dollars. And you hire him?"

"Oh, we keep an eye on him. But he's honest, now. He was living over his head, trying to keep his greedy-ass wife in Birkins and Bentleys."

"Why, though?"

"Why do that for people who hurt me?" he asked, clarifying; I nodded. "I spent years hating my family. Listen to the early stuff Bright Bones put out, you can hear it. That's years and years of hate and anger and daydreaming of revenge. But it was fuckin' exhausting, living like that. And then I found Tommy dead, and that just…" He shrugged, swallowing hard. "That changed me. And I read somewhere, while I was down in Rio, that the best revenge you can get on people who hurt you is to not let them see you hurting, to just succeed where they tried to make you fail. I took it a step further, figuring maybe the best revenge is to kill 'em with kindness. And that shit *burns*, Laurel. They don't expect it. They don't know how to handle it. It really chaps their ass, and watching 'em squirm is funny shit." He gestured at the happy family out by the pool. "This? This is gonna be the best one yet. Jeremy saved my ass, for real. He's a legit angel from heaven, and the hell he and Bex have overcome to get where they are is just unbelievable. Inspirational shit, I'm tellin' ya. That motherfucker out there clawed his ass out of the hood and into not one but *two* Ivy League universities, and graduated top of his class from both—and that's a man with bullet holes hiding under that suit. Legit. He could be at the top of a Fortune Five Hundred company, if he wanted, yet he keeps slumming it with my ass. I tried firing him so he'd get a real job, but he kept showing up, so…" A shrug. "Guess I'm stuck with him, fortunately for me."

"When are you going to tell them?" I asked.

"Right now." He put two fingers in his mouth and whistled sharply. "Jer, Bex! Come here, a sec."

Jeremy tossed the last inflated pool float into the water, over his oldest daughter's head like a game of ring toss, and headed in.

Bex glanced at Emmanuel. "Manny, *cuida a tu hermana, sí?*" She pointed at Violet, the youngest, who was splashing gleefully on the top step, wearing bright orange floaties on her arms, and pink Rainbow Brite swim goggles on her face.

"Yes, Mama," Emmanuel said, sitting at the edge of the pool, lazily kicking his feet in the water.

I brought out the folder of paperwork and set aside the unfinished portion, set a pen on top. Jeremy and Bex leaned on the other side of the kitchen island from Titus and me. Titus still had his sunglasses on; he slid them off and tucked the arm over the neck of his tank top. Spent a silent moment looking from Jeremy to Bex.

"You got something to say, T?" Jeremy said. "You're worrying me."

Titus laughed. "Nothing to worry about. I just want you to do something for me."

Jeremy nodded, answering immediately, without hesitation. "Anything."

Titus turned the stack of papers around, slid them across the island. "Sign these."

Jeremy frowned. "T…"

Titus arched an eyebrow. "You said anything. What I want is for you and Bex to both sign those. Don't read 'em, don't ask questions, just fuckin' scribble your names on 'em where Laurel has the fun little sticky note arrows."

Bex shook her head. "What do I gotta sign for?"

Titus sighed. "Did I not just say don't ask questions? Jesus. For smart people, you sure are havin' a hard time with this."

The dime was dropping, I could tell.

Jeremy slowly took the stack of papers and pulled them closer, picked up the pen, and signed his name, handed the pen to Bex. For the next minute or so, all was silent except the scratch of the pen and the rustle of turning papers.

Done, Jeremy pushed the stack of signed documents back toward Titus. "There. Now what's this about?"

My throat felt oddly tight. I ignored it.

Titus glanced at me. "Got the keys?"

I nodded, produced the two brass keys from my

purse. Placed them side by side on the counter in front of Jeremy and Bex.

Jeremy stared at them as if they'd attempted to come to life. "Titus. The fuck *is* this?"

Titus shrugged. "Those are your house keys."

Bex blinked rapidly. "*Our* house keys." She glanced around at the kitchen. "Keys to…to *this* house?"

"Well yeah," Titus said, as if it were the most obvious thing in the world. "Duh. Your house. This house— it's your house." He tapped the papers with a thick, ring-heavy forefinger. "You just took ownership of it. You own it, free and clear, forever."

Jeremy was swallowing hard. "Come on, man. Quit playin'."

Titus just smiled. "You know I don't play, Jer."

Jeremy swallowed again, blinked hard, turned to look at his kids—Emmanuel had finally forgotten to be cool and was in the pool playing with his youngest sister on the top step, while the other girls splashed each other and took turns trying to do a bigger cannonball.

He looked back to Titus, and now a tear was trickling down. "Our lease is up on Monday."

Titus nodded. "Yeah."

"You know we were saving for a down payment."

Titus nodded again. "I know I pay you enough you could afford this yourself." He did a head-tilt-shrug movement. "But I know a few other things, too. I know you been paying down your student loans, and I know you send several grand a month to Bex's family in Venezuela, and I know you pay for your mom's dialysis. You two won't ever spend on yourselves, so…" he shrugged, gestured with a broad sweep of both long arms at the house around us, "here we are."

Bex was sniffling. "My cousin was in a car accident, and he was the main earner for my family, so—"

"Bex, I know." Titus smiled at her. "You two been living in that little three-bedroom ranch with all these crazy-ass kids for too long. You deserve more. Now, you got more." He pointed at Bex's belly, which looked like it was about to pop any second. "With five kids, three bedrooms ain't gonna cut it. Now each kid gets their own room. Have you checked out the shower yet? It's got, like, fifty different settings. Gonna need that Harvard degree to figure that shit out, bro."

Jeremy and Bex were exchanging looks. "How can we ever thank you, Titus?" Jeremy said, his voice quiet, low.

"Don't." Titus was watching Luisa with special intensity as she did a running belly flop. "Just enjoy it. You do enough, for me, and for others." He glanced at Jeremy. "Don't think I don't know what you do Sunday mornings, bro."

Bex glanced at Jeremy. "What? What do you Sunday mornings?"

Jeremy hissed. "Goddamn, man. I was keeping that on the DL."

Titus laughed. "He's going back to his old hood and fixing up houses. He puts bars on windows, replaces carpet, fixes stairs, puts in new windows, new appliances, shit like that."

Bex was frowning at him. "Why you didn't tell me?" She whacked his arm. "You told me you were playing ball with friends."

"I *do* play ball," Jeremy said. "After I do other stuff."

Bex rattled something off in Spanish, and Jeremy replied, more slowly and with a distinct American accent, but in otherwise passable Spanish.

Bex crossed her arms and rolled her eyes, muttering something that sounded like, "macho asshole got a heart too big for his stupid head."

Titus glanced at his watch. "Well, I gotta go."

Jeremy frowned. "Where? You don't have anything on your schedule today."

Titus winked at me and slid his sunglasses on, pushing away from the island. "I do now." He pointed at me. "This lady needs brunch. Her stomach is growling like crazy over here."

I stared at him. "It is not." And cue my stomach gurgling so loud they probably heard it in Orange County. "I have to take this paperwork back to the office."

"No problem." He twirled his keys around a finger. "How about I meet you at your office and we go from there. There's this great food truck down in Santa Monica that has the best fuckin' spicy-ass tacos."

Bex arched an eyebrow at him. "Not better than *my* spicy-ass tacos, I hope."

Titus went around the island and wrapped her up in a brotherly hug, swaying side to side with her. "Of course not. Your spicy-ass tacos are the gold standard against which all others are measured."

"What I thought," Bex mumbled. "Thank you, Titus. You're too good to us."

"Nah, just good enough." He let her go and did a man-hug with Jeremy, who mumbled something muffled against Titus's shoulder. "I got you, Jer. No worries." He ambled for the door, pausing to shoot a look at me. "You comin' or what, Laurel? I'm hungry."

I tucked the folder under my arm and smiled at the couple. "Congratulations on your new home. If you have any questions, call me—I know the builder personally." I slid my card to them. "Enjoy. And congratulations on your baby, too."

They thanked me, and insisted on hugging me, walking to the door with me.

Titus paused, standing halfway in his truck, pointing at Jeremy. "Oh, I almost forgot—the movers will be at your place Monday at nine. They'll do everything, all you gotta do is move your personal valuables and yourselves. You'll be settled in by Tuesday morning." He grinned. "Also, another truck is coming here Monday afternoon—they're gonna take away your shitty-ass thrift store bullshit furniture and replace it all with new. It's a big house, gotta fill it with something, might as well be nice stuff. Anything you don't like, they'll bring you something you do."

Jeremy sighed. "Any other surprises?"

"Um?" Titus pretended to think. "Not that I know of. I'll let you know."

They just shook their heads, still looking stunned at what had just happened. I got into my car and headed for the title company office to drop off the paperwork, Titus's huge red truck behind me.

And I wondered what I was going to do now.

Rich, gorgeous, talented, hung like a horse, incredible at sex, easy to talk to and be around…*and* he did stuff like this?

Gah, how's a girl supposed to retain her hard-won emotional frigidity?

Not liking this guy just got a lot fucking harder.

CHAPTER SIX

A<small>ND</small> I <small>WAS TIPSY.</small>

Tacos at the Santa Monica food truck had led to chips and guac and Dos Equis at a pier-side cafe. Which had led to us being outside under a big red umbrella for the past two hours, our table now littered with empty bottles, our laughter raucous and wild. We were trading war stories, him of his crazy life as a rock star, me as… well, me. Spoiled rotten, the daughter of spoiled rotten parents who let me run amok and do whatever I wanted, funding my every whim without a word or blink…or a hug, or rules, or structure, or anything. It made for some fun stories, at least.

Finally, Titus paid the bill and we continued our wandering, rabbit-trail conversation while strolling the Santa Monica pier.

The funny stories faded, and I felt him revving up for a serious question.

"So, boarding school in Europe," he said. "Was that, like, year-round?"

"Well, I came back for summers…usually. There was the year I turned sixteen, I spent that summer in Greece with my friend and her family—she was the daughter of the Greek president at the time, so I spent most of that summer at the presidential palace in Athens." I thought back. "And, junior and senior year both I spent in Spain, as a guest of the princess."

He made a face. "So that business about the princess was true?"

I laughed. "Oh sure. That was actually in reference to a different princess. The school I went to is where pretty much all the royal children from across Europe and most of the world went, along with the kids of anyone with the right wealth and connections."

"Damn. That must have been interesting."

I cackled. "Interesting, yeah. That's one word for it. Also applicable: neglect, and abandonment. For me, at least."

He seemed unsurprised by this. "The others too, I'm guessing."

"Well, some yes, some no. I went home for the summers with my friends because even though they got shipped off to boarding school same as me, when they went home, there was at least a pretense of familial love and affection."

His eyes were sad for me. "Not so much for you, huh?"

I snorted. "Yeah, no. I was a nuisance at best, mostly. They bought me whatever I wanted as a kind of apology for not giving a shit. And then once I was older, it more like, could you maybe just go live on your own? We're busy. Here, have fifty thousand dollars a month. Not enough? Try a hundred thousand a month."

He blinked. "Jesus shits."

I laughed. "That was when I was twelve. My spending allowance by the time I was seventeen was roughly equivalent to that of a third-world country. It's honestly embarrassing." I sighed, waved a hand. "If I was home, I was in the way. They'd have swinger parties, these big crazy orgies where people would just be fucking in the hallways and in the pool and every bedroom, in the kitchen, just trading around, everyone fucking everyone else, with my parents presiding over it all like they were a god and goddess at a bacchanalia in their honor. It was gross. They have no dignity whatsofuckingever."

"Then why did they even have you?" He winced. "Shit, I'm sorry, that sounded—"

"No, it's true. I wondered it myself. I don't think they meant to, if you want to know the truth." I snorted a derisive laugh. "I asked Mom, once, and she just laughed at me and walked away. I'm not sure my dad is my father, if you know what I mean. I don't look like him, and knowing what went on at those parties, it could have been literally anyone. There's no way to know, and they're not telling. I've stopped wondering. It doesn't matter, honestly. He raised me, sort of. By which I mean, I raised myself and he funded my existence. So if the man who accidentally donated his sperm to my mother is the man who I call Dad, if it's someone else, it just doesn't matter."

"That's rough," he said.

"Could have been worse." I gestured at him. "You said your dad used to hurt you. That sounds worse, to me."

"Yeah, that wasn't great. He'd go on benders every couple weeks and anyone who was in the room with him would pay for it. Then he'd feel bad and try to go dry and he'd be miserable and ignore me. And in the meantime, Mom was just…she was a colossal bitch, verbally abusive, emotionally manipulative, all that. Just to balance out Dad knocking us all around. She and my dad hated each other, but they came from this old-world tradition where you just don't divorce no matter what."

"What kind of old world?" I asked.

"They're both first-generation Americans—Dad's Italian, and Mom is Albanian. I guess when Grandpa, my dad's dad—came over, he got a dictionary and figured out the translation of his name and changed it to the English word—Bright. Used to be 'Chiaro' or something like that."

"And where did they come up with the name Titus from?"

He laughed at the question. "Mom. Back when they had me, Mom was into going to church, hoping it would help out with my dad's drinking issues, and I guess she just liked the name Titus, from the book at the end of the Bible."

"So what you're saying is, Titus Bright is your real, actual name?"

He snorted. "Sure is." He dug his wallet out of his back pocket and tugged his license out and showed it to me. "You know I must like you if I'm showing my license, which has my middle names on it—most embarrassing middle names ever."

"Giuseppe Adnan?" I asked, reading. "Your name is Titus Giuseppe Adnan Bright?"

"Sure is."

"Nothing embarrassing about that. Giuseppe a perfectly common and ordinary Italian last name. Adnan I'm not familiar with."

"My dad's father was Giuseppe, my mom's dad was Adnan. It's Albanian." A shrug. "It's not embarrassing, but it's not rock star."

I laughed at that. "Well, one could argue that since *you're* a rock star, it is therefore by definition, rock star."

"You have a point."

We walked in silence. "It's amazing, what you did today."

"Nah." He paused at a bench, glanced at it, at the ocean, and sat down. "I have a plan to give away everything I've got, eventually. I've got it all planned out—all the charities and everything. I mean…" He paused, swallowed. "Assuming there's no one else to give it to, you know? Like, I couldn't possibly spend it all in my lifetime even if I tried, and I'm not inclined to try."

I heard a lot he wasn't saying. I didn't ask about any of it. I liked him enough as it was, and that was bad, because I wasn't about to let myself go falling for anyone. You had to have a heart in order to fall for someone, and I was fairly certain I didn't. I'd never felt anything to tell me the opposite, except for where the girls were concerned, and that was different.

"So you're gonna give it all away like Warren Buffet, huh?"

He laughed. "Yeah, pretty much."

"Not going to give it to your family?"

"If by family you mean the people I was born into, hell no. I did my part by them, I got no interest in anything else. I don't talk to 'em, I don't see 'em, nothin'."

"What about your brother?"

"Nope." He waved a hand. "He's an ungrateful bastard. Had the gall, after I fixed his disaster of a fuckin' life, to ask me for a car, for another handout, for more and more, like I owed it to him. He never did shit for me except make my life hell. He led the charge in teasing me, bullying me at school, all that. I know I'm all big rock star guy now, but back then I was a skinny dweeb who played the violin and listened to weird music. Tommy was my only friend, and Bright Bones was originally just us fucking around in his garage. We didn't even have a name for ourselves. This guy drove by on a motorcycle one day, heard us, and asked us to play at his bar. He was like, you guys are eighteen, right? We were like, fuck yeah, because we weren't. And then when we got there, he was like, you're twenty-one, right? And we were like fuck yeah, because free beer. And that's how Bright Bones started. Playing at a closing set at a biker bar at sixteen."

"I always thought that story was apocryphal or whatever."

"I don't know what the fuck that means."

"It means…told as true even if no one is sure if it really is."

"Oh. No, it's true. We were sixteen, not thirteen like some of the stories say, and we didn't get brought into the back room after our first set by prostitutes."

I laughed. "Yeah, I heard that too. That one I assumed was true."

He grinned. "Nah. They weren't prostitutes, just horny biker chicks."

I cackled. "So it *is* true!"

"Hell yeah. Lost my virginity that day, and I was hooked on the rock star life from then on."

"I can see why."

"Free booze, nobody asking how old you are, people jamming out to your music, girls flashing their tits at you and begging you to screw them in the back of wherever, all the drugs you could ever want and then some, and then when we signed with the label, fuckin' buckets of money? Hell yeah. Of course looking back, it was way too much way too soon, but as a kid, you don't think that. You just roll with it."

"I mean, obviously. Who in their right mind would say no to that? Especially when it got you away from a home life that sucked?"

"Right. The label got us a tour bus and suddenly we were traveling the country, and eventually the world. Me and Tommy, poor little redneck bastards from fuckin' Shitsville Kentucky? It was glorious."

"Kentucky? I always heard Chicago."

"Nah, that's just where we blew up first. We were from Kentucky. Outside Louisville. For whatever reason, when we first started touring in a shitty old van, Chicago was our big spot, where we developed a following. It was our home base for years, so we always said we were from Chicago, because we were both embarrassed about being from Kentucky, dumb vain bastards that we were."

"You get embarrassed about weird things, Titus."

"Image is everything, to a rock star. Especially when you're twenty, twenty-three or whatever and the whole world hangs on every word, every picture."

I sighed. "I may not be famous, but I do understand image being everything. I understand that on a visceral level."

"Explain, if you would."

I kicked off my Louboutins and hooked them in my fingers, strode into the sand toward the water's edge, stopping when the water licked at my toes and arches. I felt Titus beside me.

"It's that kind of a thing for you, huh?" He was holding his flip-flops in one hand, digging a hole in the sand with his toes. "You don't have to answer—you can tell me to go to hell."

I shook my head, staring at my feet and watching as ocean foam swirled around my toes. "It's…embarrassing, and hard to talk about."

"Dude, I get it."

"I know you do, *dude*," I said, teasing him with a look. "That's why I guess I'm willing to talk about it with you— because I guess you'd really get it." I paused a moment, then two, gathering my thoughts. "My mom, I think I mentioned at some point, was—is—from a family that goes back to the earliest days of Hollywood, like from the silent film days. My great-grandfather was one of the first silent film directors, and my great-grandmother one of the first actresses. Octavius Miller and Darlene Oldfield—look them up, sometime."

Titus chuckled. "No, I know them. Who doesn't?"

"Right. So then my grandfather, Albert Phineas Miller, he was a writer, director, actor, producer, all that."

"No shit. Everyone knows him. One of the greats from the Golden Era."

I nodded. "And an insufferable bastard, truth be told.

Everyone hated working with him, but he was a genius. And he married my grandmother, Amelia Loop, when she was eighteen and he was forty-nine." I held up a finger. "There is a point to all this Hollywood history, I promise—it's not just me being snooty and name-droppy about my ancestry. So Albert and Amelia had several kids, most notably my mother, Elise Miller. You probably know her."

"For sure." He gave me a grimacing grin. "I had a poster of her taped to the inside wall of our van."

"The one from *In With The New*? Where she's wearing the tiny white bikini and holding the gun? Yeah, every teenage boy of a certain age had that poster."

"I guess I didn't realize that was your mother. You said she was Hollywood royalty, but…"

"Yeah. She married the director of that movie, *In With The New*—Calum Crane—when she was twenty, and they had a son, my half brother, Davy Crane."

"You have a half brother?"

"Had. He died of a brain tumor when I was four. I never really knew him. That broke them up, Calum and my mom. She divorced him, quit acting, moved to Paris, and studied art. By which I mean became a wino and spent my grandparents' money." I sighed, waving a hand. "There's a through line in all of this that I haven't mentioned yet. Famous parents who were children of famous parents, and so on for three generations—everything was scrutinized. Image was everything. By the time

Mom moved back to LA, got back into acting, and met my dad, she'd been the subject of so much tabloid speculation, had been affiliated in some way or another with dozens of different men. Her mom, my grandmother, had been the same. And as my grandmother got older, she went to increasingly nutty lengths to stay relevant, to stay beautiful. My grandfather obviously ended up with a series of mistresses who were increasingly younger as he got older. But Grandma Amelia? She had to do crazy stuff, surgeries and crazy diets and all that to stay young and beautiful looking. She did a Playboy centerfold at fifty-eight, to prove she was still sexy. Mom did that *Caligula* remake a few years ago, at sixty-one, where she appeared fully nude, full-frontal, the whole thing." I shook my head. "So what does that mean for me? Image is everything. It was drilled into my head that my value to them, to anyone, was in my appearance. My appeal—my sex appeal. Mom told me, when I was thirteen and we were having her version of the birds and the bees talk, that unless I was sexy and stayed sexy, I'd never amount to anything."

"She said that you? That you'd never amount to anything if you weren't sexy."

I nodded. "Sure did. My value as a woman is in my sex appeal—that was the lesson of my life. The driving factor behind everything." I swallowed hard. "I did do some modeling when I was young. Overseas, for European magazines." I couldn't believe I was telling him this. No one knew about this, since it hadn't gotten American media publicity; if I went to Europe, however, I'd still get recognized now and then.

He eyed me. "When you say modeling. Something tells me you're not talking about dresses."

I laughed. "No, not dresses. Not nude, like it wasn't some Euro version of Playboy, but I wasn't clothed either, not all the way. I'd reached full maturity, breast-wise, by seventeen, and…I needed attention. I'm psychoanalyzing myself retrospectively, you understand. But I got an offer from an agent to do some modeling, and I figured it was obvious. My whole family did stuff like that. I'd seen Grandma Amelia's centerfold, and most of Mom's early roles had been scantily clad at best. So it was kind of a duh that I'd get approached to model, and it wasn't at all surprising that they'd ask me to pose topless. Over there, nudity isn't as big of a deal as it is here. But still, it leads into everything."

"At seventeen?"

I nodded. "They thought I was eighteen. Or, assumed, conveniently, and didn't bother asking for confirmation." I considered. "I did twenty-some shoots, in varying degrees of nudity for a variety of magazines."

"Clearly, that didn't lead to acting or better modeling gigs."

"Clearly. What it led to was…me feeling like that was the only way I could leverage my looks for attention. Which led to using my looks for attention and relevance in other ways, from a very young age. It's all I'd seen, all I'd ever had modeled for me. And it worked. I was popular in school. I got invited to all the best parties, got invited on expensive vacations with famous kids of famous parents. There were no rules. I was given as much alcohol as I could drink and left to wander the streets of Milan and Paris and Prague and Rome and Athens and Lisbon and Madrid with my friends, and unlimited credit. Sounds like every teenager's dream, right? I thought so. Like, this is the fuckin' life, man. But you know what came with it? The men at the parties. The princes and dukes, the sons of CEOs and prime ministers, and the CEOs and prime ministers themselves more than a few times, who assumed, correctly, that they could ply me alcohol and cocaine and get me to perform for them. Take off my shirt and dance for them. Wander around the party in nothing but my underwear, carrying around a ten-thousand-dollar bottle of eighty-year-old champagne, dancing with men twice my age." I dug my toes deeper into the wet sand. "And that meant, obviously, being taken into the bathroom and guest rooms for other performances. Willingly, but drunk and high—willingly, because these were the richest and best and most famous men on the planet. It was actors, rock stars, producers, princes, all that. I was their plaything, because I was young and sexy and nubile and had been told all my life that I had no other role and no other value in life but as the plaything of wealthy men."

He was silent a long time. "Fuck, man." He kicked

at the sand. "You're pointing a finger right at me, you know. I was that rock star, in those hotel rooms all over Europe, at those parties, with the girls just like you, and I took what was offered and never thought twice about it, as long as they could tell me they were willing."

"We may have even been at some of the same parties," I pointed out. "God knows neither of us would likely remember it if we'd met at one."

"No shit," he murmured. "I was blasted off my rocker for pretty much all of my twenties and thirties, up until…you know. My shit came crashing down." He finally looked at me. "So, what changed you?"

I laughed. "Zurich, Switzerland, 2001. October tenth, just past three a.m."

"You know the exact time and date."

"Not the kind of thing you forget." I glanced at him. "It's heavy. Like, heavy as fuck."

"I know about that shit, trust me."

"I'm sure you do." I sighed, closing my eyes. "I was invited to a party. A ritzy, swanky sort of one. Started out as a black-tie sort of thing, fancy hors d'oeuvres brought by servers in tuxedos, a string quartet, dancing, all that. Then, as the night wore on, the party moved up to the penthouse suite of the hotel where the event had taken place. It went from a swanky, classy, stuffy *event* to a real party. The expensive wine went away and out came the bottles of booze and the bags of coke. It was mostly upper management for financial institutions, you know, the places that deal with money but aren't banks, and stocks guys and such. A real good ol' boys club, just the European version."

I had to pause again.

"I've never talked about this. Ever. With anyone."

"Understood."

"The party dwindled as the night went on, people leaving here and there, and somehow I just never managed to be one of them. There was always one more conversation, one more shot, one more line. And then, suddenly, it was just me and four or five guys."

"Oh, shit."

"Yeah, oh shit. You can probably guess where this is going. I don't really remember much. I'd had so much to drink, snorted so many lines it's honestly a wonder I survived that night at all. I remember being sort of herded into a bedroom. It was dark. I was confused. I remember my clothes, such as I was wearing at least, being pulled off. Being touched. Saying no. Trying to fight. I was just so fucked-up, and there were four of them, or five, maybe even six, I don't remember. It goes kind of fuzzy after that, for which I'm honestly kind of glad." I swallowed hard, and again, but the hot lump wouldn't go away. "I remember bits and pieces. A face above me, and then a different one, and a different one, and so on. I remember it hurting. I was far from being a virgin, obviously, but they weren't, you know…nice about it. I remember it going on for a long, long time."

"Fucking hell, Laurel."

I knew he simply didn't know what else to say. But shit, what *was* there to say? Not a damn thing that meant anything. "When they were done, they left. Just left me there, a hundred different kinds of fucked and fucked-up." I blinked away a tear, savagely shoving it all back down. "I never told anyone. I went home, took a bath, and spent the next couple months getting even more fucked-up, just never alone with men. Eventually, I just sort of decided I was over it. I never went back to parties, though. I did my partying alone. At first, I would have flashbacks, during sex. But up to then, I'd honestly enjoyed sex. I'd been a kid, right? Thirteen and unsupervised in Europe, what else was going to happen? That party in Zurich marked my coming of age, I guess, in my mind. I was no longer a teenager, no longer a girl. I was a woman. And I was going to own my body. I wasn't going to let being gang-raped stop me from enjoying my body, my sexuality, and my life. So, I forced myself to get over it. Such as one can, I suppose."

"How the hell do you even…" He shook his head. "How do you force yourself to heal from that?"

I cackled bitterly. "I said I forced myself over it, I didn't say I *healed* myself of it. Oh no. There has been no healing, sir. Just a lot of forgetting and suppressing and ignoring."

"And you never talked about it with anyone? Never pressed charges?"

"Hell no. Those guys would have just bought me off. Paid whatever it took to silence me, one way or another. I was voiceless, I didn't matter. I was theirs to take and use as they wish. And what would talking about it have done? Opened up the wounds I was working so hard to ignore. So no, I haven't. You just…deal with it. Fake being fine until eventually you just sort of reach some semblance of actual fineness."

He gazed steadily at me, no pity, just sadness, sorrow, commiseration. "I'm sorry that happened to you."

"Me too. And thanks." I smiled at him. "So. Tell me something funny."

"Something funny?" He regarded the waves, the afternoon sunlight glinting yellow orange off the green-lead-blue sea. "Okay, I got one. But this is one you can't repeat."

"I'd never repeat anything you tell me."

"Except to your girlfriends?"

"Well, maybe. Depending on the story. But we're tight, and things between the six of stay between the six of us."

"Figured as much." He chuckled. "So, we—being Bright Bones, me, Tommy, Rick the Dick, and Froot Loop."

I cackled. "Rick the Dick and Froot Loop?"

"Rick Maroni, bassist, and Zander Smith, rhythm guitar—he pretty much lived off of Froot Loops cereal, like he ate that shit for breakfast, lunch, dinner, and midnight snack. I swear to fuck he kept a little pouch of them in his goddamn pocket and he'd eat them on stage. It turned into his thing, at the end of our sets and encores, he'd pull that bag of Froot Loops out and toss them at the crowd. Eventually, he used the cereal tossing as his way of indicating which girl he wanted. He'd toss them the red Froot Loop. If you got a red Froot Loop from Zander, you were his pick for the night."

"That's kinda…"

He laughed. "Kind of a dick move? No kidding. That's not the story, though."

"Wait, hold on. Why Rick the Dick?"

"Because it rhymed, and because he's a dick. Hell of a bassist, which is why any of us put up with his ass. Man could shred that bass like literally no one I've ever met in my life. But he was a colossal dick. I don't even want to repeat some of the shenanigans he pulled. We actually kicked him off the tour on two different occasions because of the shit he pulled. Had to get his guitar tech to fill in. But we always brought him back because the fans just went bananas for his bass solos."

"If *you* don't want to repeat it, then I think I'm fine not knowing."

"Yeah, you are. Trust me." He took my hand and walked with me along the sand. "So, it was after a show in Dallas. Usual postshow nonsense. We had three dates in Dallas, so we'd booked suites, right, and we partied it up. Girls, drugs, booze, the usual bullshit. Well, we all passed out. This was after the last show which meant we were leaving the next day for a pair of dates in… Albuquerque? Flagstaff? Don't remember, and it doesn't matter. I woke up in my suite, and I was buck-ass naked. Not too weird considering the kind of nonsense we got up to that night, but what was weird was I couldn't find any of my clothes. And my phone was gone. And it was, like, two in the afternoon and we had been scheduled to leave at eleven. So I called the other guys' rooms… no answer. Called the front desk and they told me we'd been checked out hours ago."

"Oh my god."

"The fuckers stole my clothes, took my phone, checked out, and left me in Dallas, bare-ass naked and without so much as a red cent on me. Took my wallet, my cards, everything."

I was laughing, now. "That's brutal."

"No kidding."

"What'd you do?"

"Fortunately, I'd memorized my agent's number. I called him and he handled it. Got clothing sent to me, got a car for me, and I made it to the show on time."

"Did you get them back?"

"Fuck yeah, I did. Now, don't judge me—I was a prick back then, all right?" He chuckled. "I laced their drinks a few weeks later with knock-out drugs. Like, they were out for the *count*. I stripped them all naked, and me and a bunch of the roadies brought 'em to a park in the middle of the city—St. Louis? No, it was…Des Moines, maybe. Shit, it's hard to remember—all the cities blur together after a while. Midwest somewhere's all I know. We dumped them naked in the park, and we drew mustaches and glasses on them with Sharpies. And we fuckin' left 'em there. Ohhhh man, were they mad. It was all over the place, photos of 'em, videos, everything. Someone got a recording of them waking up—being woken up by police, actually. God, were they confused. They didn't speak to me for a week, and our shows were shit because we were all out of synch and pissed off at each other. Rick would mess up his solos on purpose, and then I'd do something, and then Tommy would intentionally change the beat count, and we'd all get messed up. Eventually we got over it. It was Tommy, of course, who was like, ya'll, we gotta snap out of it or we're gonna break up, or worse, get canceled because our shows are going to absolute shit. So I told 'em, you prank me, I prank you. And we agreed from then on, no pranks."

The mention of Tommy sapped the humor from his face, as it always seemed to do.

"Just wondering, here, but where'd you get the date rape drugs?"

He shot me a sardonic look. "I'm Titus Bright." A shrug. "I told my buddy Hank, the lead roadie, that I wanted to prank them and what I was thinking, and he handled it. So I guess the answer is, I don't know, I just trusted Hank to handle it. And to answer the question you're not asking—no, that was never, *ever* our MO with women. We didn't need to. They wanted us, and they came willingly to the slaughter, so to speak. The reason we kicked Rick off both times was he had violated that code, that we could take what girls offered, but were cool about it. We didn't leave 'em out in the cold when we were done with 'em, and we didn't treat 'em like objects. Rick would say or do shit that made Tommy and me especially super angry and we'd give him the boot. We threatened to permanently replace him if he pulled that shit again, after the second time we had to kick him off. But we never allowed anything…sick, I guess. Rick's whole deal was feeling entitled. Pressuring girls into shit and then being a dick to them after he'd gotten what he wanted." A shrug, a sigh. "But, looking back, the fact that it was so easy to procure something as nasty fuckin' evil as that…I'm not proud of it, even if I just used it as a prank on my buddies."

I patted his arm. "I honestly didn't consider the idea that you'd ever do something like that." I glanced at him. "Actually, Autumn was slipped a mickey or whatever you want to call—just after she'd met Seven. She went on a date with another guy who'd responded to The Ad, and he gave her something, or had something put into her drink somehow—we're still not sure how. But any man who could and would do shit like that?" I shook my head. "He can die in a hole."

"And I'll put him there," Titus growled. "If you can't

get ass for yourself the honest time-honored way of hitting on girls and getting shot down until one feels sorry enough for your stupid ugly face to pity-fuck you, then at least have the goddamn dignity to pay for it, which is the other time-honored tradition. And by that I mean, someone who's in that line of work voluntarily." He huffed. "That shit pisses me off."

"I can tell."

He rolled a shoulder. "There was this girl who followed us around. Shannon. Sweet, beautiful girl. She was connected to one of our crew, somehow, none of us were ever quite sure who or how. She was just always around, at every show, and she'd just make herself useful. She wasn't some desperate groupie, you know? Like she loved us, loved our music, but never was like, please please one of you any of you please fuck me. She just… followed us. She'd help set up and tear down, she'd help out with catering, make sure we had water bottles in the green room for after the show, she'd roll joints for us, help make sure that once playtime was over, the girls who'd partied with us got where they needed to go safely. Honestly, Shannon was a godsend and an angel, and we eventually took notice and started paying her to just be who she was, to do what she was doing. We just got used to Shannon being around."

He sighed heavily, bitterly.

"Then, at a festival in Idaho, she was hanging out and partying after our set with us and some other boys from various bands. I saw some guy messing around with her, but she was an adult, you know, so I just kept an eye on her. We all got pretty protective of Shannon. And she could party, okay? She could take care of herself. But something was off that day. She knew how to pace herself, and she never got wack, like so bombed she was falling over herself. I mean, we all got that way once in a while, and we'd take care of each other if it happened. And I figured maybe I'd missed her take some shots or something, or maybe she'd smoked something while we were on. I wasn't sure, but she was just acting…off. I don't know. Too out of control for how Shannon got even wasted. I didn't like it. So I kept an eye on her. And sure enough, she wandered off and some dickhead from a new band playing their first festival was following her. I caught up right as he was trying to drag her behind a gear trailer, yanking at her clothes and muffling her mouth. I beat the unholy fuck out of that guy. I mean, it was *bad*." He shook his head. "But she was, like, our sister, you know? You just didn't fuck with Shannon."

I bumped his shoulder. "You're a truly decent person, Titus."

He snorted. "Dunno if I'd go *that* far. Not tolerating rape doesn't make me decent, it just makes me not a piece of shit."

"I meant decent in the old version of the word, not as in, okay or merely acceptable. Like, good and decent. And I meant it."

He laughed. "Thank you, Laurel." He glanced at me. "Wanna head out?"

"Sure."

⁓

He pulled up into my driveway—and seemed puzzled. "This is you, huh?"

"No, *this* is me," I said, holding out my hands in a *ta-da!* gesture, then pointed at my house. "That's my house."

He snorted. "Smart-ass."

"Better than being a dumbass," I retorted.

"Har-har-har," he deadpanned.

"Not what you expected, is it?"

He regarded my home, and shook his head. "Honestly, no. I figured you'd live in a fancy condo downtown, a penthouse maybe."

My house was a two-bedroom, two-bathroom ranch, utterly unremarkable and in an utterly unremarkable neighborhood of suburban L.A. I owned it free and clear, had paid comically little for it and had—probably surprising to pretty much anyone who didn't know me very well—done a lot of renovation to it myself. It was brick—once drab tan, now painted white—and I'd had the roof replaced with a green metal roof, and had added solar panels which killed that utility bill entirely. The front yard was small, small enough that I mowed it myself with one of those old-school manual push-reel mowers. There were box shrubs under the front picture window, and a large planter filled with daisies and irises and whatever else piqued my fancy each spring. The walkway from sidewalk to front door had once been cracked and crumbling cement, and I'd had it ripped up and replaced with flagstones. The front door was green to match the roof, and matching shutters.

The driveway was a project I'd meaning to get around to for a couple years, but never quite did—it was the last thing in the exterior that I hadn't updated yet, and was old, cracked, and crappy. Detached garage, also updated to match the rest of the house, with a lovely new wooden fence and gate.

He huffed in amusement. "Yeah, no, this is not what I expected when I thought, *I wonder where Laurel lives,* you know?"

I laughed. "I know, nobody does. But I grew up in a huge fancy Bel-Air mansion with eight rooms and ten bathrooms and a pool house and just about everything you could imagine. And weird I know it may be, but I just was always curious about neighborhoods like this. I was always drawn to cute little houses like this. And when I first started selling real estate with Lizzy and Kat, we were the new girls on the block with our own brand-new brokerage and we built our brand selling places just like this. Eventually we moved up in the world, started selling more and more expensive places, and for a long time I did live in a condo exactly like you're probably imagining.

But I found this place once—listed it, as a matter of fact because I just loved the bones of it, and felt like it was just so cute, had so much potential. And Lizzy was like, if you love it so much, buy it yourself. I'd been complaining about my condo, anyway. Like, no yard, no privacy, no solitude. City living was wearing on me. So I did. I bought it, and I fixed it up." I hopped out of the car and headed for the side kitchen door that was my usual entrance, unlocked it, and led Titus inside. "And if you want to be really surprised, listen to this: I did probably eighty percent of the renovation in here myself. I myself knocked down the wall between kitchen and living room—upon the advice and guidance of a professional contractor, of course. And I myself demo'd the whole kitchen, all the floors, and both bathrooms. I myself combined the master bedroom with the formerly unattached bathroom to create an en suite master. I installed all the floors. I put up the drywall. I mudded and sanded and painted. I had the cabinets and counters installed because, frankly, I was simply not strong enough."

Titus looked around at my kitchen. White cabinets with brushed nickel pulls and matching faucet, top-of-the-line stainless steel GE Profile appliances, a dark navy island, and pale gray quartz counters with nice touches of gentle, subtle movement. Flooring was vinyl, sturdy and wide plank, made to look like wood but a fraction of the price, in alternating light and dark shades to complement the counters. The whole effect was a kitchen that was clean, simple, comfortable, balanced, and timeless. I was very proud of it; I'd also been careful to not spend so much that I'd never get the cost back in resale value. The flooring was carried through the house, with antique, handwoven rugs under the dining room table, the couch in the living room, and in each of the bedrooms. The theme of gentle, timeless, monochromatic base colors with pops of color for accent carried through to the rest of the house as well.

Titus took it all in. "You did all this?"

I nodded, pleased and flattered at the fact that he was obviously impressed. "Damn, girl. You got skills."

I shrugged. "I've been around enough renovations professionally that I had an idea how things worked, and I knew I could do most of it. And I always had my friend Mark in my back pocket—he's my go-to contractor that I refer clients to, and if I was stuck or wasn't sure what to do or how to do it, I'd call Mark, and he'd walk me through it without mansplaining or taking over. I'm very proud of my home, but I understand why you'd think it's not what you expected from me."

"No, it's beautiful. For real. Comfortable. Feel silly using this word, but it's…cozy."

I laughed. "Oh, you're too macho and cool for something to be cozy?"

He snorted. "Yes. I'm Titus fucking Bright—I don't do cozy." He laughed. "It's honestly not that. Or maybe it is. But I grew up in a shithole, and then went from that to a P-O-S, rusty as fuck, twenty-year-old Econoline work van, and then tour busses and hotels, and then finally the rig I got now." A shrug. "I dropped out of school and left home at sixteen, and I've never had a home that wasn't on wheels since."

"You dropped out of high school?"

He nodded. "Yup. Finished ninth grade and we dropped out to play full-time halfway through our sophomore year."

"Wow."

He grinned. "And then there's you, miss I went to USC."

I rolled my eyes. "UC Berkeley, actually."

"Nice." A pause. "So. Can I see your room?" Titus murmured.

I swallowed hard. Nerves rifled through me. "Uh, sure."

I led Titus Bright to my bedroom, my *sanctum sanctorum*. No one saw my room. No one—certainly no male.

So…why was I leading him to my bedroom? Why was I allowing this man to see this part of me, this private, vulnerable side of me?

I really, really hoped I wasn't going to regret letting Titus see this part of me.

CHAPTER SEVEN

K ING BED, PALE LAVENDER FLEECE QUILT, FLUFFY WHITE pillows, white walls with abstract black-and-white photography, another of my antique hand-woven rugs. Part of the reason I'd chosen this house was that the master bedroom featured a closet that was abnormally massive for the style and age of the house.

He paused to look at a photograph on the wall—an aged, cracked wooden pier pylon up close, framed so it was hard to tell what it was. "Who took this?" He glanced at me over his shoulder. "If you say you, I'm gonna have an existential crisis."

"Why?"

"Because no one should look the way you do, be as successful as you are, as cool and down to earth and funny, as sexy, *and* be able to renovate a house on your own, *and* be a talented photographer."

"It's a hobby," I said, shrugging. "I think Lizzy is the only one who even knows I do photography."

He sighed, sounding actually annoyed. "So you *did* do the photography in here?"

"Guilty as charged. I discovered it in college. My friend had this old black-and-white antique camera, and I was messing around with it, and he later developed the roll I'd been screwing around with, and was like, *girl*, you're really good. You should keep doing this. So I did. I got myself a camera and once in a while when the mood strikes, I'll go bum around downtown or something and shoot a few rolls. I have fun with it, but it's not something I'd quit my day job for."

He examined the other pieces on my walls. "I dunno, this shit is pretty legit. I'd buy it."

"It's legit, huh?"

He nodded. "Legit." He turned in place. Swaggered toward me—prowled, really. "You are somethin' else, Laurel McGillis."

I was nervous—why was I nervous? I'd already fucked him. I knew it'd be good.

Too good, and maybe that was why.

Either way, my knees shook. My hands shook. My mouth was dry. My heart was thumping. I had to swallow a dozen times, and still couldn't make my throat any less clogged.

"Something else, huh?" I echoed, inanely.

He took my hips in his hands and tugged me to himself, slowly and inexorably. And I went, blinking up at him.

"I can't fuckin' handle you, Laurel. You're too much of too many different things."

Something in those words lanced straight to my core—and not in a sexy way. "Yeah, I get that a lot. It's why I ham up being the stereotypical shallow dumb blonde LA girl. It's easier."

He shook his head. "Bullshit. That's the cowardly way out of being your real bad-ass self."

"But you yourself just said you can't handle me. I'm too much."

He snorted. Touched his lips to mine. "You can't tell sarcasm when you hear it?" Another kiss. "I dunno if sarcasm is the right word. A joke. Saying the thing you don't mean, to emphasize how much you don't mean it."

I felt his lips touch mine, again and again, delicate, dry little half kisses peppering my mouth, my upper lip and then one corner and then the other, each one making my heart skip a beat, skip a beat, skip a beat.

"So you *can* handle me," I breathed.

He slid a hand around my waist to cup my buttock. "I dunno, Laurel…*can* I handle you?"

I huffed a laugh, tilting my head up to bare my neck for his descending trail of kisses. "Such an idiot."

He laughed, not at all offended. "Yup." His touch slid down over my backside, the hem of my skirt, and then found the bare backs of my thighs. "This fuckin' skirt, though—this what I can't handle."

I pulled his beanie off, and his thick, curly black hair

fell around his face; I gathered it in my hands and held the back of his head as he pressed kiss after kiss down my throat to the generous expanse of cleavage above the buttons of my shirt.

"What is it with you rock stars and these out-of-season beanies?" I asked, breathless.

He laughed, backing away to focus on undoing the top button. "It's a whole look. I dunno. It is kinda stupid. My head gets hot and then my hair gets sweaty and turns into a frizz bomb. But it looks cool, so…" A shrug, as he undid another button. A few more in quick succession. "Did your tits get even *bigger* than the last time I saw you, or what?"

I played with his hair, laughing. "Push-up bra magic."

"Well, I approve." He had my shirt open, and sat back to simply stare at my chest. "Goddamn. You make me want to do some seriously dirty shit to you."

I let him search my waistline for the zipper of my skirt, which was on the side rather than the back. "Oh? Such as?"

He found the zipper finally and lowered it, and now my skirt was open but on, to match my shirt. "Gross things that you wouldn't like."

I laughed as he reached under and around the back of my shirt to unhook my bra. "What *are* you doing? And again I say, like *what*? I can be dirty."

He shook his head, ignoring both questions. Pushed

my shirt backward, letting it fall off, and in the same movement, slid the straps of my bra off of my shoulders so that garment fell off at the same time, and then without missing a beat knelt and dragged down my skirt and the skimpy black thong I wore under it.

And just like that, within the space of a single breath, I was naked.

He knelt at my thighs, hands gripping my ass cheeks and pulling me to his mouth. "Can't get enough of this." A lick, a kiss, sending lightning searing through me. "Of you."

I gasped, and my hips flexed. "God, Titus. I can't get enough of you doing it to me."

He shook his head, sighing, groaning. "I can't stop." A flick, a lick, a kiss, a hot breath, fingers now inside me, tongue drilling me and driving against me. "I like you too much."

Oof. That…made the anxious, nervous hammering of my heart all the worse.

This felt good, too good, and I wanted the dirty. I wanted the rough. I didn't want his tender words. I didn't want to know he liked me. He was a rock star. He was famous for his errant sexual promiscuity, infamous for the stories of threesomes and more, for letting girls desperate for him line up outside their bus so they could get a turn with him, and his willingness, stamina, and impossibly short refractory period to please them all.

I was fine being another conquest, another of the

many girls to get a sample of Titus Bright's intensity, his glorious body, his sinfully killed mouth, his wondrously massive cock.

I was fine with it. Totally fine.

I was *not* looking to be the girl who thought she could tame him, who thought she could capture his heart along with his body, not to mention his fidelity.

I didn't think that. Didn't want that part of him. This was just sex. Nothing more.

God knew I wasn't about to go handing out the keys to my heart to *anyone*. Mainly because there *were* no keys—or, more accurately, the keys led to a vacant space, a black hole, an empty cavern where no light existed.

There was nothing there to give.

I had no business pretending otherwise. No business even wondering what it could be like to…

He interrupted my thoughts with a renewed assault on my sex, which shook me, left me gasping and heaving. He got me to the edge and drove me over without mercy, without slowing. I came with a hoarse cry, and my knees gave out.

He let them.

Caught me, and tossed me onto my bed with a bounce. Knelt over me and set about devouring me all over again, until I was quaking with the fury of a second climax, hard on the heels of the first, and then a third moments later, until I was sweating and crying and screaming, thrashing under him.

He let me down from the mountain, then, but only because I begged him to.

"Stop, Titus, stop. Let me…god, fucking god, Titus," I gasped. "You're crazy."

"Feeling that sweet pussy come all over my mouth is the best fuckin' drug I've ever had," he murmured, crawling up my body, still fully clothed. "And I've tried 'em all."

I had to touch him. Had to make this dirty rather than sweet. Yanked at his shirt. His shorts. Fumbled awkwardly at his underwear until he laughed and kicked them off, and then he was beautifully naked above me. I grasped him, caressed him. Fondled his balls and used both fists on his length until he was growling.

I scooted backward, up the bed, away from him. Lay on my back and cradled my breasts between my arms for him. "Tell me the dirty things you want to do, Titus. Better yet…show me."

He crawled up the bed after me, cock swaying heavily, hard and thick and long, plump fat head leaking, weeping. "You really want to know?"

He knelt over me, straddled me, staring down at me, his gaze rife with appreciation.

"Do I look like I'm teasing?"

He caressed my breasts. "You look like the most goddamn gorgeous creature on the fuckin' planet. You look like I want to steal you and hide you in a cabin in the mountains for a fuckin' month so I can keep you to myself, so I can have my wicked fuckin' way with you all night and all day until neither of us can fuckin' walk."

I sat up a little more, and he straddled me, towering over me, his hips at chest level. "That sounds like the best idea I've ever heard."

He pressed his thumb against my lower lip, then against my nipple. "These fuckin' tits, though, Laurel. I want to fuckin'…" he groaned, sitting down on his heels to cup my breasts in his hands. "I want to lick them and kiss them and taste your nipples…" He lowered to do exactly that, moaning at the taste of me. "And I want…" He lifted up, onto his knees. "I want to fuck them, Laurel."

I cupped my breasts and pushed against him, clasping his thick hard cock between the mounded globes of flesh. Lifted my chest and sank down, plunging his shaft between my breasts. "Like this?"

He groaned, watching his cock vanish between the globes of my tits, feeling the soft silky flesh around him. "You know the fantasies I've had about doing this?"

I smirked. "Consider me the source of all your fantasies come true, then."

He shook his head, biting his lip as he shifted his hips. "You don't want that."

"Don't tell me what I want, Titus. You don't know what I want."

"So tell me."

"What if I told you I wanted to know I'd made your fantasy come true?"

"You don't get it. I'm not talking about some on-going thing, like I sit around in the shower jerking off thinking about randomly titty-fucking someone." He plunged upward again, to sprout up between the tops of my breasts, and I couldn't help but bend over to fit my lips around the tip as it appeared. "Jesus, woman. You're gonna kill me, here."

"Good. That's what I'm going for. Murder by orgasm. And you thought you were dirty." I lowered around him, so he sprouted up again and I let the flat of my tongue slide against his tip, tasting his leaking essence. "So then what *is* the fantasy?"

"You." He growled wordlessly as I kept him in my mouth and used my hands to plunge my tits around him. "Fuck, fuck, *fuck*, Laurel. *You're* the fantasy. You, doin' this." His hips were moving, then, flexing. "Coming all over these tits. Flipping you over and fucking from behind until you're crying for it, and then coming all over your perfect ass. Fuck, Laurel. You want to know the dirty truth? I wanna fuck your mouth. I wanna bury my hands in all that blond hair and fuck your mouth until you take my cum down your fuckin' throat."

"Oooh, Titus," I breathed, smirking up at him. "You *are* dirty."

"Told you."

This was familiar territory. I understood this. It was safe. Dirty, sexy, flirty, naughty, I could do.

"You'd better pick one, then." I rose up and plunged

down, taking him into my mouth on the upstroke. "Since you're already here, might as well start here."

"Laurel, I didn't mean…" He trailed off as I sped my efforts. He had my headboard in a death grip, the wood frame crackling under the power of his hands. "Fuck, you feel good."

"Yeah? You like this?" I whispered, my breath huffing on the tip of him, took him into my mouth and then back out again. "You like fucking my big fat titties?"

He grunted a laugh, an affirmative. "You have no idea, Laurel. None."

He was grinding against me, now. Hard, fast. I just held myself around him, mouth open above the opening between my breasts so each thrust put him into my mouth. Faster, faster. Grunting, groaning.

"You gonna come all over me, Titus?" I whispered. "Paint my tits with your cum, Titus. Let me have it."

He didn't stand a chance. My trap had been set the moment he saw me in this outfit.

"Fuck, Laurel," he snarled. "Fuck, fuck."

"Yeah, baby," I whispered, watching him lose control, watching his jaw clench, watching his beautiful razor-sharp abs tense, watching his hips pump and plunge his cock through the gap of my tits, watching the hard angles of his V-cut sharpen with each thrust. God, he was beautiful.

Granted, I got nothing whatsoever from this, on a physical level. But watching Titus Bright—*the* Titus

Bright—helpless above me, face a rictus of crazed plea-sure…that was fucking *fun*. Pleasurable in itself, knowing I *had* him, right where I wanted him, too blasted into the dazed wonder of ecstasy and knowing he was getting it from *me*, that was a reward it and of itself.

Bonus: the fact that he was too distracted to level me with his unexpected sweetness, his impossible to resist genuineness, his emotional vulnerability, his openness with his past…

Dammit, woman, stop. Stop thinking about him like that.

Focus on the dick.

He was close. I could tell at a glance. Throbbing, eyes closed for a moment then wrenching open to watch himself against me. His movements were sporadic, his rhythm faltering.

"Laurel…" he groaned.

I just moaned, for his benefit. Moved to complement his thrusting. And then as he went frantic with the rapidly rising edge of orgasm, I abandoned the pretense of using my tits, took him in my fists and wrapped my mouth around his thrusting head and sucked, took the thrusts and swallowed around them and then backed away and plunged my touch around him faster and faster until he jutted his hips forward hard, once more, flexed there, head thrown back, up on his knees, gasping, groaning. He dropped his chin to his chest as he reached release.

I took the first shot in my mouth—as much on my

lips as in my mouth. He growled and thrust and came again, shooting another thick gout onto my chest—I clenched my arms around my breasts to pile them up for him, letting him take over jerking him, squeezing them together as he spurted yet again, now painting his thick white cum in a stripe and puddle on my squeezed-together nipples. When he began to sag, I let go my breasts and gathered his shaft in my hands and plunged down on his still-pulsing erection, mouth latching around his cock and sucking the last droplets from him until he sank backward and fell to the bed beside me in a dazed, heaving heap.

Covered from lips to tits in his sticky, cooling seed, I watched him gasp. "You alive over there, Mr. Bright?"

"Nope. Dead." He was gasping raggedly, as if he'd just sprinted a football field. "I can't believe you just let me do that."

I patted his chest. "It was hot, trust me."

"I think I owe you at least a dozen orgasms."

I laughed. "I'll accept that. But it *was* hot."

"Hold on, just…just hold on. Let me catch my breath, and then I'll clean you up and start paying you back."

I raked a gentle scratching touch over his belly. "Later. I'll just jump in the shower."

I didn't give him a chance to argue, I just slid out of bed, away from him, away from that mouth of his. I relished what it could do between my thighs, but I feared what it could do between my ears, my heart—such as it existed, at least.

I closed my bathroom door and twisted on the shower water. Regarded myself in the mirror. Cum dribbled down my chin, smeared across the valley between my breasts and trickling down between them, coated my nipples in a thick sticky white glaze. All over me. I tasted it. Felt him all over me.

I wasn't about to tell him this, but in all my sexcapades in Europe and since, I'd never let anyone do that to me. BJs, handjobs, crazy sex in weird and wild places— everything I'd shared with my girls was true, and then some I'd never dared tell even them. But this? This was new. Unique to Titus.

And it had felt like crossing a line.

I didn't regret it—it *had* been hot. Sexy as fuck, and I'd do it again. But the reason I'd done it… that was the line I'd crossed. The act itself was not something I was or would ever be ashamed of. I'd done it because I wanted to, of my own volition, and not due to any pressure from him. If anything, I'd drawn him into it. But I'd done so to avoid letting our interaction turn any more personal.

I just couldn't fucking handle anything deeper. Not after all we'd already shared. The stories I'd told him—the truths previously long-buried, which not even Lizzy or Kat knew…I couldn't believe I'd told him that shit. I'd never told anyone. Not my parents, not my friends at school, certainly not any authorities. The only people who knew were me and the men who'd done it to me.

Had I been defaulting to old habits, after talking about it? Maybe. Once I'd gotten past the blunt trauma of it, I'd devolved immediately into a party girl of all-new proportions—no more drugs, no more overindulgence of alcohol. Just enough to kill the inhibitions and loosen up, and then I'd chased sex. Sought out any male who could make me feel good.

I'd sought pleasure as my only reason for existence. Hoping to fill the void. Hoping to fuck away the memories that haunted me. Hoping to fuck away the pain I'd felt, when I had woken up and knew what had happened, the hazy understanding that I'd been violated numerous times by numerous men. I'd turned into someone who used sex as my escape instead of chemicals. Used pheromones and oxytocin rather than vodka and oxycontin and tequila and THC and wine and cocaine.

I'd succeeded, to some degree. Never thought about that day.

Or rather…rarely.

Never had bad dreams about it…almost ever.

When I thought of sex, I thought about good things. The great sex I'd had in the years since. I'd refused to let those assholes ruin it for me.

The bathroom was wreathed in a dense fog of steam; I'd spaced out. I adjusted the temperature to a heat I could stand, climbed in. Rinsed off, scrubbed away, somewhat reluctantly, the last vestiges of Titus. Washed my hair, conditioned it.

Refused to think about the man on my bed.

I expected him to be gone when I emerged—I'd been in there more than half an hour. But, when I opened the bathroom door, wrapped in a towel with another around my hair, he was naked on my bed, sipping a beer he'd helped himself to from my fridge.

"Hope you don't mind," he said, lifting the bottle. He had another one on the nightstand; he twisted the top off and extended it to me. "Here."

"Yeah, Titus, I mind—you can fuck me, but you can't have my beer." I sipped. "Thanks."

He laughed, his eyes on me. "How can you be even sexier just out of the shower than you were in a killer mini skirt and all made up?"

I shook my head. "You're crazy."

He took a big swig of his beer, then slid to the edge of the bed, his eyes hungry. "For real. Every time I see you, every different outfit, wearing nothing at all, with makeup on, no makeup on, like this in just a couple'a towels? You're fucking sexier than ever… It's crazy as hell and I just don't understand it."

"I think it's just you," I said. "You must have done something to your brain."

He shook his head. "Nah, honey." He reached for me. "You've earned a little payback, I think."

"We started with payback, Titus," I said, reticent to start anything else—emotionally, I mean, not physically.

He sensed it. "Yeah, I guess so. But what you did was…fuck, man, it was crazy." His eyes hunted mine. "I wasn't expecting it."

I shrugged, trying for a breezy, sexy grin. "You never know what you're gonna get with me."

"No kidding. You keep me on my toes."

He stood up, and the intense sexiness of his body was so overwhelming I wanted to ignore my emotional and mental imbalance and just have my way with him again. Those fucking abs. That V-cut. Jesus, that cock. I wanted it inside me. God, he'd made me feel so good.

He towered over me. Stared down at me. "Laurel, what's up?"

I shrugged. "Nothing."

"You're a shitty liar."

I huffed. "Why do people keep saying that? I am not!"

"Maybe I can just tell, then. So." He trailed a fingertip over my breastbone, through errant droplets of water. "What's up, Laurel? Talk to me."

I guess maybe he deserved a little more truth. "It's just that, actually—the talking." I swallowed hard. "That stuff we talked about—what happened to me. I've never talked about it. I've never spoken of it with *anyone*, not with Lizzy or Kat or anyone. Not once since the day it happened. And I guess I'm just…" I shrugged, honestly not knowing *what* I was.

He nodded. "I get it." He gestured to the bed. "I can go, if you need to be alone. I'm just not the type of guy to…" A shrug as he tried to find the right phrase.

"Ejaculate and absquatulate?" I filled in, with a snort.

"Abs-skwa-what?" he said around a burst of laughter. "What the fuck does that even mean?"

"Absquatulate. It means to flee, or leave abruptly. My friend used to say it, back in college. She came across it in a blog post about little-known words and thought it was fucking hysterical. And she used to complain about guys who would, you know, hump and dump, pounce and bounce, or, ummm…oh, I know—nail and bail. There's a million, each worse than the last, and when Evelyn came across that word, it became her go-to. Ejaculate and absquatulate." I shrugged.

"God, I'm gonna have to remember that one," he said, still laughing. "But yeah, that. I've never been a guy to ejaculate and absquatulate."

"It's okay, Titus. I'm fine. I just…" A shrug. "I guess maybe I just need some time."

He nodded. Dressed quickly. Held his beanie in his hands. "Laurel, I still feel like I'm missing something, here."

"You're not. It's really fine, Titus."

"See, I've always been of the opinion that when a woman says *fine*, it's never a good thing."

I laughed. "I am definitely one of those women, I admit. I can put a hell of a lot of different meanings into 'fine,' depending on the situation. But in this moment, I swear, I mean it in the literal sense. I am *okay*. Today was just a lot."

"As long as you're sure." He twisted the beanie into a tight roll. "Because honestly, I don't really want to leave, you know. I like you. I like hanging out with you. Doesn't even have to be anything else."

If he stayed any longer, he'd end up calling me a shitty liar again. Just hold on to the lie a little longer, I told myself. He can't see through it.

"Titus," I sighed. "I don't know what to say."

He bent, cupped a hand tenderly around the back of my neck, and kissed me.

God *damn* the man.

How dare he be able to kiss like that?

He backed away, leaving me utterly shook, breathless. Because that kiss had been a *statement*.

"I see you, Laurel McGillis. I may not have much of an education, but I'm not stupid. I *see* you." His fingers grazed my cheek. A smile graced his lips. "I'll give it to you, and no arguments. For now."

I swallowed. Words had abandoned me.

He backed away another step, toward my bedroom door, eyes narrowed, jaw tensed, the smile gone, a billion thoughts burning on his beautiful face. "Fuck," he snarled.

Launched himself across the space in a single stride, slammed up against me, and his arm circled my waist, and his lips slashed across mine. His tongue slid against my teeth and I had no choice but to open for him and his hand was raking at the towel in a turban around my hair, tugging it free. My damp hair fell around my shoulders in cold strings, stuck to my cheeks and back. He yanked my towel off and tossed it aside to leave me naked and cold, only to warm me with his own body heat. He dragged me harder against him, hand in my hair and the other clutching at my ass to clutch me in a fierce, wild, crushing embrace, and his mouth devoured mine, tongue slashing, lips greedy.

I felt him hardening against my belly, felt my instinctual need for him rising in me like a flood tide.

If the kiss before had been a statement, this one was...

Him screaming from the rooftops.

And then, all at once, he was gone. My front door slammed closed before I even knew he'd moved, and I was naked and aroused and confused.

And alone.

"Fuck!" I snarled, my tone a nearly exact mirror of Titus's, moments before.

CHAPTER EIGHT

"**A**ND…YOUR KEYS!" I HANDED MY CLIENTS A KEYRING jingling with a set of keys to the house they'd just purchased. "Best of luck in your new home, and if you have any further questions at any point, call me—and thank you, from the bottom of my heart, for the opportunity to do business with you!"

The clients each shook my hand and left the title company with huge grins on their faces. I finished up the paperwork with the girls from the title office, and then walked back to Six Chicks, which, conveniently, was just down the street a few doors. I filed the paperwork, and was preparing to look over my slate of clients and potential clients. The front door jangled; I wasn't expecting anyone and I hadn't seen or heard from Titus in almost a week, as he was up in Canada for a series of pop-ups, so I assumed it was for someone else in the office.

"Not gonna say hi?" a deep, rumbling voice said, from a foot above my head.

I started, clapping my hand over my chest. "Holy shit, Titus, you scared me."

He plopped down in one of the chairs opposite my desk, kicking his feet up on the edge. He wore a pair of battered Converse, a pair of khaki Dickies cut off below the knee, and a plain black ribbed tank top, with what I was coming to understand was his favorite headwear, the black beanie. "Whatcha doin', hot stuff?"

I leaned forward, pushing a pen tip against the sole of his shoe. "Feet off my desk, you heathen." He pulled his feet down and crossed an ankle onto his knee, and I gestured at my computer. "Well, this being an office, and it being daytime, I'm working."

He rolled his eyes. "Okay, then, smart-ass, a better question would be, can you stop working and come hang out with me?"

"Hang out with you."

He nodded, scratching at his jaw. "Yeah. Hang out. You, me, doing, you know, stuff."

"What kind of *stuff*?"

A smirk. "Butt stuff." He cackled. "Kidding, kidding. Actually, I rented out an arcade."

I gave a frowning smirk. "You rented out...an arcade."

"Yeah. I woke up wanting to play Skee-Ball. So I gave this arcade like ten grand and they're gonna stay closed for us. Figure we could go play Skee-Ball, and drink some beers, and just...hang out."

I shook my head, laughing. "Yes, Titus, I can quit for the day and come play Skee-Ball with you."

He lit up, grinning. "Really?"

I put my computer to sleep and grabbed my purse. "Yes, really. I just closed on a house today, and I don't have anything else scheduled. I was going to work on putting together some staging pieces for a new listing, but I can do that tomorrow. It doesn't even go up until next week anyway."

He clapped his hands on his thighs. "All right. Let's go throw balls at holes!"

I laughed. "I think you roll them, actually."

"You roll the balls, do you?" he said, snickering.

I groaned. "Oh my god, you're horrible." I couldn't help a cackle, though. "Yes, Titus. You take the big hard round ball in your hand, and you roll it down the tube and into the hole."

He laughed, head thrown back. "Ball jokes from Laurel. I win."

We were both still laughing as we climbed into his truck and headed for the arcade. The owner was an elderly man wearing yellow plaid pants, a brown button-down, bowling shoes, and a derby.

"Mr. Bright, welcome, welcome," the proprietor said. "I'm Louis, and it's my pleasure to host you and your friend this afternoon. Anything you want, just ask. I've turned all the games so they don't require coins.

They'll still give you tickets, but of course, anything from the gift shop you want, it's yours."

Titus shook his hand. "Thanks, Louis. I appreciate you doing this for me." He gestured at me. "This lovely lady here is my friend Laurel McGillis."

Louis took my hand and kissed the back of it. "A pleasure, Ms. McGillis." He pointed at the counter where you exchanged your street shoes for bowling shoes. "I'll be there if you need me."

Titus looked like he was as excited for this as if he were ten years old again. "A whole arcade and bowling alley, all to myself."

I laughed, resting a hand on his arm. "Is this, like, a lifelong fantasy come true?"

He nodded, zero irony in his expression or voice. "Absolutely. When I was a kid, we couldn't afford the arcade. Then I was too busy touring, and then I was too famous, and also too busy."

"Well, here we are. What are we doing first?"

"Skee-Ball. Definitely Skee-Ball."

The next hour and a half, Titus lost in Skee-Ball to my clearly superior ball-handling skills. He never lost his good humor, though, laughing harder and harder as it became obvious he wasn't going to win—I sank ball after ball into the highest point holes, my string of tickets reaching ever more comical proportions, while he struggled to sink a single ball. By the time he decided it was time to do something else, my pile of tickets was so long I had to carry it in my arms.

Titus cackled as I tossed the pile of tickets on the prize counter. "So, you're good at Skee-Ball."

I pointed at the giant pink stuffed bunny rabbit. "I want that." Louis got it down for me, and I laughed as I took it from him—the thing was bigger than I was. "I played softball in high school, and my group of friends in college used to go bowling every week." I smirked at him. "Also, I'm just really good with balls."

His voice dropped to a husky murmur as he took me by the hand and dragged me across the building toward the arcade area. "Yeah, you're good with balls. I'm still thinking about the other night."

"Hey, that makes two of us thinking about that night."

"Well, I doubt we're thinking about the same thing," he said.

"Oooh, I love this game!" I dragged him across the arcade to a vintage Ms. Pac-Man game. "There was a pizza place near my apartment in college, and they had a Ms. Pac-Man, and I'd play it all the time." I sat down and started a game, while Titus stood behind me, watching with his hands on my shoulders. "What part of that night are *you* thinking about?" I asked, focusing on my game rather than looking up at him.

"All the payback I didn't get to do."

I snorted. "Funny, I for sure figured you'd be

thinking about, you know, how I let you cum all over me."

His fingers tightened on my shoulders. "Don't get me wrong, here, babe—I'm thinking about that. I think about that shit all the fucking time. Several times a day, if you want the truth." His hand slid from my shoulder to my throat, and then down, over my breastbone, above my cleavage. "My cum all over your lips, all over your tits. Yeah, babe, I think about that. But what I think about even more? Getting you off. Licking your sweet pussy until you come so hard, so many times you don't know which way is up."

I barely avoided getting eaten by a blue ghost. "You're gonna make me lose, butthead," I mumbled, thighs pressing together. "I never know which way is up when I'm around you, even when you're not making me come."

He glanced over his shoulder, presumably at Louis, who for the most part had been behind the bowling shoes counter watching a TV in the bar area, on the opposite side of the building from where we were. Then, sneakily, his hand slid down, down, fingertips edging under the neckline of my dress and under my bra to cup my breast.

I wiggled under his touch. "You're gonna make me mess up, Titus," I breathed.

"You already kicked my ass in Skee-Ball," he muttered. "Gotta make it even."

"Oh, you think you can beat my score in Ms.

Pac-Man? Even distracting me like that, I guarantee you I'll still kick your ass."

His other hand stole under my garments to cup my other breast, fingers tweaking and rolling my nipples. Damned sensitive nipples—it was intensely distracting. I tried like hell to tune out the yummy, tingly warm scratch of his hand on my naked skin, to focus on the yellow round…thing, eating its way around the screen. When he began twiddling both nipples at the same time, my breath caught and my attention wandered…

"Dammit!" I sat back, grabbing his wrists but stopping short of yanking his hands away—his touch *did* feel good, after all. "You're gonna pay for that, Titus."

He laughed. "All right. My turn." He noted my score, and I scooted out of the seat so he could take it. "Prepare to lose, Laurel."

I waited for him to pass level one, level two…waited until he was really cranking on level four, and then I sidled between his arms, sat on his lap.

"Hey," he laughed. "No fair. I didn't actually get in your way."

I straddled him, facing him, and began planting kisses on him, starting at the side of his neck where the thick sinews met his shoulder. "Oh, is this distracting?"

He huffed. "Nope."

I slid my seat on him, grinding back and forth as I kissed up his neck, over his jaw, behind his ear. He remained admirably focused as I ground and kissed, but his undoing was when I stuck my tongue in his ear.

He leaped up out of the seat, laughing and shouting at the same time, bringing me with him. "Cheater!" he cackled, tossing me onto my feet and coming for me with clawed fingers. "That was cheating."

"Cheating? There has to be rules for it to be cheating. You distracted me, I distracted you." I darted out of his reach, glancing at his score as I circled around the Ms. Pac-Man unit. "I beat you, by the way. By a good two hundred points. So far, I'm winning this date."

He lunged for me, and I dodged around a deer hunter game. "Only because you cheated!"

I barely avoided his grasping fingers—I had good reason to stay agile in this game, since I hated being tickled. "Oh, I cheated at Skee-Ball, did I? And did you specify any rules for *how* I could distract you? No, you didn't. There was no cheating. Just good old honest womanly wiles."

"I'm gonna catch you and I'm gonna wile you, woman." He dodged the other way around the deer hunter game, but by that point I was screeching in laughter as I sprinted—as well as I could in three-inch heeled sandals—between rows of games and putting a giant four-person motorcycle racing game between us.

"Oh, you're gonna wile me, are you?" I laughed, breathless, as I faked one way, and then another. "What does that even mean, anyway?"

"I don't know, but you're about to find out." He watched me fake this way and that, then pulled a fake of his own…which my dumbass fell for hook, line, and sinker.

He had me in two steps, then, catching me in his arms and lifting me clear off the ground, one arm keeping me held aloft while pinning my arms to my sides, while the other sought my ticklish spot—he found it in a matter of seconds: my ribs.

He proceeded to hold me pinned and off the ground, helpless, and tickle me until I was laughing so hard I couldn't breathe. I finally resorted to kicking his shins and begging for mercy.

"Okay, okay!" I gasped, tears of laughter on my cheeks. "Mercy, ohmygod stop, stop, stop!" He let me down and backed away, warily. I smoothed my dress and glared at him. "I *hate* being tickled."

He made a sarcastic face. "Well, you *were* laughing."

"It's an automatic response."

I held the glare. "I *was* going to suggest we sneak into the bathroom and see what kind of…*trouble*…we could get into. But now, I'm rethinking that plan."

His face went from sarcastic to comically tragic in an instant. "In my defense, I didn't know you didn't like being tickled. And you *were* playing hard to get."

I let a smirk finally cross my face. "You were chasing me. I was supposed to, what? Just let you catch me?"

He shrugged. "I mean, I wasn't planning on tickling you until you started playing keep away."

"Oh?" My voice sounded breathless and sultry, even to me. "What were you planning on doing, then?"

He swaggered toward me. "Well, we'd have to sneak into the bathroom, for that. But it involved finding out whether you're wearing panties under that skirt."

"Wouldn't *you* like to know?" I teased.

"Of course I want to know," he muttered, taking me by the hand and tugging me into motion. "Thus me suggesting I find out, in the bathroom."

We neared one of those video game pods that's partially enclosed, to create a more immersive experience, or something. I pulled him into it and sat down—it was facing in a direction which meant Louis, even if he'd been looking this way, couldn't see anything going on. And we were the only ones in the arcade, so…

It was a *Jurassic Park* driving game sort of thing, and I pressed the button to start it. The machine began grinding, humming, and jolting as the music started, and the voice-over began.

Titus glanced at me. "Jurassic Park, huh?"

"Yup." I grinned at him. "And I've got a hungry dinosaur."

He snickered. "Ohmygod, Laurel, you've got a hungry dinosaur? Really?"

"What? Like you've never made a terrible dick pun before?"

"Of course I have. I just didn't peg you for the type to make terrible vagina puns. You come across as this classy lady, and all." He was only nominally pretending to pay attention to the game.

I cackled. "Titus, babe—if you think *I'm* a classy lady, then you really need to get out more and meet some actual classy ladies, because I am *not* one."

I glanced this way, and that. The coast was clear, as Louis had by now fallen asleep kicked back in his chair, feet up on the glass counter, *Wheel of Fortune* reruns playing. I think I heard him snore, actually.

"For one thing, a classy lady wouldn't even dream of doing this in a public place." I tugged the hem of my dress up, inch by inch, baring my shins, then my knees, then my thighs.

Titus had abandoned all pretense of playing the game—whatever the objective seemed to be; it appeared to be more of a ride than an interactive game. Not that it mattered. We weren't in this pod to play a game, after all.

At least, not a video game.

I tugged the hem up one last inch, and my black thong was revealed. "There. Now you know. I'm wearing panties."

He inhaled deeply, slowly, chewing on his lip as he let it out with a growl. "Take 'em off."

I smirked, winking. "Is this the payback you were referencing, earlier?"

He blinked lazily, eyes roaming my body, down from

my eyes to my cleavage, to my thighs, to the black cotton over my sex, damp with desire and sticking to my skin. "Could be."

The game was at the end of the experience, and he started it over. Leaned past me to verify our host was still zonked out.

"You want it to be?" he asked, his voice low as his fingers trailed over my thighs.

"Well, I've never done anything like this in an arcade before."

"Me neither." He slid his finger over the damp cotton. "Off, Laurel. Let me see you."

I shimmied out of the thong, handing it to him. "There. Now what?"

He shoved the black thong into his hip pocket. "Now, you come on my fingers before the game ends."

I leaned back against the seat, sliding down, spreading my thighs for him. "If you're challenging me, then I'll up the ante—can you make me come twice before it's over?"

He brought his fingertip to my sex, dragging the thick digit through my slick folds. I was already shuddering—when his touch slithered against my clit, I had to bite down on a gasp, chew on a whimper. When he thrust two fingers inside me and smeared my own wetness against me, I had to bite down on my lip and close my eyes and swallow around the scream in my throat—roughly fourteen seconds had passed and I was already hurtling past the first orgasm, rocking raggedly against his fingers as they swirled against my sex, the pressure of his fingers precise and perfect, his speed exactly calculated to bring me maximum pleasure, his rhythm torturously designed to keep me at the thrashing edge of climax.

He kept me there, just past orgasm, with nothing but two fingers lightly drilling against my clit, until I began shaking and trembling and a shriek escaped my clenched teeth and I was riding his fingers. On the screen, a pixelated raptor made a sound that rather effectively mimicked my screams. The second orgasm battered me into quaking jelly, left me gasping as the game credits rolled and the screen flashed "insert $1.50 to start game."

"Two orgasms before game's end." He let his fingers halt, but didn't remove his touch. "What do I win?"

"I thought…" I had to pause to get my brain function back. "I thought that was payback for the other day in my room."

He laughed. "It was. And I owe you at least two or three more."

I shook my head sloppily. "Nah, I think we're even."

We just sat, for a moment, watching the intro screen of the game cycle. He had something on his mind, I could tell. I didn't want to ask. I was having fun, and I didn't want it to be anything. Just a fun date with a hot guy who could make me come twice in a matter of minutes with nothing more than a couple fingers.

His eyes cut to mine, and our gazes locked. I saw the things in his eyes, the unasked questions—the nascent desire for something I wasn't sure I was ready or willing or able to give.

"Bet you I can beat you at the deer hunter game." He withdrew his touch, and my skin mourned the loss of his heat, his rough touch.

I laughed gratefully as I tugged my dress down and exited the game. "Now that, I'll give you. I've never shot a gun of any kind in my life."

He eyed me incredulously. "You haven't? Not even, like, a BB gun?"

"Nope. You'll probably go apoplectic when I tell you this, but I actually was once invited through some mutual friends to spend a summer in Scotland with some royals from the UK. Like, at their famous summer castle, the one in the show, *The Crown*. They took me hunting, and skeet shooting, but I was too nervous around them, and couldn't shoot. I held a big double-barrel shotgun, but I chickened out."

He grunted in disgust. "Pathetic." He laughed, to make it a joke. "I don't shoot a lot, actually. I don't own a gun. I've been shooting with friends, though. Some dudes I know have this big fuckin' ranch down in Mexico, like thousands and thousands of acres, and they took me down there and we went hunting. Pretty cool, for what it is, but hunting is kinda boring for me."

I laughed as we started the game and pulled the fake

orange rifles out of their scabbards. "Thank you! Like, when I went with the girls, in Scotland, it was *so* boring. Just crawling around in the dirt, walking for miles, waiting in absolute silence for some poor deer half a mile away to just blithely walk into a bullet. I don't get it. I didn't tell them that, of course. I acted like I was having the time of my life."

"Of course. What one does when one is hunting with English royalty."

"Rawwwwther," I drawled, in a passable affectation of a posh English accent.

Conversation was light, then. We played pretty much every game in the arcade at least once, and Titus beat me at most of them.

Finally, Louis woke with a start, and checked the time, and realized he was supposed to have closed an hour before. The poor old guy looked just absolutely done in, exhausted from his long nap, and it *was* pretty late, so Titus made sure Jeremy had paid for the day, and we took our leave.

Next stop was a pizzeria—it was a tiny corner place, the dive bar version of a pizza joint, with a handful of tables covered in red-and-white checkered cloths made of that weird not-quite-rubber material. There was a group of four twenty-something girls at one table, and the moment Titus and I walked in, they went silent, staring, only to huddle together and start whispering fiercely.

Titus grinned at me. "You order. I'm gonna do the rock star thing." He jerked a thumb at the table of girls.

"What do you want?"

He shrugged. "Whatever."

I cackled. "Isn't that supposed to be my line, here?"

He affected a high-pitched voice. "Oh, just order for me, darling. You know what I like."

"Anchovies and onions, coming up," I said, laughing.

"Pepperoni and bacon, how about that? I'm not picky." He paused. "Well, anchovies and onions are both pretty gross on pizza."

"Pepperoni and bacon sounds good to me." I couldn't help it—in the presence of four drooling, lust-agape, starstruck young women staring thirstily… at *my* man?

I kissed him…but *good*.

I about passed out, mentally, when I realized I'd thought of Titus as my man.

He chuckled as he pulled away, touching my chin with a thumb. "Territory marked, huh?"

I wasn't sure how to answer. Just shrugged. "I just wanted to kiss you."

He backed away. "Shitty liar, Laurel. You're a shitty liar. But again, I'll give it to you."

"I'm not jealous!"

He held up his hands. "I think it's hot, so don't argue for my sake."

I huffed, and turned to the counter. "Just go be a rock star while I order our pizza."

He cackled, turning around only a few steps from the table of girls. "Hi, ladies. How are we doing this fine evening?" He grabbed a nearby chair and did the hot guy thing where he spun it around and leaned against the back of it.

He spent the next few minutes flirting with them, taking selfies, signing shirts and receipts and such, while I ordered a large pizza and a milkshake to share. The teenaged kid behind the counter was actually wearing a Bright Bones shirt under the open button-down shirt sporting the logo of the establishment. He was shy, though, afraid to make eye contact with me and finding it hard to look anywhere except my chest, because teenage boy—the only other place his eyes went was Titus, and there was hero-worship in his stare.

I took a table in the corner and sipped at the milkshake while Titus took his leave of the girls, who were giggling and comparing selfies and discussing which filter was best as they exited.

Titus was about to sit down with me when I glanced up at him, humming a negative as I swallowed a sip of milkshake. "Mmmm-mmm. Not done being a rock star yet, big boy." I glanced meaningfully at the kid behind the register.

Titus saw the shirt, and nodded. Dug in his pocket as

he headed for the counter. "What up, buddy. Nice shirt. Where'd you see us play?"

"Uh, here. LA. One of your last shows."

"Sweet, man." He pulled something out of his pocket—a much-folded piece of paper. "So, answer me a question. How big a fan are you?"

"I have every album you've ever made, on CD, digitally, and vinyl." He shifted uncomfortably. "I'd been saving my allowance and job money to buy a car, but when I saw you guys were doing a set of shows in LA, I used it to buy front row seats."

Titus set the folded piece of paper on the counter. "So, this is pretty special." He eyed the kid. "What's your name, buddy?"

"Cal."

"Cal, this here is actually the set-list for a show in Minnesota, one of our very first shows outside Chicago, actually. Written in Tommy's own hand." He pulled his Sharpie out from behind his ear, uncapped it, signed the paper. "I've been carrying it around for years, but I think it's time it went to someone else."

The kid looked about ready to shit his pants. "For real?" He traced the paper with a fingertip. "No fuckin' way."

I got choked up, watching Titus do something that sweet, so spontaneously. Damn him. Damn the man. It was easy to stay objective and detached when it was just fun and sex. But when he did something like that? God, how could I *not* fall for him?

Shit, shit, shit.

Did I just think that?

I wasn't falling for him. Was not. Absolutely not.

Titus realized I was distracted the moment he sat down, but he didn't push it. Didn't angle to get invited in when he pulled into my driveway. Just…kissed me, quickly, lightly, and cupped my cheek with a rough paw.

"I'll see you soon?"

I blinked at him, distracted by my emotions—namely, the freak-out I was shoving down, holding back. "Uh, yeah. Yeah." I rallied, momentarily. "I had a really great time, Titus. Really, really great."

He touched his thumb to my chin. "Good. I had fun too." A pause. As if he was about to ask me what was wrong. Don't—don't—don't. "Um. Yeah. I'll call you?"

I smiled at him, leaned in and kissed him—I had to. "Yeah. Call me. Soon, okay?"

He nodded. "Promise."

I went inside, watched him leave through the blinds of my front picture window…when he was gone, I promptly called Lizzy and demanded an emergency meeting, all hands, alert, alert, code red, major freak-out.

I was falling for Titus.

Lizzy slammed the empty wine bottle down on my coffee table. "I hereby call this emergency meeting to order."

I laughed, already tipsy. Or, tipsy again, since I'd already been tipsy once today. "First on the agenda, I'm not talking about it."

Teddy huffed. "Yes, you are. You called us, remember?"

Zoe was still taking the many cartons of Chinese carryout she'd brought from the paper bags. "You know, for all that you never stop talking, Laurel, I'm realizing how little you ever actually *say*."

Kat was uncorking the next bottle of wine. "For real. The last year and a half or so, ever since Lizzy met Braun, I've learned more about you than in all the years I've known you before. And it's making me realize how little I actually *know* about you."

Teddy helped Zoe with the food, arranging opened cartons, stacks of paper-wrapped chopsticks, and packets of soy. "You're a master of obfuscating, is what you are, and avoidance. And changing the subject. But as I said, you called us upset and said you needed some support. And in the years I've known you, you've never asked for help for anything. Which means it's serious. But now that we're here, you're gonna be all like, *oh no, I'm not talking about why I'm freaking out, even though we all know it's because I'm falling for Titus Bright and I don't know how to handle it.*"

"I am *not* falling for Titus Bright." I slugged wine.

Lizzy grabbed my wrist. Her eyes locked onto mine. "Listen, Laur—we'll sit here all night and get drunk with you, as drunk as you want to get, and we can all take tomorrow off. But you have to *talk* to us."

I groaned, flopped my head forward onto my palm. "Feed me. And then ply me with me copious amounts of alcohol, and prepare to be horrified."

And so they did. We destroyed a couple hundred dollars' worth of Chinese food, washed it all down with glass after glass of red wine, all shot through with jokes and levity and banter and acting like this was just another girls' night in.

But then.

Oh, but then.

Food gone, floating with a full belly and a heady buzz, I leaned back in my favorite comfy chair and twisted the stem of my wineglass, watching the light sparkle through the ruby liquid.

And I told them everything I'd told Titus.

And more.

I told them, in candid detail I'd never have shared with any man, all the things I'd done to erase the memory of that night. How I'd also used shop therapy to fill the hole, to staunch the wound. Thus, the fact that my spare bedroom was a secondary closet, filled with hundreds of thousands of dollars' worth of purses, shoes, dresses, skirts, tops, jackets, jewelry, and lingerie.

I told them everything.

How I suspected my dad wasn't my father, the gross things I'd witnessed regularly as a child that had made sex to me always seem like no big deal. How I'd never had a sexual relationship that meant anything. How I wasn't sure what that even looked like, how one would do that. How to…do that.

I told them everything.

Except one thing.

The one thing I'd not told Titus either.

Autumn would understand, I think. She'd suspect, if she were here, but she and Seven were still in the Caribbean.

When I was finally done talking, no one had much to say.

"Damn, Laur," Teddy said, eventually. "I guess it all makes sense, now."

"No shit," Kat said.

Lizzy patted my thigh. "And you told all or most of this to Titus?"

"Yes."

"And you'd never spoken of it before, to anyone?" she clarified.

"Right."

"And then you and he came here," Teddy said, twisting an empty bottle on the coffee table, "and the sex happened. Except you freaked out and made it not sex. Because feelings are hard and you don't think you have a heart to give."

"Right."

Kat munched on a fortune cookie. "If it wasn't sex, what was it?"

"And did he buy it?" Zoe asked, as a follow-up.

I closed my eyes and scooted down in the chair, feet up on the table, resting the wine-glass on my chest. "It was…just fucking around. You want to know the dirty details? Fine. He happens to be an absolute god among men at going down, by which I mean he gave me three screaming orgasms in a row without even trying, just to fucking warm me up. And then I let him fuck my tits and come all over me. And then I took a thirty-minute shower, expecting him to get the hint and leave. Only, *apparently* he's not the *type* to ejaculate and absquatulate, and I had to be all like I'm fine, I just need time because talking about all this is a lot. And then he started to walk away, like he got it, but then…*but then* he decided to kiss me like I've never been kissed in my entire fucking life. But wait, there's more! He walked away again, only to stop, launch himself *back* across the room, rip the towel off my hair and away from my body and kiss me like…" I swallowed hard. "Like…I don't know. I don't fucking know. Like he was saying something he didn't have the words for. Like I was *his*. Like that first time we met. And before he kissed me, he said he *saw* me." I blinked hard. "So I don't know if he bought it. I don't think he did. And I'm worried. I'm scared it was…I'm scared I'll lose him, and I'm scared that I think I *had* him to lose, and I'm scared of not wanting to lose him, I'm scared of being with him, being around him at all because he just gets me—he can get me to just *open up* like nobody I've ever met and I don't understand how or why, and if I have sex with him again it'll be…I don't fucking know, something I don't know how to handle. And I'm fucking scared."

Lizzy took my wine from me, set it aside, and curled up in the chair with me—*on* me. "Honey pie. Listen. I know this is scary. I know it's hard, it doesn't make any sense. But take it from me, okay? It can be worth it."

"Yeah," I sniffled. "But what if it isn't? Braun turned out great. You have a guy so great he's at home right now being Daddy to your little one so you can be here with my dumbass. That's great. And it worked out for Autumn, so great for her. I'm really, really happy for you. But…I don't know *how*. I've never seen it. Love, I mean. That's what we're talking about, right? Love? I don't know how to do that, how I can…be the woman who…" I trailed off. "See? I can't even talk about it and make any kind of sense."

"I think you just have to give him a chance," Kat said.

"Because so far," Teddy said. "He's got all the re- alness points in the situation. And I say that with love."

I frowned at her. "Did you hear what I let him do? I feel like that's pretty real."

She shook her head. "No, babe, that was classic avoidance technique and you know it. You did that so you wouldn't have to have actual sex with him and risk an emotional bond and connection. You know it and I think he knows it. He said he *sees* you, right? That means he knew exactly what that was, and he's not gonna let you get away with it."

I squeezed my eyes shut tighter. "How can he not let me get away with it?"

"I dunno—that's for him to figure out. But it means you have to decide if you have the courage to *try*," Teddy said.

"God, you're such a matchmaker."

"Always the matchmaker, never the match," she quipped. "Still true. What I said, I mean."

Lizzy kissed my temple. "She's a hundred percent right. You have to figure out what you want. Him, or emotional safety. And by safety, I mean safe in the little bubble of emotional isolation you've been living in your whole life. Which we all get, honey. We do. Shit, Kat is still in it herself. And we all know why. And she knows she's on the shortlist for getting matched."

"Won't work," Kat said, "I don't have the damage Laurel has—I'm just not interested."

"Bullshit!" Lizzy sang. "But this is about Laurel here, not you, so I'll let it slide."

Kat just rolled her eyes.

I looked around at my friends. "I wish Autumn was here. I miss her ass."

"You miss her *ass*?" Zoe asked, snickering. "Is there something you need to tell us?"

"Oh my god, Zoe. Grow up, woman, seriously." I reached over and grabbed a fortune cookie off the side table and chucked it at her. "So immature."

"*You're* immature," she shot back. "She does have a great ass, though, doesn't she? Lucky Seven, that's all I've got to say."

"God, Zoe. That's your sister!" I groaned another laugh. "What did I do to deserve such friends?" I grinned at her, at everyone. "I love you guys. I still have no clue what I'm gonna do, but I'm glad I have you guys. I may crash and burn and fall into little pieces, but at least I'll have the five of you to be there when it happens."

"Yes, you will," Lizzy said. "What you're gonna do is you're going to give Titus Bright a chance. Because if you don't, I'm not sure even best friend and girl code will be enough to keep Kat from trying to get her hands on him."

Kat rolled a shoulder. "I mean, that man is the finest thing to walk this earth, and if you don't find a way to keep him, you'll regret it forever, and you'll be the dumbest person to ever live, and I may never forgive you, and we can't be friends anymore." A huff. "But, I would never take a shot at him if it didn't work out with the two of you, as much as it would hurt to let such a snack go. I love you too much."

I sighed. "This is scary. He left. Because I…I guess I

maybe pushed him away. What if…what he's like, nah, not worth the rejection."

"You didn't reject him," Lizzy pointed out. "You just iced him out emotionally."

"After sharing your deepest, darkest secrets with him." Kat reached out and held his hand. "Which I totally understand, because I'm the same way. If I open up even a little, it's immediately followed by a complete shutdown."

"I just…" I rubbed my face. "Now that he's gone and I'm thinking about things and you guys are all like, don't be dumb, take a chance, I'm wondering if I fucked up and if I'll get another chance. But then I think about taking that chance and it scares me shitless. I have serious abandonment issues, you know? Like hardcore. There's just never been a male in my life that I've ever trusted. Not one, ever. How do you go about reversing thirty-nine years' worth of not ever trusting men, ever, for any reason? How do you…how do you overcome the trauma of being gang-raped? Sure it was a long fucking time ago, but still. I can say with frankness that I don't think I'm healed from it."

"Didn't you hint to Autumn that you did talk to someone?" Teddy asked.

"That was…about something else." I swallowed hard. "I can't get into that. I have seen a therapist, but I kept those conversations narrowed to one particular issue."

"Laurel…" Lizzy murmured. "It's *us*."

I shook my head. "Not now. Please. It's been too much of a day. I'm nice and pleasantly drunk and I'm feeling good with you guys and I don't want to talk about that."

"Okay, honey." Lizzy hugged me, and then I was being buried under an avalanche of best friends, all hugging me and smothering me with their love. "Another time, then."

Late afternoon, at home, a few days later. I was doing laundry and listening to a podcast on recovering from unhealed trauma, when my doorbell rang.

I finished folding the skirt in my hands and headed for the front door, replacing the earbuds in their case. I opened the door to find a short woman on the far side of middle age, her graying brown hair in a cute bob, dressed casually in jeans and a white blouse; she carried a large purse, the open top revealing a clipboard with a yellow legal pad clipped to it. She wore thick-framed glasses, and her smile was friendly.

"Hi, Laurel McGillis?"

She seemed official, or something. Nerves shot through me. "Yes. How can I help you?"

She broadened her smile, perhaps sensing my nerves. "My name is Dr. Katherine Hines, I'm a psychologist specializing in sexual trauma."

I swallowed hard. "I see." I frowned. "One of my friends sent you, I'm guessing?"

"Actually, not the friend you're probably thinking." She reached into her purse and withdrew a torn slip of paper with writing scrawled on it, handed it to me.

Laurel,

Dr. Hines is the most highly regarded specialist in the country for this particular issue. I know this is not my place. I get that you may be pissed off at me for making this huge assumption. But I'm willing to piss you off if it will help you, because I guess I figure what else do I have to lose. Please understand where I'm coming from. Just talk to her.

TB

I swallowed hard, chewed back my inclination to shut down, to resort to anger. "What did Titus tell you?"

She shook her head. "Nothing at all. He paid in advance for me to come here and spend a couple hours with you. He only told me that you're his friend, he cares about you, and that he felt like you may need help with some past issues that you've been…avoiding, perhaps, in my area of expertise."

I bit back a laugh. "Titus Bright paid you, a licensed therapist, to come to my house. I didn't think you guys did house calls."

She chuckled. "I don't. This is the first time for me."

"But here you are."

"Here I am. It's my calling to help people, and he hinted that you may be resistant to seeking the help you need. I want to help you." Another chuckle. "And it doesn't hurt that he was very…generous…in compensating me for the unusual request."

I sighed. "Well, you're here. Come on in."

We sat down in my living room, and she settled in with her notepad and pen. "Why don't you tell me about yourself. Just…to break the ice a little."

Hesitantly, at first, I told her my background. She asked subtle questions, I noticed, which got me to keep opening up. And if I attempted to gloss over something, she always caught it. By the time an hour had gone by, I'd explained most of the messy garbage from my childhood with my parents and the parties they hosted.

"So, that's a lot," she said, at the end of ninety minutes of me gorging on old pain. "I think it would best serve you if I came back next week and we carried on from there." She handed me a business card. "I am willing to come back here, if it's easiest for you. But my office is also rather close to you. Less than half an hour from here."

"We didn't even get to the good stuff, Dr. Hines," I said. "The real reason you're here in the first place."

She nodded. "I know. But Rome wasn't built in a day, right? I think it would overload you to get into all that right now. We're just establishing a baseline today, okay?"

I nodded. Considered. "I can come to you. And I can pay you myself."

She just smiled. "Mr. Bright has covered my time for at least another session, especially if you come to my office. We can discuss options beyond that." She put her clipboard and pen in her purse. "Laurel, you're doing the best thing possible for yourself, by addressing this stuff. I know it can be hard, when it's something you've kept repressed for a long time. But if you want to have a healthy future, you need to heal. And with this stuff, with severe sexual trauma as Titus hinted we're dealing with, it can take a long time and a lot of therapy to help you heal from it. Don't expect overnight miracles. But if you trust me, and you're honest with me, and you do the work, I promise, it'll be worth it."

"Thank you for coming, Dr. Hines." I did feel…a sense of relief; and I did know therapy could help.

"Mr. Bright…" She smiled at me. "He cares about you. It takes courage to do what he did, sending me here."

I nodded, chewing on the inside of my cheek. "Yeah, it does. Anyway, thank you, again." I led her to the door. "So next week?"

She glanced at me on the way down the steps from my front porch. "Yes, I'll contact you tomorrow with a day and time, once I have my schedule in front of me."

"Sounds good. Bye, Dr. Hines."

"Bye, Laurel. See you next week."

She drove away, then, and I stood on my porch with my front door wide open, trying to fathom how I was supposed to feel about Titus, now.

Complicated, that was how.

He'd sent a therapist to my house. Clearly, he felt I needed to address the issue in my past. How presumptuous of him. But…he wasn't wrong. Stubborn me, I'd refused for years. Refused to talk about it, pretended my fucked-up way of dealing with it was just fine. It wasn't fine.

I mean, clearly I had issues with trust and intimacy. Look at what I'd turned things into with him, the other day.

I owed him a conversation, didn't I?

If only I had any clue how to find him, how to get ahold of him.

꩜

"So, Laurel." Dr. Hines gave me that kind, professional smile. "Now that we've had a few sessions to really dig into what happened to you, let's spend this week discussing its effects on you."

Almost three weeks had passed since I'd seen Titus. He'd had flowers delivered to my house, twice. An edible arrangement of fruit, once. He'd hired out a day spa for a full day, for the girls and me.

There'd been a note, as well:

Laurel,

I'm on the road this month for a series of pop-ups on the East Coast. I'm not ghosting you, I swear. But I think you need time before we can really see each other in the way I would like. I hope some of the things I've done have shown you that I'm looking at things with you as being more than just a hookup. A lot more, potentially. I'll be back a week from today, and if you're interested in spending time with me, let me know.

I like you, Laurel McGillis. I want more than just…what it's been between us, so far. I guess I'm asking you to just give me a chance.

TB

I'd shown the note to the girls, and there was fawning and oohing and aaahing, and a lot of blunt statements that if I fucked this up, I'd regret it the rest of my life, so don't fuck it up.

Give him a chance.

TRY.

Thus, I'd actually had two sessions a week with Dr. Hines in the three weeks since that first one, because the more I got into it with her, the lighter I felt. Talking to Titus had sort of broken the seal, so to speak. Now that it was all coming out, I was feeling better about myself, and I was genuinely thankful that Titus had done what he did.

In today's session with Dr. Hines, we did indeed get into the various and many ways I'd been affected by both my childhood and the traumatic assault I'd experienced as a teenager. Which…it turned out, was a lot.

At the end of it, Dr. Hines poked her chin with the clicker of her pen, regarding me steadily as she formulated her thoughts. "Laurel…" She trailed off, paused, started again. "At some point, you have to learn how to develop an intimate, vulnerable, trusting relationship with a man. If you don't, the rest of your life will be…" she gestured with her pen, "what it has been, up till now. If that's what you want and what you're okay with, then that's fine, right? But…if it's not, at some point, you have to just take a chance on trusting someone."

I swallowed. "Yeah, I know what you're getting at." I sighed. "Titus."

She nodded. "I am absolutely not here to give you relationship advice or play matchmaker. But from what you've told me, and considering he risked your understandable anger in hiring me on your behalf, and unbeknownst to you at that, I'd say it seems pretty apparent he cares deeply for you."

"How can he? We barely know each other."

An understanding smile. "That's not…it's not really how love works, though, Laurel."

"It's not?"

"Nope. For example, I've been married to my

husband for forty years. I'm fifty-eight years old. Do you know what that means?"

I did the easy math. "You married at eighteen."

"Right. We met at school, fell in love, and we knew that was it. Our parents, our aunts and uncles, all of our teachers, everyone we knew was like, you can't possibly know what you want at seventeen. You're too young, yada yada yada. We didn't believe them. We'd known each other a total of four months when we got married. We ran away and lived in his car until we turned eighteen, got married by a justice of the peace, and that was it. Is that feasible for everyone? Obviously not. But I knew, and Jake knew, and it didn't matter how young we were or how long we'd known each other. When you know, you know."

"I *don't* know, though, Dr. Hines, and that's the issue."

She nodded, twirled the pen between two fingers. "So, let's imagine for a moment that he changes his mind from what he said in the note you shared with me. Let's say he does 'ghost' you, as he put it." She used air quotes around the emphasized word. "You never see him again, you never hear from him again, that's it. Over and done. What then?"

My heart pounded, and my chest got tight, and it was hard to swallow. "I would be devastated. I haven't seen him in three weeks, and I won't see him for another week, and I…" The lump in my throat was hard to swallow past. "I miss him. I feel like I messed up the last time I saw him and I haven't spoken to him since then and I…I miss him."

"Have you ever missed a man before?"

I cackled at that. "Hell no."

"You say that with such vehemency, as if the very concept is laughable."

"Because it is, Dr. Hines. I use men—use 'em and lose 'em. I'm guilty as hell of treating men like little more than walking penises, essentially. I've never…there has never been a man in my life *to* miss."

"And Titus?"

"For the first time in my entire life, I see a man as a person, as someone worth knowing. He's more than just sex to me."

"But?"

"You're relentless, you know that?"

"It's my job." She smiled encouragingly.

"But…it's scary. Because…because I don't feel like I have anything to offer him." This was nearly a whisper.

"Laurel, you're smart, you're beautiful, you're successful. And he clearly sees something in you."

"I don't mean like that—I know I'm all those things."

"So then when you say you don't have anything to offer, what *do* you mean?"

I swallowed, but the tears trickled down anyway. I tapped my chest, over my heart. "I meant here. I don't have anything in here to offer him."

She frowned. "You mean emotionally."

"Right."

She was silent a moment. "Laurel…what is love? To you. In your own words. What is love?"

I shook my head. "I don't know."

"Has anyone ever told you they love you?"

"My girlfriends."

"Okay, so…who was the first of them to say it to you?"

"Lizzy."

"When Lizzy told you she loved you, how did you know she meant it? What did you think? How did it make you feel?"

I laughed. "I got angry, actually. I didn't believe it. I didn't know what to think. Like, yeah, we're friends. Yeah, I care about her. But bitch, you *love* me? The fuck does that even mean, between two straight women?"

"And?" she prompted.

I sighed, shook my head again, tugging my ponytail to the other side. "And what?"

"And what does that mean? Anyone can *say* they love you, but how do you know Lizzy *means* it? And what does it look like?"

I groaned. "She's there for me. She doesn't put up with my shit—she tells me when I'm full of it, tells me when I'm being stupid. She laughs at my antics, which can be pretty ridiculous. She takes care of me if I'm sick or something, and gives me grace when I'm being a bitch, which is often. I can be me with her, and not apologize or explain—and she's done so for years even though I haven't been precisely forthcoming about my past. She just…*accepts* me."

Dr. Hines smiled at me, and that smile had a way of making you *think*, making you realize what she was leading you to. "Sounds like you *do* know what love is."

"But it's different, with men."

A tilt of her head. "Is it?"

"I don't know—*you're* the expert, here."

"Not on love. I'm an expert on healing from severe sexual trauma. But I *have* spent the last forty years being loved well and truly by a good man, through many different phases and seasons of life. That doesn't make me an expert, though."

"So is that different from being loved by a best friend?" I asked.

She chuckled. "Hey now, I ask the questions around here." She arched an eyebrow. "What do *you* think?"

I groaned a laugh. "In psychologist school, is there a class on how to turn everything into a question, and every question back onto the subject?"

Another dry chuckle. "Yes, there is—it's called psychology."

I cackled. "Smart-ass."

She laughed, clicked her pen, made a note. Glanced at me. "I will, in this instance, give you what you would call a straight answer, but being a psychologist, I'm going to do it in the form of a question. Are you ready?"

I rolled my eyes and laughed. "I can't wait."

"In what way is a romantic relationship with a man different from being best friends with a woman?"

"I mean, they're completely different."

"Are they?"

I huffed. "Well now that you ask *that*, it makes me rethink my answer."

"I'm not say anything either way—I want *your* answer."

"You make my head spin, Dr. Hines." I considered the question. "How is a romantic relationship with a man different from a platonic friendship with a woman? Um. I don't even know how to answer that. I've never had a romantic relationship with a man."

"Never? Not even close?"

"No."

"Every interaction you've *ever had*, with every male in your entire life, has been either professional or purely sexual?"

"Yes."

"And to define: purely sexual means you don't have pillow talk, for example, or see each other outside of sex. Purely sexual means you meet in whatever way, go somewhere, have sex, and as soon as the deed is done, one or both of you leave to go your own way. And you rarely if ever see that person again, rarely if ever even have sex with the same person twice in a row, excepting in the same evening. Do I have that mostly correct?"

I nodded. "Yeah, that's about it."

"You've never gone on a date with a man, as in been picked up, had dinner where he paid. Never gone for a long walk on a beach, holding hands and talking about absolutely nothing of any importance whatsoever? You've never watched a sunset with a man you cared for? You've never woken up at first light and made love and watched the sunrise together without needing to talk? You've never just been held at night, without the expectation of sex?"

I blinked hard. Swallowed harder. "No." I had trouble speaking in a voice loud enough for her to hear. "And that sounds like a completely different thing than being friends with a woman. Apples and...not even oranges. Apples and baseballs."

"It does, doesn't it?" She smiled at me, handed me a box of Kleenex. "But it's not. It's red apples and green apples, Laurel."

"Well you're gonna have to explain that one to me, Doc. Because I call bullshit."

"The only difference is sex." A pause, to let that sink in. "It's another facet of the relationship, and it adds complexity, yes. So maybe it is apples and oranges—I guess I have to admit I'm having trouble continuing that metaphor in this context. But think about that, okay? The only difference between a long-term, monogamous, romantic relationship and a platonic friendship is sex. When you really break it all down to individual components."

"Keep explaining. I still call bullshit."

A sigh. "Think about it, Laurel. You and Lizzy—are you physically affectionate with each other? Hugs, sitting close to each other or even *on* each other, adjusting the other's outfit, maybe even holding hands?"

I shrugged. "Sure. We don't really hold hands, but other stuff."

"So you're comfortable with each other and comfortable enough in your friendship that you show physical affection in various ways."

"Yes."

"And you have each expressed, in so many words, that you love each other."

"Yes."

"You do things for each other without expecting it to be returned, meaning you don't keep track of who paid for drinks last, or who owes the other money for dinner, things like that. Maybe you do other random nice things—close up the office so she can meet her husband for dinner after a showing, cover some paperwork because she had an emergency, housesit while she's on vacation, things like that. Not because it's expected of you, not because she's your boss, not because you think she'll buy you a present or give you a bonus, but because you care about her. You love her. She's your friend and you *enjoy* doing things for her, so she knows you love her. Because it makes *you* feel good to do those things."

Fuck.

Now it was starting to click.

"Yeah," I whispered. "All that is true."

"You do those things, as I said, because you *want* to. But, the flip side is, you do those things also because you feel safe doing them. You know they're appreciated. You know she'll be there for you. You know, too, that she has, does, and will those things for you. You each give to the other without the expectation of repayment, knowing your needs in that friendship will be met." A smile. "It's not perfect, of course. She makes you mad, you make her mad. But you've learned how to communicate, how to resolve conflict. You forgive each other and don't hold grudges and move on."

I nodded, swallowed hard, dabbing at my eyes with a tissue. "Yes." I tried to smile and failed. "I think I get it."

"Maybe. But let's really drive this home, huh?" She clicked her pen, which I was learning meant she had a doozy aimed at me. "If you were to kiss Lizzy—or add any other kind of physical touch from the sexual end of the spectrum, what would that mean?"

"It'd mean…we'd be lesbians."

"Try saying it a different way."

"Politely, you mean."

"Just a different way."

I sighed, adjusted my hair. "It would make that a romantic relationship."

"Right." She clicked the pen again, made a note. "Just to be clear, one kiss doesn't constitute anything. Sexuality is a spectrum, not a duality, an either-or thing. But you see what I'm saying, right? Jake, my husband, is my best friend. I don't need to have sex with him to know I love him. I can show him in other ways. He shows me in other ways. At the end of the day, that's the first thing we are, and the most important: best friends. Soul mates. My sexual relationship with my husband *is* an integral, important part of our relationship. It connects us. Bonds us. It's an expression of our physical intimacy. But it doesn't *define* our relationship. You see what I mean?"

"Yes, Dr. Hines, I see what you mean."

"Let's bring this full circle, now." A pause, her eyes serious, searching. "If you can love Lizzy—if you can say it, mean it, show it, do it—and if you can *be loved by* Lizzy in return, accept her love, her affection, her gestures, her words, and believe she means it and be comfortable in it…what makes you think you can't do the same with Titus? You have no problem believing you have something to offer Lizzy, right? So my point is, the only significant difference between letting yourself love Lizzy and letting yourself love Titus is that with Titus, there would be a sexual element."

"You make it sound so fucking simple."

"It is, Laurel. It is simple." She leaned forward and

touched my knee. "That doesn't make it *easy*. You've never seen a healthy romantic relationship. Never had one, never even tried. But you *do* have an example—six examples!—of healthy platonic friendships."

"Lizzy and Braun's marriage is amazing." I looked up, blinked, dabbed at my eyes. "They love each other. They communicate. It's...I'm jealous, honestly. I'd never admit that to anyone but you, and you're legally not allowed to tell anyone. But I am."

"My point in this entire session, Laurel, is that you *don't have to be jealous*. You can have that." She set aside her notepad and pen, took my hands and squeezed them. "Do you hear me, Laurel? *You—CAN—have—that.*"

I was weeping openly now, not even worried about my makeup. "What if I can't? What if I'm too fucked-up? What if...what if he doesn't want that with me? What if we have that and then he leaves? He cheats on me? He... he fucking dies? Jesus...it's just so terrifying. What if... what if I tell him I love him, and...and he rejects me? I don't think I'd survive that."

"There are just as many opposite what-ifs, though." She remained where she was, facing me, hands around mine. "What if he's already in love with you? What if you take this risk—and it is a risk, make no mistake—and you offer him yourself openly and truly and with complete vulnerability, and he accepts you, exactly as you are? What if you develop a relationship as amazing and fulfilling as Lizzy and Braun have? What if you spend the next thirty, forty years together, happy and in love? You're not even forty—you could easily live to at least seventy or eighty, and that's a whole lifetime of love for you and Titus to make together. What if you're exactly perfect for each other?"

I nodded. "What-ifs go both ways, is your point."

"Right, exactly. You can ask as many negative what-ifs as you want—and they're endless. Or, you can ask as many positive what-ifs, and those are just as endless."

She leveled a long, serious look at me. "The real question, here, Laurel, is which are you going to focus on?"

CHAPTER NINE

I T HAD BEEN A VERY, VERY LONG, AND VERY, VERY DIFFICULT day. I had a listing that was currently Six Chicks' most expensive property, and I'd been trying to sell it for months without success. I'd shown it half a dozen times without so much as a sniff of real interest—today, I'd shown it to someone who'd come with fully qualified funding, spent an hour showing it to them, feature by feature. They'd expressed interest. Had talked about possibly putting in an offer once they'd seen it in person.

They'd walked away leaving me a distinctly negative impression. The master hadn't been as big as they'd thought it would be. The views weren't as impressive as the photography had them to believe. The kitchen and dining room weren't open plan to the main den.

And then, a sale that had been literally a handful of signatures away from done had fallen through due to financing issues with the buyers.

Titus hadn't called me, hadn't sent flowers in three

days, hadn't shown up, hadn't even contacted me through Alaina.

Autumn was still gone and we were all covering for her, which meant extra paperwork and extra showings and extra phone calls and extra client meetings.

I'd had a killer headache for hours.

I was horny.

I missed Titus.

On the way home, I'd run into an accident and had been stuck in traffic for over an hour, and *then* I'd finally gotten less than a mile from home, and I'd blown a tire. I didn't have a spare. I didn't have a jack. My phone was at two percent battery, I didn't have a portable charger and my very cool and hot classic Aston Martin DB6 didn't feature a charging port of any kind that I could even get an adapter for.

So, I sat in my car on the side of the road, a mile from home, and just cried for a few minutes.

And then I'd called Lizzy.

"Hey, you," she answered. "What's up?"

"I'm a mile from home with a flat, no spare, no jack, and my phone is about to die. I've had the worst day. I need help."

"On it," she replied. "Girl power to the rescue."

Twenty-five minutes later, a flat-bed tow truck arrived. The driver was burly and smelled like cigarettes and was super nice, in a gruff, businesslike way. "Been taken care of," he mumbled to me, an unlit cigarette dangling from one corner of his mouth. "Takin' your baby here to a buddy of mine, he'll fix her up and bring her back to you."

I frowned at him. "Is that how this stuff usually works?"

A shrug. "Nah, course not. But you got friends who like you, I guess." He gestured at the passenger door. "Climb on up, missy, I'll run you home. You'll have this pretty little ride of yours back in an hour or two."

He dropped me off at home and gave me a two-finger salute. "There you go."

"I feel like I should tip you or something."

He waved a hand. "Nah. I'm being well compensated. If I've got it right, your friend's husband is friends with the owner of the company I work for."

"Well, thank you. I didn't even ask your name, I'm sorry. I've had a really horrible day."

"Name's Rob. And you're welcome. See ya, now."

He rumbled away in a growl of diesel fumes and noise, and I headed inside. By the time I was in the kitchen, my heels were off and my purse on a counter. By the time I hit my bedroom, I was naked, leaving a trail of clothing down the hall. I may or may not have had a bottle of champagne in hand, from which I was drinking directly.

I started the bath, setting the bottle of champagne on my vanity as I somewhat frantically yanked my hair out of the complicated braid-bun; makeup wipes, meet face. Once the water was hot and filling the tub, I tossed in my favorite bath bomb, which gave off crazy bubbles and a divine lavender scent.

I lit a good half dozen different candles while the tub filled, and then danced and swigged my way into the kitchen where my purse was, so I could grab my phone—I put it on a charger and connected it to my Bluetooth speaker for some relaxing music.

I was searching for the right playlist, standing naked in my kitchen with the champagne bottle in my other hand—now a third empty and nearing the halfway mark.

I hadn't selected a song to play, yet, so I was rather confused when I heard the soft, delicate strains of a guitar being played.

"Home," Michael Bublé.

Wait, what?

I checked my phone, but it wasn't coming from there.

Where was the music coming from?

Granted, I'd slammed almost half a bottle of champagne in less than ten minutes, but should I be hallucinating music?

Oh. It was coming from outside. Next question: how? Or rather, why?

Shit, the tub. I ignored the mystery for a moment longer and shut off the water, because it was in danger of overflowing, even despite the overflow preventer.

Back to the front door, bottle in hand. I was just

tipsy enough to be aware and not give a shit that I was bare-ass naked as I opened my front door, standing in full view, framed by the storm door. Hair loose and wild and kinked from being a braid all day, no makeup, naked, champagne bottle in one hand.

I must have been quite a sight.

For Titus.

He was parked in my driveway, tailgate facing the door, front end facing the street. Tailgate down, sitting cross-legged on it. He had his favorite acoustic—a famous guitar, that one; it was his first guitar, a Yamaha he'd bought used at fourteen years old, and it had been old then. It was scratched and battered, covered in bumper stickers, and did not have a strap.

One leg hanging off the tailgate, foot kicking in time as he picked the melody. Wearing faded blue jeans cut off below the knee with fraying white threads, unlaced black combat boots, wearing a plain black ribbed tank top, and that stupid fucking beanie. Aviators. The rings on his fingers, tattooed and pierced and rocking a now-unkempt beard. Beautiful. Rugged and imperfectly perfect.

He whipped his sunglasses off his face with his fretboard hand and tossed them aside without missing a beat. Began singing the lyrics in that rough, dark, beautiful voice. His eyes never left me. He barely blinked as he sang the song to me. I leaned against my doorway and sipped, my own gaze never leaving him.

When he finished the song, the last note still hanging

in the air, I nudged open the storm door with my foot. "Maybe you ought to finish the serenade in here," I said.

He clutched the instrument by the neck and hopped off the tailgate, pausing to reach back with his free hand and grab something. He kept it behind his back, hidden from view as he approached the front door—I backed away, toward the bathroom, as he entered, staying out of reach as he prowled for me.

Into the bathroom, where I stopped my retreat from Titus as the back of my knees reached the tub. My heart hammered for some unknown reason, as he stalked and swaggered toward me.

Bought his free hand around, and held out a single perfect red rose. Didn't say a word.

I took the rose. Pressed the silky petals to my nose, inhaled its scent.

I couldn't contain myself any longer—I threw myself into his arms, the champagne sloshing in the bottle. He dipped at the knees and I heard the humming thunk of wood and strings hitting the marble floor, and then he had me, held me aloft, my thighs clenching around his waist, one arm around his neck.

I gazed down at him. "Hi."

"Missed the shit out of you, Laurel," he murmured.

I kissed him, by way of answer. When our lips finally parted, both of us were breathless. I brought the bottle between us and touched it to his lips, tilted. He took a sip, then pulled away.

"Rather be drunk on you," he growled.

"Well, if you don't help me with this, I'll be drunk on champagne *and* you."

"Fine by me." He kissed me, and then slowly lowered me into the water.

I hissed at the heat, holding on to him as I descended under the bubbly surface. "Gonna get in with me?" I asked. "Room for two."

He grinned. "I was gonna serenade you some more."

"How about a Titus Bright song? I've always liked his music."

He grinned. "Have you really?"

I nodded, dead serious. "Absolutely. I've been a secret fan for years."

He blinked. "Wait, you're serious?"

I giggled, sipped. "Yup. I saw you in concert, Bright Bones I mean. One of the last shows of your last tour."

"I wouldn't have pegged you as a heavy metal fan."

"Don't you know by now that nothing about me is what you'd expect?" I shrugged, grinning at him over the rim of the bottle, my voice disappearing into the glass. "I have as many layers as Shrek."

He cackled, and hopped up onto my vanity, guitar propped on his thighs. "Here's a little song I'm actually still working on. I started it last week. I was on the last leg of the pop-up tour, going from Billings to Butte, in the middle of fuckin' nowhere in the middle of the fuckin' night, couldn't fuckin' sleep for shit."

I slid lower in the water, letting the bottle dangle over the side; I realized I'd had enough, now that Titus was here, so I leaned out and set the bottle on the floor. "Is that fuckin' right?"

"Sure fuckin' is." He started a melody, low chords in a slow, melancholy progression. "Laying awake in that big-ass bed in my trailer, all alone, staring at the ceiling. And I was thinkin'…"

He seamlessly transitioned into song:

"There's this girl,
Don't really know her,
But I think I'm in love.
Montana's got mountains,
Plains of Texas, sun and heat
Nebraska's got corn
Maybe it's wheat,
New Orleans, New York, New Jersey,
Philly and Fargo in winter and fall,
I've been to 'em all,
Seen everything everywhere a time or two.
But there's this girl,
Sorta just met her,
Don't really know her,
But I think I'm in love.
She's got these eyes so bright
They're not really blue
Unless the sun hits 'em right
Not really gray

Unless she looks at me a certain way.

Hair like the sun,

Shines like gold loose or up in a bun.

She makes my heart sing,

Gives it a song,

Sends my soul on a wing

Makes right what was wrong.

You see

There's this girl.

Sorta just met,

Don't really know her,

But none of that matters,

Because I think I'm in love."

The last notes quavered, his voice and the guitar fading, echoing in the beautiful acoustics of the bathroom.

"Still a work in progress," he muttered. "Some of the lines are dumb as shit, like real first-grader rhymes. But lyrics were always Tommy's strong suit, not mine."

I couldn't answer, because I had my hand over my mouth, eyes shimmering. "Titus," I whispered. "You mean that?"

"Yeah, I usually did the music, and Tommy—"

"No, you big dumbass. The song." I tried to gather myself, but didn't really succeed. "What you said."

He laughed, raked fingers through his beard. "Oh, right." He slid off the counter, set the guitar down, and knelt beside the tub. "Yeah, Laurel. I meant it."

I swallowed hard. "How do you know?"

"Spent my whole life on the road. Started touring full time at sixteen." A hard sigh. "Never looked back, you know? Home has been tour busses and hotels, my whole life." He cupped my jaw in a rough hand. "How do I know I love you? Because now when I think *home*, I think of you."

I whimpered, a sad, pathetic sound. "Titus." It was a sob.

"Talk to me, Laurel."

"I've seen Dr. Hines twice a week since you sent her to me."

"I was half sure you'd never speak to me again, after that."

I huffed a laugh. "Me too. I was so shocked that you'd send me a fucking *therapist*. Like, *who* does that? Am I *that* fucking broken?"

"Only because I am, so like recognizes like, you know?"

"It was something I needed so badly. I don't think you can understand."

"So you're not mad?"

"No, Titus, I'm not mad. I'm grateful." I grabbed his beard, which was just long enough to tangle my fingers in, now, and pulled him to me. "I am *so* scared, Titus."

"Of what? Why?"

"You—this. Us." I touched my lips to his. "Dr. Hines, in our last session, talked to me about how being in love with you is no different than loving Lizzy as my best friend. The only difference is sex."

"Like, gender, as in orientation, or sex as in sexy times?"

"As in sexy times. It was this whole long thing, but it helped me realize my issue isn't with you. You're incredible. You've been nothing but incredible since I met you. My issue is trust. My issue is men."

"Understandable, considering."

"But unless I want my life to look the way it's always been, I have to choose differently." My fingers, still dangled in his beard, dribbled suds down the soft curly black tendrils. "I have to choose you."

"Easier said than done, though, huh?"

I nodded. "Yeah, it is." I blinked tears. "I'm sorry about the last time we saw each other."

He frowned. "Why?"

"I was avoiding...*this*." I sighed, tugging gently on his beard. "Avoiding intimacy. And you deserve better."

He nodded. "Thank you. I don't want to seem like I'm not grateful as fuck for every moment I ever get with you no matter what it looks like, because I am. But, that day—I really did want...more. Something more than just...*fucking*, I guess. I don't know how else to put it. That day at the house you showed me. That didn't feel like a typical hookup, to me, and that's how I knew..." He trailed off. "It was different, it was more, and that was the moment I knew this whole thing with us was going to be different. I wanted different, Laurel. I want different now. I wanted different that day here. But you didn't, and I could tell, so I just…" A sigh. "I don't know how to say it. I guess I just let you turn it into something else. Don't get me wrong, it was fucking hot, like…seriously fucking hot. I still think about it. But on an emotional level, it's not what I really wanted."

"I know." I closed my eyes. "I know. I knew then. But I was too scared."

"I won't hurt you, Laurel." But even as he said it, I thought I saw a flicker of shadows in his expression; it was there and gone so fast maybe I dreamed it.

Maybe I was projecting. Because I myself still had one last secret I wasn't ready to let go of.

He took my hands in his. "I have a kind of crazy idea."

I laughed, a tear-sodden sound. "Okay?"

"What if we don't have sex for a while?"

A shocked cackle burst out of me. "What?"

"Well, you said being in love is just friendship but with sex."

I frowned. "I mean, I guess that's the gist of it, yes."

"I don't have many friends—Tommy is one of the very few truly close friends I've ever had. Rick and Froot Loop weren't really my *friends*, they were my bandmates. You'd think after twenty-some years together we would be like brothers, but…it just never happened that way. I know them better than they know themselves, but we never bonded the way Tommy and I did. There's Seven, and a few others that I'd say I'm close with, mostly other dudes in the industry."

"Okay?"

"I've never been friends with a woman. Alaina is my assistant, and she's thirty years older than me. We're not friends—she's my employee. And Bex, Jeremy's wife…" A sigh. "She's my manager's wife. I care about her, but I have to be careful. I've got a reputation, both deserved and not, but still, a certain reputation, you know? One out-of-context photo, one snippet of conversation, and things could blow up. So I can't be her friend." His eyes met mine. "You're my friend, Laurel. And if what you're saying, if what Dr. Hines told you is true, then maybe the best chance we have of making this relationship work is to take sex out of the equation so we can focus on being friends."

"That sounds really fucking difficult."

He snorted. "You're telling me? You're the one who answered the door buck-ass fucking naked."

"We could take sex out of the equation after we have sex one more time? I missed you, Titus. I missed you a lot, and I thought about you literally all the time."

He growled. "It's been a month. I want you so fucking bad. I've jerked off two or three times a day, thinking about you. Thinking about these fucking gorgeous tits of yours. How they looked wrapped around my cock."

I moaned, lifting up out of the water so the bubbles

streamed down my curves, leaving them covered in a thin scrim of white froth. *"Titus."*

He stood up, backed away. "Much as I fuckin'…want isn't the right word—need, I fuckin' *need* you, Laurel. But as much as I need you, want you, can't bear not touching you, I want this to work. I've never wanted that before. I've never loved anyone, ever. Except Tommy, and he was my brother in all but blood. Not my parents, not anyone. You're it. And I want it to fucking *work*. So that means we have to learn how to be friends."

I was sitting up, blinking at him. "You mean it."

"Yeah, I do."

"How is it even possible?" I scraped bubbles off of my breasts. "How can we see each other every day or however often, and not fuck each other senseless? I'm *this* close to literally assaulting you right now, you do realize that? I've jilled off every day and sometimes more than once, thinking about you and all the things I want to do with you. My poor vibrator has gotten more use the past month than in all the years I've had him."

"Him?"

I grinned. "It's big and purple, and his name is Grimace."

"Like the weird-ass fuckin' purple potato with arms thing from McDonald's?"

"Yeah."

"You masturbate with something you call Grimace?"

"Yep."

"You're so fucking weird." He grinned. "I love that about you."

"You really want to do this?" I sank back down in the water, if only to make it easier for Titus to have a conversation with me. "You really want to try to have a friendship without sex?"

"Yeah." He sat with his back to the tub, and his chest lifted, shoulders broadening, and then he sighed. "I mean, do I *want* to see you every day and not have sex with you? Fuck no. My dick already hates me for having the idea. But…it just feels like the right thing to do, if you and I are going to have a real legit shot at a successful relationship."

"And that's what you want. With me."

He nodded. "I do." He plucked at the strings at the hems of his shorts; I heard his teeth clicking against his lip piercing. "The last month I was…" He laughed. "I was about to say on tour. Old habits die hard. I don't want to call it a tour, but I don't know what else to call it. Anyway, the month I was gone doing the pop-ups, I had a whole lot of time alone to think. I'm forty-one, and I've never had a home. Never owned anything. Never had roots. Never had family, except Tommy, and without him, I…" A choked breath. "I've been half alive, since I found him. That shit really fucked me up. I've been going through the motions, you know? Like, I spent those years in Brazil, but eventually I just got so bored I had to come back and make music again, because if I didn't, I was gonna…" Another sound, almost a sob; I twisted in the tub and wrapped my arms around him from behind, soaking his shirt with sudsy water. "I almost killed myself. I sat on a hill in the forest overlooking Rio, a gun in my hand, contemplating suicide. To this day, I don't know what stopped me. Cowardice, maybe, or call it courage, I don't know. Some weird combo of both. I just couldn't. I had more music to make, and it was the idea of never…never being on stage again, never seeing my fans go fuckin' nuts when the lights hit me up…that's the shit that brought me back. But even then, I was just surviving." His hand covered mine. "And then I saw that ad on Jeremy's Instagram."

I laughed. "Wait, *what*? The Ad? It *was* the fucking ad? I thought you…" I wasn't sure how I felt. "I thought you saw me for the first time at the wedding."

But then I remembered the words he'd said to me that day, heard them in my head as clearly as if it was an audio recording: *You're even more fuckin' stunning than I'd imagined you would be, Laurel McGillis.*

"The fucking ad." I laughed.

He seemed puzzled. "Why do you sound pissed-off?"

"I didn't post that. It's a thing with the girls."

A snort. "Oh. So…"

I pressed my nose to his ear, inhaled his scent. "So you *did* see The Ad."

"I was hanging out with Jeremy and Bex and the kids. Jeremy was scrolling through Instagram as we talked. I was sitting next to him and he passed the ad.

Scrolled past it without even seeing it because I mean, he's got Bex, and he loves the shit out of that woman. I grabbed the phone from him and went back to the ad."

"I haven't actually seen it. I just know what it says."

"I'm confused."

I laughed. "It's a long story. It all started with Lizzy— The Ad is how she met Braun, and it's how Autumn met Seven."

"I see. Well, I saw the ad. It's a photo of you, probably an older one, from a few years ago. It's a naked selfie, but not showing anything, know what I mean? The arm-bar thing, turned to the side. You look so fuckin' sexy, so beautiful. And I saw that, and I was like—in my head I was like *that girl is going to be mine.* It was this thought, clear as day, and I've never ever in my life thought anything like that about a woman, ever. Not even remotely."

"So, how'd you end up at the wedding?"

"Through what Jeremy calls social media stalking. You, Lizzy, Autumn, the other girls are all the only people that account follows, and Jeremy went to the various pages for all of you girls, and discovered that Autumn had Seven all over her feed. And I've been buddies with Seven for twenty years. Every so often we connect here in LA and hang out for beers or whatever, and every year around the first week of summer we all meet down in Moab for some off-roading, a whole big group of us. So, I saw Seven on Autumn's feed, or rather Jeremy did, and was like, you have Seven as a mutual friend. So I called Seven and asked if he knew you, so I could figure out how I could meet you. And he was like, funny you called me, because I was legit about to pick up the phone to call you. He was about to get married and wanted me to play their backyard wedding. So I was, of course I will. Just curious, though, will your girl's friend Laurel be at this wedding? Because I *have* to meet her."

I swallowed. "So you were at the wedding just to meet me?"

"Well, call it killing two birds with one stone. Seven is one of my very few real friends, so I would have played his wedding regardless, but I also had to meet you. So yes, you were the main reason I was there, other than as Seven's friend and being the wedding music."

Silence.

"So, dumb question maybe," I said, tracing the ridge of his breastbone where it met his shoulder, "but how does this work, then? If we're not going to have sex for who knows how long, what do we, like, *do*?"

He chuckled. "I dunno. We'll have to figure that out."

"I mean, you get what I'm saying, right?" I moved, and water sloshed out of the tub. "If I even go on a date in the first place, it's always been with the sole and express purpose of deciding if I want to have sexual relations with the individual in question. What does a date just to hang out even look like? And what do you do afterwards?"

He shook his head. "I don't fuckin' know, Laurel, I really don't. I'm no expert at nonsexual relationships by any stretch of the imagination. And you being naked right now is making this *really* fuckin' hard, let me just say that right now."

"Making *this* hard, like the situation, or making *you* hard?" I ran my hand under his tank top, over his tattooed chest.

He groaned. "Goddammit, woman."

I mirrored his groan of frustration, swishing away in the water and sliding under the surface; I stayed under for a moment or two, and then resurfaced, scraping my hair back away from my face. "I'm sorry," I murmured. "I'm just used to thinking with my dick, metaphorically speaking."

A laugh. "Same."

I lifted the drain plug. "I want it too, Titus," I whispered.

"You do?" He twisted in place, eyes narrowing in on mine. "You really do?"

I nodded. "Yeah, I do." I searched him. "Titus, just…" I swallowed hard, my voice barely a whisper. "Just don't…don't change your mind about this—about me. Okay?"

His mouth met mine with rough demanding force. "I won't, Laurel. I promise I won't."

CHAPTER TEN

S OME DAYS, WE HAD TO TAKE IT HOUR BY HOUR. FOR TWO people who'd never bothered even trying to have a nonsexual relationship with a member of the opposite sex, let alone a meaningful romantic relationship, this was fucking torture.

We took it week by week, too. Sometimes, we had to plan our dates to be in places that precluded any shenanigans. Which, as I discovered, was somewhat problematic, since my boyfriend—**gulp** I had a boyfriend—was *the* Titus Bright.

We'd go to dinner, and half the dinner would be Titus taking selfies and signing things, and he was always gracious. Walk down the streets of downtown LA or Rodeo Drive, shopping or whatever, and he'd get stopped a dozen times in a quarter mile. Once, memorably, we got surrounded leaving a coffeehouse early in the morning by a swarm of paparazzi and fans, like you'd see on TMZ or whatever. It was awful. They were all shouting questions at us, cameras were flashing in a blinding barrage, crowding us and crushing in on us, and they wouldn't leave us alone. Finally, Titus wrapped his arm around me, pressing himself in front of me.

"Hey!" he shouted. "I don't want to be an asshole here, but if you don't let us through, I'm gonna start swinging."

Immediately, the crowd backed off and parted.

He moved us out of the circle of the crowd, and then glanced at me for a moment. Back to the crowd of paps. "Okay, guys, here's the deal. This is the only statement I'm going to make." He glanced at me again, and I knew he was about to out us as a couple publicly; I squeezed his hand and nodded with a smile. "This is Laurel McGillis. She's my girlfriend, and I love her. End of statement. Get your photos, and then leave us alone. Please."

I turned my body into his and smiled my professional smile, holding it and then adjusting my position and my head and my smile and holding that again—I knew the drill from my brief stint as a model.

Titus turned us to face this way, then that, letting the other photographers get their shots, and I played along, and we ignored the shouted questions about marriage and babies and how did we meet and will Titus ever do a normal tour again.

Finally, Titus held up a hand. "Okay, ya'll. We gave you the scoop, and this is exclusive, okay? You guys know

I'm private, so take this as the gift it is. Now leave us the fuck alone. It's all you're gonna get from me."

And then we were hustling away, his arm protectively wrapped around my shoulders, fast-marching us to where my car was parked.

There were long days alone, showing houses and going through closings, while Titus traveled for pop-ups in various places. He'd show up at my house in the middle of the night, sometimes, and I'd leave the side door unlocked for him and he'd climb into bed behind me, half dressed, and wrap his long arm over my side and sidle up behind me and I'd be half awake, and suddenly safer simply because he was there.

There was a movie premiere he was invited to, since he'd done a couple songs for the soundtrack—he'd recorded them a good year before we met, while the movie was still in production. This was exciting for me—I got to buy a fancy dress and get it tailored, and Titus somehow got me a jewelry set on loan, a pair of massive diamond earrings and a matching necklace worth a shuddery, *gobsmacking* amount of money, even to me, who'd grown up with a diamond-crusted spoon. There was a Rolls-Royce limousine, and the red carpet and the gauntlet of flashing cameras as I hung on to Titus's arm for dear life, ignoring the shouted barrage of questions. We were posing for photos in front of the media wall.

"Do you think the reporters ever get tired of

shouting questions and being ignored?" I asked him, doing my best attempt at ventriloquism.

He snorted. "I guess not. Mainly because every once in a while, we'll answer one." He smirked at me. "Case in point. Yeah, you, second row. With the white tie. What was your question—can you repeat it?"

There was a brief hush as the chosen paparazzo asked his question again, more loudly. "Titus, do you think you'll ever propose to Laurel?"

Titus smiled at me, speaking to me rather than the reporter. "Yes, I do." He laughed. "Now, don't go getting your hopes up, I'm not proposing right now. But yet, someday in the near future, I will propose. It won't be public, though, so don't get to thinking you'll be able to get spy shots of it happening. Trust me, it'll be private. But it will happen, and soon."

My heart leaped. Jumped, twisted, soared.

A promise—that was him reassuring me, promising me.

As we moved away from the media wall through the throng of reporters and gathered celebrities—most of whom Titus seemed to be on wave-and-a-chin-nod familiarity with—I pressed my lips to his ear for a private word.

"Titus, I hope you know I'm not expecting that. A proposal. I'll never try to tie you down."

He stopped dead in his tracks, twisted to face me, nose to nose. No smile, here—serious, piercing. "It's not tying me down, you goose. It's choosing roots. Choosing home." A soft kiss. "I know you didn't ask. You don't have to."

"I just want you to understand that I love you and I'm fine with the way things are now."

A grin, then, finally. "Yeah, well, maybe I'm not."

I let it go, then. We made it into the theater, where we hobnobbed with A-list celebrities and I pretended to not be starstruck as I met household name after household name. There were quite a few curious looks at us, at the perennially single Titus Bright, whose name was, once and for a long time, synonymous with the rock star life, with alcohol and drugs and women and crazy antics, who had been a tabloid darling for the absolutely insane pace of his life, who had been seen and photographed with a who's who of gorgeous women—none of whom he'd ever been seen or photographed with more than once; that Titus Bright, now very publicly in a relationship with a noncelebrity.

Thank god for him I cleaned up well, wasn't afraid of publicity, and didn't get scared of cameras being in my face.

I felt like the luckiest girl in the world.

∽

Ten in the morning, Six Chicks office—I was pounding coffee and wishing I'd had breakfast, ignoring my growling stomach, and missing Titus. He was only halfway through one of the longest series of shows he'd done in months: eight shows in four weeks across the Southwest and into Texas, two in Vegas in two days, three in Lake Tahoe, Sacramento, and San Francisco, respectively, and then a whole further series of eight more shows in the Pacific Northwest, working his way through Oregon into Washington State and up into British Columbia.

He was slated to be gone almost two and a half months.

The upside of his unique way of doing shows was that he could spread the timeframe out, so the schedule wasn't as grueling; in the old days, touring the traditional way with Bright Bones, they'd have done eight shows in eight days in eight states, and that would have been just the first leg. Titus's way, as Bright Star, he could take his time, and if he felt like adding a show or two in a particular location because he felt the city in question wanted more, he could do it on a whim. No stadiums to book months ahead of time, no ticket sales to worry about. The downside was, he was gone almost as much as a traditional tour schedule, but he performed fewer shows. It was the nature of the beast, I knew. Now that we were together, he was spacing his pop-up tours farther apart than before, so he'd have a month or two home with me before he had to leave again.

It never got easier, him being gone.

Today was a bad day, for me. I missed him. I was cranky. I was horny. I had bombed a showing the day before—not really my fault, as I'd done my job as well as ever, it was just the prospective buyers were what we called house hunter tourists. Wealthy, qualified buyers who *could* afford the home in question, and who were, ostensibly, looking for a second or third or fourth house. But they weren't *serious*. They just took these vacations that basically consisted of looking at expensive houses as a form of entertainment. Wasting my time, my resources, getting my clients' hopes up that a sale was imminent, and then… "Oh, we'll be in touch." Translation: nada.

The worst.

I heard a diesel rumble but ignored it—this was a busy stretch of road, and you heard all sorts of vehicles.

"Um, Laur?" Teddy's voice.

"Yeah."

"I think that's for you."

I blinked. "What? What's for me?" I looked at Teddy, who pointed at the storefront windows.

Giant black semi, taking up half the road. Was something that massive even allowed here? I sat at my desk in confusion. That was Titus's rig, obviously, but he was still on tour. What was he doing here? Why bring the rig?

There he was, my man, in full rock star regalia: tight black jeans, ripped to the point that it was a wonder they had any structural integrity left, high calf-length combat boots laced all the way up, and a loose, flowy, gauzy, white linen button-down left unbuttoned almost all the way, showing his ripped torso and all those tattoos, sleeves rolled up to his elbows. Hair loose, wild, glossy black. Mirrored aviators. Leather bracelets, hemp bracelets, and rubber bracelets running up his right wrist, and a wide leather band, with a heavy gold watch on the right.

"Jesus, Mary, and Joseph," Teddy breathed. "That man is sex on a stick."

I cackled as I leaned back from my desk and watched him approach. "Yes, yes he is."

"I can honestly and legitimately say I do not in any way, shape, or form comprehend how in the ever-loving sam hill you're staying celibate around him." Teddy was damn near drooling—I didn't blame her, I was too.

I sighed. "I don't want to talk about it."

She laughed. "So what you're saying is, it's as hard as I think it is?"

"Harder. Literally, the most difficult thing I've ever done in my entire life." He was striding across the room, then, with that long-legged cocky swagger of his.

He didn't stop when he reached my desk, but rounded it and before I knew what was happening, he was scooping me out of my desk chair and holding me in his arms, one arm under my knees and buttocks, the other around my shoulders.

His lips slanted across mine, eager, impatient, wild. Kissed me breathless. "Hi."

I grinned, expecting him to put me down. "Hi. Guess you missed me, huh?"

He just stared at me. "More than you know. Touring *is* the business, but now that I've got you in my life, waiting for me, it's just…it just sucks without you."

I held on to his neck and shoulders, took the opportunity to kiss his neck, his throat, his stubbled jaw. "Well, I wasn't expecting to see you today, but I'm glad I got to. I was missing you, I don't mind admitting."

He smirked. "You were missing me, huh?"

I sighed, nuzzling against his chest. "So bad."

"Well, good news. I rearranged my schedule."

"So you're home?"

"Nope."

I frowned. "I'm confused, then."

Instead of putting me down, he carried me across the office toward the front door. "You're coming with me." He kicked open the door and angled through it.

I frowned at him. "Coming with you where?"

"On tour."

"Titus. I have to work. I have showings all this week and next. I'm closing in a couple weeks on a property. I have to stage—I have meetings with prospective clients."

He didn't slow, or put me down. "No, you don't. It's all be rescheduled. I worked it all out with Lizzy."

"I don't have anything packed."

"I sent Bex to your house. She packed for you."

I huffed as he ascended the three small steps at the side of the trailer, up near the front, meaning toward the tractor part. Inside, it resembled a swanky modern high-rise penthouse: spacious, clean, sleek lines. From the outside, the exterior looked opaque, glossy black—within, the entire length of the trailer was windows, tinted or mirrored or something to prevent anyone seeing in while still letting in light. A couch ran one entire wall, curved around the back end, terminating in a J-shape at a kitchen area midway along the far side opposite the entrance, with a built-in table, booth-style. Instead of a single TV screen, the entire wall—the wall of what I considered the front, nearest the tractor part of the tractor-trailer—was turned into a giant screen via at least a dozen smaller TVs programmed to function as a single screen. The entrance, on the side near the front, admitted you into the kitchen and living area, but if you went straight it led you up a short, steep flight of steps that turned a ninety-degree angle and led, presumably, to the bathroom and bedroom. Yeah—when I said the trailer was huge, I meant *huge*—the upper half would be big enough for him to stand up in as easily as the lower half, and Titus was not a short man.

"Damn." I blinked as he set me on my feet. "This is...amazing."

"Custom designed and built. Don't even ask how much I paid." He laughed. "But, it's home."

"You mean, it's your home away from home."

He kissed me. "Exactly. Home away from home." He gestured at the stairs which led up. "Your bags are up there already."

"You said you rearranged your schedule?" I asked, as I moved through the living area, taking in the high-quality luxury finishes with an expert eye—the phrase, *no expense was spared* certainly applied, here. "Meaning, what?"

"Meaning, I moved things around so our route took us this way, so I could come pick you up. You're gonna be with me for the whole Northwest leg."

"You and me, alone, on a tour bus or whatever you want to call this, for two and half weeks?" I gave him a look that was half smirk, half frown. "That sounds amazing, and like a lot of temptation when we're supposed to be eschewing sexual relations."

He held me by the arms. "It's not about avoiding sex, Laurel. It's about building our relationship. And a road trip is a great way to do that." He quirked an eyebrow at me. "Unless you don't think you're up for it. Being that near me, for that long, without sex."

I huffed. "Of course I'm up for it." I was wearing a miniskirt, and I swished the hem of it teasingly. "The question is, are *you*?"

He growled. "As long as there's no teasing, yeah."

I held out my hand for him to shake. "No teasing. Just a good old-fashioned celibate road trip."

He shook my hand, and then yanked me up against him, wrapping his arms around me in a tight embrace. "I really did miss you."

"Every moment of every day, Titus," I breathed. "I'm glad you did this. Surprised, though."

"Well good—it was supposed to be a surprise."

We took our seats and the giant rig went into motion—I'd have thought there would be more sway and sense of movement, but it was shockingly smooth. It turned out to be easy, being with Titus on the bus. Once you're used to ignoring the hormones and the desire, it becomes easier to sink into just…enjoying his presence. Being near him. Soaking up his energy, his warmth. He sprawled out on the couch, one foot on the floor, the other along the couch-back, and I lay between his thighs, my head on his chest, and we watched movie after movie.

My life was typically very fast-paced, busy from wake up to pass out. Especially when Titus was gone—I filled my days even more full when he was gone just to keep myself from thinking about missing him.

This was…slow. Delightfully boring, in the best way. Nothing to do at all for hours on end but cuddle with Titus and watch movies. He had a mobile Wi-Fi hotspot built into the rig, of course, so he had access to all the streaming services. And he let me pick the movie, nine times out of ten—and never complained when I picked girly rom-coms or silly reality TV. I'd concede to his masculinity every once in a while, of course, and he'd pick a shoot-'em-up action flick or something like that, usually an older one from the glory days of action movies. Rarely did anything we watch get steamy, because that was just playing with fire, right?

Portland, Oregon. His first show was an acoustic

pop-up in a park. Just Titus, a stool, a mic, an amp, and a guitar. The morning of the show, Jeremy started posting all over Titus's socials about it—he liked to make it a kind of scavenger hunt. He'd post hints of the location, and force the fans to figure out where it would be. By the time Titus plugged in his guitar and sat on his stool, the park was packed. People had brought chairs, blankets, picnic supplies, beach balls. There was a group of guys playing frisbee, people passing joints around…it felt like a festival.

I was sitting on a blanket a few feet away from Titus, to his right and near his feet, where I could gaze adoringly up at him as he sang love songs to me.

Which…is what he did.

"Today is gonna be different," he said, by way of introduction, as he strummed chords and adjusted the tuning. "I may play some favorites toward the end, but hopefully you guys will be cool with this, but I was thinking I'd do some covers. I almost never play covers, if you know me, you know that." He gazed down at me. "But I've got someone special with me today—my girlfriend, Laurel. So, today is about her." He grinned at the crowd. "If anyone gets a good photo of her looking up at me like she really, really loves me, tag me in it." He winked at me. "Okay, this one is 'Love me Tender.' If you don't know this song, well…I can't help you."

The man could do Elvis, that was for damn sure. He did his own arrangement of it, a slow deep croon in that rough beautiful voice of his, fingers picking the melody with an occasional show-off run of fingerstyle wizardry. He did "Unchained Melody," "Can't Take My Eyes Off You," "Wonderful Tonight" (for which he traded his acoustic for an electric, and did incredible justice to the original guitar licks by Eric Clapton), "I Wanna Be Your Lover," "I Don't Want To Miss a Thing"…if there was a hot, sultry, sweet, or romantic love song from the past fifty years, he covered it. And yes, his Instagram feed was overrun with photos of me, sitting on the blanket near his feet, not taking my eyes off him for a single moment.

He did end up doing acoustic or solo versions of his top five or six hits, the ones that get requested on the radio most, the ones that traditionally would be reserved for encores, since they always got the crowd pumped up and singing along.

The show ended, and we went back to his rig. I expected him to want to go out and celebrate a successful show, but the moment he got onto the rig, he kicked his boots off, tossed the shirt aside, and flopped onto the couch.

"Hold me," he murmured.

I'd never seen him immediately post show, before—I always figured he'd be pumped up, manic.

Instead, he was…

Exhausted.

"You wouldn't think a sitting-down acoustic show would be that draining, right?" He gazed up at me as I slid behind him, taking his head onto my lap and stroking his hair. "But it does. It's the being on, you know?" He closed his eyes and just breathed a moment. "I'm not actually an extrovert. I'm a homebody. I like being alone, or with a small number of people."

I hummed a small laugh. "Really? You seem so confident, so full of energy when you're performing."

"It's a weird thing. I *love* performing. But…once it's a real crowd, more than like a few dozen people, it kind of stops being…*people.* I don't know how to put it. It's a different part of my brain. It's not individuals, at that point, it's a crowd. A part of me turns on, right? I'm *on*, I'm not Titus anymore, I'm Titus Bright. I'm Bright Bones. I'm Tommy's legacy, those songs we wrote together and performed every night for twenty fucking years. I put it all out there, all of me, every performance. Whether it's fifty people in a coffeehouse, or two thousand in a park like today, I'm all the way on, putting on the best show I can."

"I can tell," I said. "And so can your fans."

He smiled. "Thanks. But once I'm done, I'm just… beat."

"I did kind of expect you to be more jazzed-up afterward."

He shrugged. "With a full band, a sold-out stadium, fifty thousand people on their feet and screaming for two and a half hours? Yeah, there's a rush afterward. Especially when it's four of you all meshing, jamming, just in the zone, you know? You get this…yeah, a jazzed-up energy, you feel kinda crazy when it's over. It can be hard to come down from it, honestly, and that's part of why people in this industry have substance abuse problems—you crave that high when you're not performing, but then once the high is over you can't come down from it, so you end up using uppers and downers and all that…on top of the fame and no one to tell you no and just the lifestyle."

"Your way seems better," I said.

He nodded. "It's not as crazy. You're not in a different city every night. Not as big, not as loud, not as much pressure. I don't get the rush quite as much, which I do miss, honestly. There's nothing like nailing a show in a sold-out stadium. Nothing in the world. But this is better. I can manage this. The trade-off is, the energy and the pressure of the performance is all on me. And I'm just beat afterward, I guess." A glance up at me. "Hope that's not a disappointment."

I continued stroking his hair. "A disappointment? Hell no, Titus." I bent forward and kissed his forehead. "I'm a homebody myself, actually. You know how I grew up, I told you everything. Well, it meant I never really felt at home. I never had a home. Even when I *was* home, it wasn't…*home*. It was a house where my parents lived, but they didn't really give two shits about me, not really. I never felt safe, I never had anywhere that was *mine*, that was safe. So, when I got out of college, the first thing

I did was buy a condo. And that was *my* place. I never let anyone in, not my friends, not my hookups, no one. Ever."

He blinked up at me. "Really?"

"Oh yeah. I'm still that way. Obviously, I have the girls over sometimes. They've all been to my house, but very rarely do they ever go into my actual bedroom. Sometimes to help me pick an outfit, but…yeah. My room especially is…" I shrugged. "It's sort of…sacred, I guess, I don't know a better word for it."

He went still. "So that day you brought me to your house, and let me into your room?"

"That was a really, *really* big deal."

"And that's why you sort of freaked out. And giving me regular access to your home, giving me space in the closet, a key…"

I laughed. "It's unthinkable. If you'd have told me a year ago I'd be giving up closet space and making a key for a *man*? I'd have laughed until I passed out."

"I actually know what you mean. You, here, on this bus with me? I still call it a bus even though it's not, but anyway—like you said, I'd have laughed you out of the room. I stopped the whole backstage girls thing years and years ago. It was exhausting. If I wanted to…meet someone, it'd be another time. At a bar, or a coffee shop. I'm just never in the mood after a show." He tangled his fingers into mine, into the fingers of my hand that wasn't stroking through his hair. "I like to be alone after

I'm done performing. Especially this style of show and tour. So having you here? I'd never have imagined I'd be even comfortable having anyone on this bus with me, let alone a woman. But you're…you comfort me, in a way I didn't know I needed or wanted…in a way I didn't know was even possible."

I leaned over and kissed him upside down, a slow sweet intimate kiss. "You're my comfort too, Titus."

"I honestly don't know how we ended up here, you and me, but I'm glad. I've never been so happy in my life as I am with you in it."

That got me choked up. "You already won me, Titus. You don't have to keep sweetening me up."

He laughed. "I'm not! I'm telling you how I feel."

He twisted with me and suddenly, somehow I was lying on his chest and we were stretched out on the couch together and breathing, and my chest was tight, my throat hot.

"I've never been this happy, either. I honestly didn't know I could be."

Like I said—luckiest girl in the world.

CHAPTER ELEVEN

Two months later

I WOKE TO THE SMELL OF COFFEE.

"Wakey-wakey, babe." That voice, rough and rumbling. "Time to get up."

He'd been gone for a week and a half, doing a series of pop-ups on the East Coast. It was Sunday, early.

We had continued to abstain from sex, and while it hadn't gotten any easier, we'd found some habits and patterns that made it doable—and the strength, depth, and intensity of our emotional relationship had proved the value of the experience. Made it all worthwhile.

"Why." My voice was hoarse, sleepy, raspy. "Too early."

"It's ten a.m., babe." A laugh. "I haven't been to bed yet."

I scooted up to sitting position, heedless of the fact that I'd taken a bath late last night and had fallen into bed naked and damp. So I was naked, and my hair was still half wrapped in a hair towel.

"Fuck, babe, why you gotta be naked?"

I tucked the sheet under my arms. "Sorry. Better?"

"No, it's not better. I'd rather see them sexy tits of yours."

I dropped the sheet, baring the body parts in question. "Well, then, don't complain."

"I wasn't. Just getting hard to resist you."

I smirked at him. "Babe, I'm waiting on *you* to call it. I'm ready to ride that dick whenever you are. Say the word, and I'll jump your bones so fast you'll be coming inside me before you know what hit you."

He snarled and paced away from the bed. "I have a plan for that." He turned back to me, handed me a to-go coffee. "Get some clothes on. We got shit to do." A growl and a huff. "I'll be waiting in my truck."

I laughed at cranky, sex-starved Titus as I hauled my ass out of bed and stuffed it into black leggings, a T-shirt, and a hoodie, with my hair pulled through a trucker hat. I mean, I understood the crankiness, because hell, I was getting cranky about it, too. My girls had all pointed out over the past few months that a sex-deprived Laurel was *not* a fun or pleasant to be around Laurel, sometimes. Was it worth it, knowing Titus and I were establishing a good strong foundation of friendship and trust? Hell yes. Did I *like* the fact that I hadn't had sexual intercourse or even any fun times with hands or mouths in the past three and a half months? No, no I didn't. Not at all. I wanted his cock. I wanted his mouth on me, I wanted that talented tongue that could give me six orgasms in as many minutes. I wanted to be naked in bed with him. I wanted to kiss him until neither of us could breathe.

But I wanted to know he was ready—*we* were ready.

And I was trusting him for that. Which was hard—putting that in his hands. Waiting for him. Trusting him for the status and future of our relationship. But it also felt good. It was scary, and hard, but it was also…kind of like the soreness you get after a brutal workout. It hurts, but you're proud of yourself for going hard and getting after it.

Yes, I'd finally started actually working out. Titus, it turned out, was an exercise fanatic. I mean, look at him—you didn't get a body like that sitting around eating Lays: he was into kettlebells, and running, and yoga, and push-ups, and barbells, and more running. And healthy food. Just to support him and spend time with him, at first, I'd gotten into all that stuff. Wonder of wonders…I'd discovered I loved it. If only, or at least partially, because between healthy eating, less alcohol, and regular exercise, my ass had begun to shrink back to its former glory, and my abs had tightened and come out and gotten visible for the first time since I was a teenager with that annoying metabolism I'd taken for granted.

Also, if we weren't having sex, I needed to get that energy and aggression out somehow, right? And so did he. Yeah, I was still jilling of with Grimace two and sometimes three times a day, thinking about Titus; it was way too easy to get off, knowing Titus was in his bathroom in his trailer, fist around his cock, imagining me in my bed with my fingers on my clit and a big purple vibrator deep inside me—wishing it was him.

I also knew I wasn't going to last too much longer with this abstinence thing. I needed…not just sex, although god knew I needed that. But I needed *him*. I needed Titus. I needed closeness and nakedness and connection.

I didn't want to just fuck him—but, granted, the first time we got it on, it'd be straight-up no-holds-barred fucking—I wanted to make love to him. I wanted to hold him. To *be* with him.

I needed it.

I collected my thoughts, stuffed them back into the box inside where they belonged, and headed out to Titus's truck.

He didn't drive us far, only a few blocks away. To a similar house as mine—small, Ranch-style, two-bedroom, two-bath…and listed by Teddy. Who was standing beside her car in the driveway, waving as we pulled in.

I glanced askance at Titus. "What…um. What is this?"

He shrugged. "A symbol."

"I don't know what that means."

"I'll explain. But first, I need you to have your realtor hat on."

I snorted. "My realtor hat is always on, babe. I can't take it off."

He nodded. "Good. I want your honest opinion."

I hugged Teddy as we ascended the three steps to the porch. "Still selling these, huh?"

She gave a nod and a shrug. "Sure. I move quite a few of them. I figure if it takes a lot longer to move the more expensive properties, why not spend the time in between flipping these? I can list and sell two or three in the time it takes to move a property two or three times the price. Smaller commission, of course, but more of them. And it keeps me busy."

"Smart, actually," I said. "I may steal the idea."

Teddy unlocked the lockbox and let us in. "So it's dated," she said by way of introduction as we entered. "But it has great, great bones. I already had my contractor Darren in here and he confirmed that this wall here," she tapped the one between the kitchen and living room, "*is* load-bearing, so you'd have to put up a beam, but the span is doable. There's nice original oak under this atrocious nineties carpet, and it runs throughout. You can see what it looks like in the master, because for some reason they carpeted out here but not in the master."

I was looking around, seeing the potential. "You could flip this easily." I glanced at Titus. "Are you looking at it as a flip? Flip and rent?"

He shook his head. "Neither. Let's keep looking before I give you my idea."

My heart twisted, rose and sank. "Okay."

Teddy showed us the kitchen. "This needs a total redo. I'd take it down to studs and subfloor, take out the wall, and completely reconfigure."

I took in the '90s oak cabinets with gold pulls and cheap laminate counter. "Yeah, absolutely. But there's space here, so if you open it up, you'd have a pretty killer open-plan living area."

Titus just nodded. "And we could do it pretty quick?"

"Between Teddy's guy Darren and my guy Mark, yeah," I nodded, heading for the hallway, "I think we could have this renovated in a couple or maybe three months, if there's surprises."

"That's what I was thinking," Teddy agreed.

The master was equally dated, but that was just furniture. New paint, a nice rug, and a small reno of the en suite bathroom, and it would be nice. The other bedroom and nonattached bathroom both needed similar cosmetic attention, but overall, it was a solid house with no egregious problems.

We headed out to the backyard, which was a decent size, with a nice big elm and a privacy fence. There was a tire swing hanging from the tree, and I sat on it, letting it spin me.

"So, Titus," I asked, eyeing him, "what's the plan with this?"

He smiled, eager. "I want to buy it, redo it."

"Okay. I assumed, since we're here." I swallowed hard. "But why?"

He frowned, confused. "Um, to live in?"

I held back my reaction. "Oh, I see."

Teddy held up her phone. "I have a, uh, call to make. I'll be inside."

Titus held the ropes, stopped my lazy twisting motion. "To live in. To be near you."

"That's…" I couldn't hold back anymore. "I guess I don't understand."

His frown deepened. "I don't understand what you don't understand. I'm saying not living on my rig anymore. Settle down. Be near you. Just blocks away."

My eyes were misty, my throat hot. "Yeah, no." I tried to smile, left the swing and headed for the back door. "It's a great plan, Titus. I'll make sure you get a good price, and we'll get Mark here ASAP. You can be moved in within eight, maybe twelve weeks."

He caught me, stopped me, spun me around. "Hey, what am I missing?"

"Nothing."

He growled a wordless gruff sound of disapproval. "You've never played bullshit mind games before, Laurel—don't you fuckin' start now."

I groaned. Wiped my face with both hands. "Why would you not want to just live with me?"

He rocked backward. "You—you'd want that?"

I waved a hand at the house. "Why would I want you to buy a house to live in, Titus? I love you. I've spent the last three and a half months celibate so we can start a real relationship. If that period is over, why the fuck would we not want to live together? If you want to settle down, do it with *me*! Not a house of your own. Jesus, of fucking *course* I want that, Titus. You said you'd propose. So propose! OR don't! I don't need a ring and a Mrs. to be happy with you, Titus. I just need you."

"I…" He twisted in place. "I don't…I didn't want to…to assume. To invite myself into your life—your personal space, I guess I mean."

I laughed, but it wasn't entirely mirthful. "Titus, my god. You're in my personal space already. You are my entire fucking life, do you not get that?" I held out my hands. "You showed up, told me I was going to be yours, I just didn't know it yet. Well? Now I do. I'm yours, Titus. So yes, if you need a fucking invitation, consider this it—I want you to move in with me. I'll give you half of my extra bedroom for closet space, for all your leather pants and vests, and you can put your eight hundred Grammy's on my mantle."

He rolled his eyes. "I have three, not eight hundred. And I don't actually have all that many pairs of leather pants."

"Whatever, you're missing the point, Titus."

He laughed, took me in his arms. "I know, I know. Are you sure?"

I rested my cheek on his chest. "Can we have sex, if you move in?"

His laugh was a rumble. "If not sooner."

"Promise? Because my vagina feels dusty."

"What happened to Grimace?"

"Oh, he's still around. Getting *plenty* of use, let me tell you. I've had to recharge him quite a few times in the last couple months, and let me just make clear here that until this abstinence thing, I only had to recharge Grimace a couple times a year." I gestured at him. "Point here being, a vibrator doesn't really count. The puss is still dusty from disuse. Needs a good workout, if you know what I'm saying."

He grumbled a laugh. "I think I understand. I'm not sure what the male equivalent is of a dusty vagina, but whatever it is, I've got it. Rusty dick, maybe?"

"Rusty and dusty, you and me," I laughed. "Funniest part of it all is that we did it to ourselves."

"Worth it, though, right?"

"Yeah." I inhaled the scent of his throat, the scratch of his beard. "Worth it."

"I'm sorry, Laurel," he whispered. "I didn't mean to upset you. I guess I just miscalculated."

"Yeah, dumbshit, you miscalculated." I could laugh at it, now, and did. "I can't believe you thought I'd let you buy a fucking house instead of moving in with me." I pulled back. "Or."

He smirked at me, hands on my hips—the most erogenous touch I'd received from him in months. "Or?"

"Or you buy it, we flip it, and sell it or rent it out."

He hummed thoughtfully. "You think so?"

"It's a good place, for a good price. Barring any unforeseen and unforeseeable catastrophes, which are always possible but unlikely since this house isn't all that old, we could get it demo'd and reno'd in two months if we're lucky, three if we're not. It's actually a decent market for flipping, and I know Mark would be down to split profits. He and I have talked about it before."

"Should I be worried about Mark?"

I cackled. "Decidedly no."

"Why do you laugh like that?"

"Because he's married, for one thing."

"Oh, okay."

"And his husband's name is Richard."

"Oh." A chuckle.

"They have three adopted kids, one from Ethiopia, one from South Korea, and one from here in LA. Mark is one of the best contractors I've ever met, and we've been buds for ten years. We throw each other work all the time, and like I said, we've knocked around the idea of flipping together. We just never bit the bullet."

"If you're in, I'm in. I've always wanted to try my hand at construction."

I laughed, but he wasn't laughing with me. "Oh, you're serious."

He gave a droll eye roll. "Yes, I'm serious."

"Well, knock yourself out. If you help, it'll go faster and we can move on to the next flip."

"How does flipping work?"

I shrugged. "We buy a house like this, renovate it to be attractive, sell it for max profit. Take that profit, and use it to buy another fixer-upper. Rinse and repeat."

"Oh. Well that's pretty simple."

"In theory it is. But you're guaranteed to get a lemon now and then, of course. Rip up carpet because you checked in one corner and saw some sexy wood floors, but it turns out the rest of the floors are water-stained garbage and you have to rip them all out and put in new hardwood and that eats into your profit. And then suddenly there's a wiring issue, and your tile supplier fucks up your order, and the plumber messes up a toilet install and there's a leak underneath the subfloor, and bam, you're over budget by fifteen grand and passed the deadline by a month and comps are saying you're only gonna net ten grand max, *if* there's no other issues." I laughed. "There's that."

He laughed. "There's risk to everything. But good news is, I've got cash to burn. I don't spend all that much, and with these pop-ups driving my royalties income, I'm sitting on more than you'd think, most of it cash or easily liquidated assets. So, you know. No worries."

"So you want to get into flipping with me, is what you're saying."

"What I'm saying is, let's go get my shit outta my rig, move it into your place, and then I'm gonna flip *you*."

"Ooooh," I purred. "I don't know what that means, but I'm down."

"It means I'm gonna take you home, strip you naked, and fuck you six ways to Sunday."

"Why stop at six? I can think of a dozen ways I want you to fuck me off the top of my head."

He laughed. "I love the way you think."

It took all of two hours to pack up his stuff off his touring rig, which until today, had doubled as his full-time residence. He had about a dozen Rubbermaid bins full of random shit, half a dozen contractor bags full of clothes, and some music equipment he wanted to bring home with him, rather than leave it on the rig, guitars mainly, and some mobile recording and mixing gear, as well as a keyboard.

We put it all in the back of his truck and made the short trip from the parking lot where he parked his rig while in LA to my house in the suburbs. Another hour of unpacking, while I condensed my clothes in my main closet and the extra bedroom to make room for his stuff. Which, fortunately for me, really was minimal, and only took up a small corner of my extra closet/spare bedroom.

Some shower stuff, and his music equipment in a

corner of the living room—which I actually really liked, since it gave my otherwise kind of spartan living room a more lived-in and eclectic appeal.

He filled my home with himself. His scent, his warmth, his laugh.

And that was just within the first couple hours.

Once his stuff was settled and organized, we plopped onto my deck chairs on the back porch, sharing a beer.

"Well, Laur," he murmured, as he took a sip. "I now live with you. What next?"

I smirked, and decided to play dumb. "I think you need to make my address your official address."

He swallowed hard. "You want me to? Make this my address?"

I frowned at him. "Not this again."

"I just…I've never had an actual home address before."

"Wait, you don't have an address?"

"Nope. Any official mail, anything I need an address for, I use the PO Box associated with Troubadour Enterprises, my record label and various other business-related stuff."

"So let me get this straight. You don't have a phone, you don't have an address…you're, like, barely an official person."

He snorted. "Pretty much."

"Okay, well first, yes, we're going to the DMV and

putting my address on your license, then a phone." I paused, smiled at him. "*Our* house, I mean."

"Our house," he repeated, and sounded more than a little wonderstruck. "I have a house. A home."

"Yes, you do."

He swallowed hard. "I belong somewhere. To someone."

"You do." I took his hand. "*With* me, and *to* me."

I took a sip of the beer, and handed it to him. "Shit, why wait? Let's go get that stuff done."

He held up a finger. "Can I borrow your phone?"

"Sure," I answered, and handed it to him.

He dialed a number from memory. "Jer, hey, it's me. So, um. I moved in with Laurel." A pause, a laugh. "Yes, for real, finally. I know. Amazing, is how it feels. Just happened, so I'm still sort of processing the whole thing. I just wanted you to know, so you know where to reach me, should anything come up." A pause, as he listened. "Yeah, you can call her. If I'm not on the bus, I'm with her. Nah, she's saying she's gonna get me one, but I'm gonna try and talk her out of it, because shit, I've gone forty-one fuckin years without a phone, I don't see the point of getting one now."

I just rolled my eyes. He chatted a few more minutes, and then hung up, handing me my phone back.

"You really don't want a phone?" I asked.

He shook his head, shrugging. "No point. If I'm not

with you, I'm on the bus. Who the fuck would I need to call?"

"Um, me, while you're on the road?"

"Oh. I can just borrow Jer's."

"He travels with you?"

"Sure he does. He's my manager, basically. He sets up the venue and arranges for the social media posts notifying the fans when and where the show is."

"Okay, well, program his number into my phone, then, so I can call him and get ahold of you. As long as I can reach you while you're gone, I don't care if you have a phone or not."

He frowned. "You don't?"

I shook my head, shrugged. "Nah."

"Really." He eyed me. "You don't want to, like, modernize me?"

I laughed. "I love you the way you are. I just want to be able to talk to you while you're gone. I miss the hell out of you when you're not here and I hate not being able to talk to you. And I promise I won't blow up Jeremy's phone. Just a call once a day is all I ask."

"I think I can manage that." He finished the beer and set it on the table between our chairs. "Well, I'm moved in."

"Indeed you are." I chewed on my lip and grinned at him. "So. Now what?"

He extended his hand to me. Wrapped my hand in

his and pulled me to my feet. "Now? Now I do a whole bunch of very dirty things to you."

I followed him inside. "I was hoping you'd say that."

He led me to my bedroom—*our* bedroom. "Any last requests?"

"Last requests?" I asked, laughing breathlessly as he kicked the door shut and began taking off my leggings. "What is this, an execution?"

"Yes," he mumbled. "Death by orgasm."

I tugged one leg free, then the other, and eagerly waited for him to peel my thong off. "My only request is that if I were to, for some weird reason, beg you stop making me come, just ignore me."

"Why on earth would you ever want me to stop?"

I shook my head as he made quick work of my shirt and bra, and finally, thank fuck, I was naked with Titus. "I don't know. I'm so horny I can't make sense. Just get down there and make me come already, dammit."

He dropped to his knees and gazed up at me, hands caressing my ass, then up to cup my breasts before sliding down to trace fingertips over my seam. "Yes, my love. As you wish."

I gathered his head in my hands and drew his face to my sex, and I gasped as he lapped at me. "I wish for this to never end."

"Wish granted," he growled, tonguing me slowly.

"Problem is," I gasped, hips flexing as he circled my clit with his tongue. "As much as I want you to just make me come a million times with your mouth, I equally as much need to get you naked and get my hands and mouth and pussy on your cock. Which I'm going for first, I don't know. Hands, then mouth, then pussy, probably. That makes the most sense, I think."

He rumbled a laugh. "Laurel?"

"Yeah?"

"You're babbling. Shut up and come."

I shut up and came—his fingers slid into me, one and then two and then three, curling and slicking in and out and gathering my wetness, and so needy for his touch was I that it took only moments to make me thrash, to bring me to quick shaking screaming orgasm.

Nothing and no one had ever been able to make me come as hard and as fast as Titus Bright.

Hard on the heels of the first, I felt another one rising, building, and he chased it, followed the path of my gasps and screams until he dragged the second orgasm out of me. Titus being Titus, he didn't relent, didn't give me quarter from the shredding ecstasy until I'd come apart on his wild, talented mouth twice more.

I yanked myself away abruptly, once the fourth shaking quake of ecstasy had settled within me. Caught him by the hand and yanked at him. "You, bed, now."

He laughed and shot to his feet, allowing me to pull him up. "Okay, okay. Whatever you want."

The moment he was even remotely vertical, I was ripping at his clothing, tearing his shirt off and shoving his shorts off without bothering to even unbutton them. I had him naked in record time, and pushed him to the bed, roughly shoving him backward as hard as I could. He flew backward, laughing, and let the bed catch his weight, flopping hard to the mattress and crawling backward.

I lurched to him, collapsing forward onto the back edge of the bed, wrapping both fists around the hot hard shaft of his erection. "Mine."

He groaned, laughing. "Yeah, baby. All yours."

I squeezed and caressed, petted and stroked. "Fuck, I almost forgot how big you are."

I stroked him with both fists for a moment, just plunging my touch around him and enjoying the heat of him, the thickness in my hands, the silk-on-steel feel of him, the veins, the plump fat head as it began to weep at my touch.

"And I almost forgot how incredible it feels when you touch me," he groaned. "So fucking good."

"You think that feels good?" I had so many needs. Him, all of him, in every way. But mostly, just his pleasure. His noises, his body, his cum. To be joined with him. "Then you're might just faint when I do…*this*."

I took him in my mouth, and he caught at my hair, wrapping it in his fists, groaning a snarl. "Fuck, fuck, *fuck*, Laurel. Fucking god, your mouth."

I hummed around him, and used my fist to stroke the many inches of him that wouldn't fit in my mouth, even after I had him at the back of my throat. One hand to caress those inches, the other to cup his balls and massage them, so every last inch of his manhood knew the touch of my hands and mouth.

"Fuck, Laurel, been so long, I can't—shit, shit, shit."

I backed away to lick the tip. "Give it to me, Titus. We have all night. All day. We have every day for the rest of our lives to make love every way there is." I took him deep, swallowing around him, then backed away. "For right now, baby, just come for me. Give it to me." I took him deep again. "Right now. Give it to me, Titus."

He groaned and brushed my hair away from my face, cupped my face in both hands, and with furrowed brow, jaw dropping open in bliss, fed himself slowly between my lips. "Fuckin'…I fucking love you, Laurel."

I swirled my tongue against him as he filled my mouth, my throat, and I pulled away and went deep again, and again, and then faster, and then I began pumping at his base with my fists and bobbing on the top inch or two with my sucking mouth and swirling tongue. Faster, faster.

"Laurel, god, fuck, Laurel." He gasped my name again and again. "Fuck, fuck, fuck. Laurel, my Laurel, fuck, you feel so incredible."

"Mmmhmm?"

He groaned, thrusting into my mouth, now. "I need to…fuck, I'm gonna come, Laurel."

"Mmmm. Mmmhmmm!"

At the last moment, an instant before I knew he was

about to fill my mouth, he yanked away with a snarl. "No, fuck no. I haven't had you in over four months, not since that day here. I'm not coming the first time with you since then in your damn mouth."

He flipped me to my back and grabbed my hands, pinned them over my head with one of his, and felt between my thighs, tracing my seam with a fingertip. Guided himself to me, nudging against my opening. "Can I? Bare, I mean."

In answer, I wrapped my thighs around him and lifted, sinking him into me. "Does that answer your question?" I breathed.

His eyes widened, raw emotion and pure pleasure warring in his eyes. "Laurel, god, oh my god. Are we covered?" he asked.

"I'm clean, obviously, and yes, I'm on birth control." I felt him fill me, withdraw, and fill me again, spearing deeper every time. "Fuck, you're huge, Titus. So fucking good. I love the way you feel inside me." I touched his lips before he could speak. "Yes, I know you're clean. Just…just fuck me, Titus."

He stopped, buried deep. "No, Laurel. No matter how good it is, no matter how hard I fuck you, it's never going to be *just* fucking again." He moved through me, and I quaked around him, tightening as my climax rose to meet his. "It's love. I'm making love to you. We're loving each other. I don't care how the fuck you say it. It's love. You and me, always, it's love."

"I know, baby," I murmured. "I know. Make love to me, then, and make it good."

"Yes, ma'am," he grumbled, chuckling. "How's this?"

I faked a bored face. "Meh. Could be better. Maybe a little faster."

"Yes, ma'am, right away, ma'am," he said, laughing, and arched forward over me as he quickened his pace. "How are you always able to make me laugh during sex?"

"I mean, I feel like sex is already the most fun you can have in this life—if you can laugh while having sex, it stands to reason it's even better."

"Being able to laugh with you while we're having sex is pretty much…" A pause, to find the right words. "It's pretty much heaven on earth."

I tugged his hair free from the ponytail he had it in, and buried my fingers in it. "It really is."

Faster, then, and harder. "God, Laurel."

"I know." I palmed his ass and pulled, encouraging him to give me more. "I thought you were about to come."

"I was. But then I got inside you and I had to make it last longer, so I fought it back."

"Well…don't. I got to come four times already. I want one of yours."

"Just one?"

"No, as many as I can get, until you can't get it up anymore."

"We might be here a while, then," he rasped. "Last time I jerked off while imagining your mouth on my cock, I was hard again with seconds of coming. I had to jerk off three times in a row before I could function normally."

"You beast," I whispered, gleefully. "Show me."

He touched his forehead to mine. "I just want to make love to you forever and never stop."

"Let me feel you come, and I'll finish what I started with my mouth."

He groaned and quickened his pace yet more. "Laurel, Jesus. What did I do to deserve you?"

"We deserve each other," I answered, gasping as he slammed into me. "We're made for each other."

I felt him tensing, felt his movements become staggered, the rhythm faltering.

"Laurel…" he gasped.

"Now, Titus," I whispered. Reached between our bodies and circled finger and thumb around his base where we met and squeezed, tugged. "Now, now. Give it to me. Give it all to me, Titus. Come for me, baby."

"Oh fuck, Laurel. What are you doing to me?"

I rocked against him. "Taking what's mine."

He chased it, then, his movements rough and ragged and furious, slamming deep and sagging there for a moment before pulling slowly back, only to drive into me hard yet again. And then a hoarse cry burst out of him and I felt him cut loose, felt him give way, felt him come.

I cried out with him, my own orgasm triggered by his. I wept with him, and we whispered each other's names, cried out chanting for god, for each other. Rocked together, his climax bleeding into mine, blending with mine, and I was merged with him and united in him and I understood.

I understood.

Love and fucking are not the same at all.

This, with my whole heart and my whole soul opened to his…

This was a whole new universe.

I welcomed the shattering, because I knew he could put me together again.

He came and he came and he came.

"I love you, Laurel," he gasped, when it finally subsided. "I love you."

I clasped him to me and refused to let him go. "I love you back, Titus."

CHAPTER TWELVE

M Y PHONE RANG. *JEREMY*, IT SAID.

Titus was still beside me, my iPad on his belly, a documentary playing. It was late morning, the day after he'd moved in.

I answered. "Hi, Jeremy. It's Laurel. You need to talk to Titus?"

"Yeah, it's urgent."

I handed it to Titus, who flipped the lid of the iPad closed and took the phone, putting it on speaker rather than to his ear. "Jer, what's up?"

"I just got a call from the LAPD," Jeremy said, rushed. "All they would say is that they need to speak to you urgently. Something happened and they wouldn't say what, but somehow it involves you." I caught an undercurrent of something unspoken. "I'm sorry, Laurel, but I had to give them your address."

"It's okay," I said. "When did they say they'd be here?"

DING...dong.

"Now, I guess," I answered my own question. "We have to let you go, it seems. They're here."

I left the phone with Titus and grabbed a button-down I'd stolen from Titus's closet, shrugged into it and buttoned it as I made for the door.

When I opened it, two uniformed LAPD officers faced me, stern and serious. "Hi, how can I help you?"

"Looking for Titus Bright," one of them said. "His manager gave us this address."

Titus came up behind me, clad in a pair of gym shorts. "Hi, fellas. What's up?"

There was a cruiser in my driveway behind Titus's big red Power Wagon, and an unmarked but official-looking sedan behind that, blocking the sidewalk. Something about that vehicle made my stomach flip.

One of the officers glanced at me, then at Titus. "Can we come in?"

I swallowed hard. Backed away, and Titus and I sat down on the love seat, leaving the couch to the two officers, who perched on the edge with obvious hesitation and discomfort.

"Mr. Bright, this is the kind of visit we hate having to make," one of the officers, his name tag reading *L. Murray*, began. "If you'd like this to be...private...now would be the time."

Titus hung his head. "What's this about? Just get it over with."

"You are listed as the only next of kin for Isabela Maria Hernandez."

I blinked. Who?

Titus groaned. "Yes."

"She's your daughter?"

My world went sideways. Blank. Tilting, whirling.

Whispered, then, barely audible. Not looking at me or the officers or anyone, anything, but his feet. "Yes." A pause. "Is she okay?"

"Isabela is fine. Her mother, Maria Consuela Hernandez…she was killed in a car accident this morning."

"Fuck." A choked breath. "Maria's dead?"

"She was on the way to work after dropping Isabela off at school. A delivery truck crossed the centerline and hit her head-on. Maria was killed instantly."

"My god." A glance at me, then. "Laurel, I…I'm sorry. I should have told you. It's…it's complicated."

"You have a *daughter*?" I whispered, hoarse, barely coherent.

"Yes. Her mother…Maria, we…it was a one-time thing. She…" A harsh groan. "I *wanted* to be there for Isabela. Please believe me. I tried. She wanted nothing to do with me—Maria, I mean. Refused to let me see Isabela. Kept me away. Won a lawsuit I filed in secret to get visitation. I fucking…I fucking *tried*, Laurel, I swear." A ragged sob. "I fucking tried. She'll take my money, but won't let me see my kid."

I searched him. "How? Why?"

He swallowed. "We were safe, the one time we slept together. After a show in Mendocino. Once, just *once*. I wore a condom. It didn't break. Didn't fall off. I think…I think she poked a hole in it, or something. I didn't have one, she did, and so we used hers. I shoulda…shoulda known better. I fought her for fuckin' *years*. Fought to be there—to be in Isabela's life. To see her, once a month even. Fucking *ever*. Once she had my kid, Maria went feral on me. She's…she's fuckin' nuts, man. Turned out she had been obsessed with me, or some shit. There was a whole investigation, and it showed all this shit. But the court still sided with her, since I'm just an itinerant rock star who does drugs and fucks around, which means clearly I'm no good. Not fit to be around my own kid. To even fucking lay eyes on her." Bitter, so bitter. "She just wanted to get a kid out of me. And money. I was ordered to pay three grand a month. I send ten. I send cards, gifts, all that shit for every holiday, every birthday. It all gets returned. The money doesn't. So it's what I can do—I send money, a lot of it, every month. But I've never once laid eyes on my daughter." A harsh laugh. "When we had sex that one time, she was like, talking afterward about *us*, about all these plans she had for *us*, and I'd made it clear before anything happened that it was just fun. She was like, uh-huh, I got it, I understand. Then, soon as it was over, she was talking about us, like she had this whole story made up in her head where I'd fallen for her, and she believed it, had herself convinced it was real, and when I was like, I'm sorry, there is no us and never will be, and I thought that was clear, she… she went crazy. I had to get Tommy and the other guys to get her off the bus. I thought that was it. Then a year later, I got this thing in the mail about child support, and I was like, child support? What the fuck?"

I was dizzy. "You have a daughter. And you never told me."

"I…" A hoarse clearing of his throat. "I didn't know how. I'm not in her life, I never see her, never see Maria, it's just a check in the mail once a month." A hoarse, choked sound. "I have never once even seen her face. Not so much as a photograph. And I wanted to, but I wasn't allowed."

The officer who'd spoken cleared his throat. "Isabela has no other kin. Maria's family is in Mexico and can't be reached. You are Isabela's only family."

"Where…where is she?"

The other officer spoke for the first time, jerking a thumb at the door, the driveway. "Out there. Waiting to know what you're gonna do."

"What I'm…what I'm gonna do?"

I stood up, and looked back down at Titus. "What you're going to do about Isabela. You're her father, and now Maria's wishes that you never see or know your daughter are moot. She needs a home, a family. Care."

He met my eyes. "She needs a home."

I closed my eyes. Sucked in a breath. Let it out slowly, shuddering. Walked away.

"Where are you going?"

I gestured at the spare bedroom. "I have to move all our stuff. She's going to need a bedroom, obviously."

"Laurel—"

I stopped in the hallway outside my—our—bedroom door. "I need a minute, Titus. And you need to go meet your daughter."

"I just…we just…" He looked to the officers, to the door and the hint of the other car, back to me. "My daughter."

I nodded. "Your daughter."

"How is this happening?"

I laughed, unsteady and shaken. "I really don't know, Titus." I walked back to him, took his face in my hands. "But it is. And we have to deal with it. So go meet your daughter."

"We?"

I nodded. "I'm going to need some time to process this, but yes, Titus. We. You and me. I'm mad as hell that you kept this from me, but I understand. Shit, there's something I haven't told you, yet. But I'm not going to… panic. Or bolt, or dump you, or whatever you're thinking. This fucking complicates things, but I told you I love you. I told you it was no matter what. And I meant that shit. Well, no matter what is here, it seems. So, here we go."

He stood up, followed me to the threshold of our room, took my hands. "You didn't sign up for this."

"Neither did you."

"No, but it's my mess to deal with."

I laughed. "What, you're going to bring your daughter to live with you on a fucking tour bus? Or rig, or whatever you want to call that thing you were living on? Or you're going to send her into the system because you can't deal? No, Titus. We live together, you and me. For all of, what, twelve hours? But here we are, right? And we have the room. So yeah, she's living here, I guess."

He let out a breath. Addressed the officers. "Bring her in, then."

I arched an eyebrow at Titus. "Maybe we should get dressed, first?"

Titus glanced down at himself, loose gym shorts hanging low, revealing as obvious the fact that he wasn't wearing anything beneath them; then to me, with my baggy men's button-down draped around my bare thighs, the sleeves rolled half a dozen times and hanging at my elbows. "Yeah, good point."

I shot a glance at the officers. "Just give us a minute to get dressed properly, okay? Two minutes."

They nodded and stood to exit. "We'll talk to Isabela and the social worker."

Alone in our room—god, it was so odd to say that, think that, that *my* room was now *our* room: I'd never shared a bed, a room, any space, with anyone, ever; even overseas at the academy, my parents had made sure I had my own room rather than having to share—I stood in my closet and gathered myself. Or, tried to.

I felt him behind me. "I'm so sorry, Laurel. I know—I know I should have told you. But…how? When? I just… it was never a good conversation, a good moment to be like, so hey, I have a daughter I never see. And no matter what I say, people will always assume I'm a deadbeat dad, right? It's the stereotype, and for good reason. But if she'd have let me, I'd have been there. I travel a lot, but with my pop-up system I'm usually only gone for a few weeks at a time at most. I run out to wherever I'm gonna play, do a few shows in that area, and then come home again. I'd…I'd have been there for Isabela. I wanted to be."

I turned and faced him. "Titus, I know." I could see the torture on his face. "I believe you."

He blinked, swallowed, seemed close to tears of relief. "You do?"

I touched his face with my fingertips. "You can't fake the emotions I see in you right now, Titus. And the way you talked about your own childhood, yeah, I believe that if you were given a choice, you'd have been there to whatever degree you were allowed to be." I sighed, shook my head with a toss of my hair. "I wish you'd told me—at any point. But I understand, really I do. I'm more shocked than angry."

"You don't have to tell me now, because shit, there's

enough happening right now, but…you said you had something haven't told me."

I closed my eyes. Ducked my head, let my shoulders roll forward. Swallowed hard. "I had an abortion. After the rape." I shuddered. "I've only ever told Dr. Hines, and now you. I did it in secret. Kept it secret for the last twenty years."

"Jesus, Laur."

"I couldn't—you know? Like, how could I go on with my life? How could I…I didn't want to—end it, get rid of it. I didn't want to. It felt wrong. But…*fuck*, it was forced on me. I…"

He pulled me to his chest. "I know, baby. I know."

I shuddered and shook against him. "I talked about it with Dr. Hines a lot. I'm not, like, okay with it. It's not, like, fine. But…I'm as okay and fine with it as I'll ever be. And I'm glad I told you."

"Does that make this harder? With Isabela, I mean."

I laughed. "Wow, I don't think that's crossed my mind yet. I mean, no? I don't know. Would you have told her to do that, if she'd asked you?"

A harsh sigh. "I don't know." Another sigh, more of a groan. "No, I don't think so. If she'd insisted I'd have supported her and helped her any way I could, but no, I wouldn't have wanted that, in that situation. In yours, it's different. But it would have been her choice, either way, so I would have supported her no matter what."

"It's a complicated, tricky, difficult, painful topic."

"Yeah, it is."

I turned away from him and lifted my chin and swallowed hard, shook my hands as if to wake them up. "Enough. We don't have time for that whole conversation, and it's not even really relevant. The point is, there's no more secrets, right?" Back to him, gazing up at him. "That was my last secret. If you have any more, now's the fucking time, Titus. Because when we go out there, that little girl is going to be messed-up. Confused. In pain. This is going to be fucking hard, for everyone. And we have to be on our A-game, because that little girl is going to need love and patience and understanding."

He nodded. "I got nothing. That was it. I told you about being suicidal, you know I've struggled with drugs and alcohol, and you know I'm sober—from drugs, I mean. Alcohol was just the thing you did as a rock star. I was always able to put the booze down when I needed to. The coke was a different story, but after Tommy, I have no interest in going down that road ever again."

I nodded. "Good. So we're clear." I took his hands, lifted up on my tiptoes and kissed him. "Let's do this."

He shook his head, breathing shakily. "I can't believe this is happening." He swallowed thickly. "I don't know how to be a dad."

"I think first, we just start with getting to know each other. That'll be enough, I think."

"Yeah, you're right." His eyes met mine, and he

blinked wetness away. "I don't think I could have done this without you, Laurel."

"Well, you don't have to." I grinned up at him. "I do have one little secret—I'm good with kids. One of those unexpected things most people wouldn't ever guess about me."

He just laughed. "At this point, nothing about you surprises me. I'm learning to expect the unexpected, where you're concerned."

I peeled the button-down off, folded it, and set it on my shelf of pajamas, and I noticed his eyes on me. "Down, boy."

He just laughed, shucking his shorts. "Can't blame me for looking."

We dressed quickly, then, and I dragged a brush through my hair and put it in a quick braid.

Before we left our room, Titus stopped me with a hand on my shoulder. "I have one question, real quick. Just to think about it, if not answer right now."

I knew what he was about to ask. "Would I ever consider having a baby of my own?"

He nodded. "Yeah."

I sighed, swallowed hard. "Until this moment, Titus, I would have said no. I never wanted the responsibility. I never wanted…never had anyone in my life I could have conceived of having that life with, and I never wanted to be a single mom. My next-door neighbor is a single mom, and she's a fucking hero in my book, but I wouldn't want that simply because it's so hard for her. So until you, no. I never wanted to be a mother. But now, with you in my life, with us living together, I guess…" I huffed something like a laugh, or a sigh, or mixture of both. "I guess now, I can see it happening. Someday."

He just nodded. "I see."

I put my hand on the knob. "Out with it."

"I just…I guess in the back of my mind, I deeply regret and resent being kept out of Isabela's life, that I didn't get to see any of it, of her life, and I…"

"You want a chance to do it right."

"Redemption, I guess. My own folks were shit, just absolute shit at being parents. I want to do better. Do it right."

I lifted up and kissed him. "Baby steps, Titus. First, let's meet this little girl." I opened the door. "How old is she, anyway?"

A pause, as he thought about it. "Six. She's six."

I held his hand and pulled him toward the living room. "You ready?"

"Nope," he murmured, "but I don't think I ever could be, so…let's do this."

CHAPTER THIRTEEN

THE POLICE OFFICERS WERE OUTSIDE, IN THEIR CRUISER.
On the couch sat the social worker, a younger woman wearing a colorful hijab with jeans, a blouse, and a blazer. Beside her, a small girl with wide, dark, frightened eyes. Black hair, short and straight, cut at her jaw. She was wearing pink shorts, a white shirt, and clean white sneakers. She held a well-loved and well-worn stuffed elephant on her lap.

The social worker stood up as we entered the living room, strode over to Titus and met his eyes, hand extended. "Hi, I'm Mena."

"Titus Bright." His voice was low and tight.

To me, then, and I shook her hand as well. "Laurel McGillis."

Mena's attention returned to Titus. "We have much to discuss. But first, Titus, this is Isabela."

Isabela held utterly still, wide eyes fixed on Titus. She seemed to be barely breathing.

Titus knelt in front of her, a soft smile on his face. "Hi, Isabela. I'm Titus. I'm your dad." A pause. "You can just call me Titus for now, though, okay?"

A nod, nothing else.

Titus glanced at the social worker, who remained impassive and watchful, seemingly content to see how first introductions played out.

"Um, do you go by Isabela? Or do you have a nickname?" Titus remained kneeling, and seemed to be trying to make his shoulders narrower, as if that was possible.

The little girl just stared at him. "Bel," she whispered. "Mommy called me Bel."

"Do you want me to call you Bel? Or would you rather I call you Isabela?"

A shrug. Eyes dropping. "Isabela."

"Okay, then, Isabela it is." Titus seemed at a loss. "Um. Is there anything you want to ask me?"

A long, long silence. Isabela's eyes roved over him, assessing. She reached out and didn't quite touch one of his tattoos on his bicep, a stylized depiction of a 1940s pinup model. "Is that Mommy?"

The girl depicted in the tattoo had black hair and brown skin, curvy, wearing a red-and-white polka-dot bikini and a bright, flirty smile.

Titus huffed a laugh. "No, it's...it's no one in particular. Or, I guess maybe it was a real person." A laugh. "How do you explain pinup calendars? Um. It's a drawing of someone from a long time ago. Sort of like a cartoon."

She frowned. "Is it painted on?"

Titus laughed. "No, well, kind of. It's on there forever." He rubbed at it with a thumb. "You try."

Isabela looked at him, then at the tattoo. Rubbed it gingerly with a fingertip, and then looked at her fingertip. "Weird. It looks like Mommy."

Titus looked at the tattoo more carefully. "I guess you're right. Never thought about it—I got that one a long time ago."

"How did they put it on you?" Isabela asked.

Titus considered. "Um? You ever draw on yourself with a pen or a marker?" She nodded. "Sort of like that. But it's this special kind of needle, like a handheld sewing machine, and they dip the needle in special ink, and the needle goes down into my skin, real fast, and it draws on my skin, and then it doesn't come off."

Isabela gave a disgusted look. "Like getting a bunch of shots?"

"Kinda, I guess, yeah."

"Did it hurt?"

"Yeah, a little."

She frowned. "Why?"

"Why?" Titus echoed. "Why did it hurt, or why did I get them?"

"Why did you get them?"

A laugh. "You know, that's a good question. They seemed like the cool, rock star thing to do, I guess."

A blink. "I don't know what that means."

Another laugh. "That's okay." A sigh. "What else do you want to ask me?"

A shrug. Isabela's eyes dropped to her hands as she toyed with the trunk of her stuffed elephant. "Where is Mommy? When can I go home?"

Titus blinked hard, and looked at the social worker for help.

Mena scooted next to Isabela. "Honey, remember what we talked about?"

Isabela nodded. "You said Mommy...you said she—she was hurt, and that the hurt was so bad she... she's not alive anymore. It was a accident." Her voice cracked, became tearful. "She's gone?"

Titus nodded. "I'm so sorry, Isabela. I wish I could change it."

"What about...." She blinked. "My bed, and my clothes? And what about all of Mommy's stuff? Who... who will take care of me?"

Mena wrapped her arm around Isabela. "We'll figure all that out, about your stuff and your mom's. And...you're going to stay here, now. Titus and Laurel are going to take care of you."

Isabela was quiet, absorbing. She looked at me, and then at Titus. "You're my dad?"

A nod. "Yes. I am."

"Mommy told me…she said my father was too busy to be with me. That he…that you had a job that made you go travel everywhere, and you couldn't see me. That you didn't want to."

Titus's shoulders shook. His head dropped. When he lifted his eyes to her, they were wet. "I…I can't say I understand why she told you that, Isabela, but it's not true. I do want to see you. I always did. It's true I have a job that means I travel a lot, but…I wanted to see you."

Isabela looked away, thinking. "When I asked Mommy about my dad, she got angry. Were you mean to her?"

Titus sighed, sat down heavily on the floor and folded his legs in a crisscross. "I…I don't think I was, but your mommy may have felt different. I don't really know how to…how to explain it, honey."

Mena touched Isabela's arm. "Sometimes, adults just don't get along, and it's nobody's fault. Sometimes, when adults don't get along, things get complicated, and they can be hard to understand until we're a little older."

Titus's eyes went to Mena's. "I know what the court paperwork says, but I—"

Mena cut in. "Perhaps we could talk about this in private." She looked to me, to Isabela. "Isabela, I need to talk to Titus for a little bit, about some adult stuff. Do you think you could go with Laurel for a few minutes?"

Isabela nodded, looked at me. "Are you nice?"

I laughed. "I mean, I try to be. How about I promise I'll be on my best behavior?"

Isabela nodded seriously. "Mommy has a friend who looks like you, only she's not as pretty, and she's not very nice to me. I don't like her."

I stifled a laugh. "Well, I like to think I'm pretty cool." I held out my hand to her. "Do you like clothes and purses?"

Isabela's eyes brightened, just a little. "Yeah. Mommy lets me wear her shoes sometimes, and if I'm careful I can play with her purses."

I wiggled my fingers and smiled. "Well come on, then. I have lots of shoes and lots of and purses. You can tell me which ones are your favorites."

I led her into the extra bedroom—I had no clue where it was going to go, honestly, but I'd have to figure that out later. Her eyes went wide at the racks of clothing that filled the room, the shelves of purses along two walls, and the shelves of shoes on the others, and in the closet.

"This is all yours?" she asked, awed.

I nodded. "Yeah, it is."

"You have a lot of stuff."

"Yeah, I guess I do."

She eyed me. "If I'm staying here, where will I sleep? On the couch?"

I shook my head. "No, honey. We'll clear all this

stuff out of here and put it…somewhere else. This will be your room. We'll bring all your stuff over, and it'll feel just like your own place. Okay?"

I could tell she still hadn't quite processed the reality, yet. Her six-year-old mind still half believed it wasn't real, that her mom would come get her. And I couldn't fathom how she must feel. How this would work. How any of it would work.

I'd just started wrapping my head around Titus living with me, loving him, letting him into my life. And now…this.

I looked at Isabela, who had wandered over to my purses and was examining them carefully, one at a time, not touching them. A little girl.

Here.

In my house.

In my life.

There wasn't room or time to panic, but I had to work hard to push it back, to fight it.

"I like this one," I heard her say.

My brain went sideways—she was holding my alligator Birkin. Don't freak, don't freak, don't freak. "That's my favorite too, actually." I swallowed the instinct to take it and put it back on the shelf. Instead, I settled the strap over her little shoulder. "Looks good on you."

She touched the outside with a very careful fingertip. "What is it made of?"

"Um, alligator."

"Real alligator?"

I nodded. "As far as I know."

"Did it hurt the poor alligator when they took its skin off?"

I gulped, tried to not cackle in raw panic. "Um. I don't know. I hope not." I felt compelled to explain, even to a six-year-old I'd just met. "I didn't actually buy the purse myself. It was a gift."

"Was it expensive?" She touched the material again. "Mommy has a purse made by someone named Louis, and she said I could have it when I'm older but not yet because it's very expensive and I'm not old enough to have a expensive purse like that yet."

I laughed, and carefully took the Birkin and replaced it, breathing a little easier when it was back in place; I lifted one of my old standby favorites from its place, a vintage Louis Vuitton that my mother had bought new before I was born and passed down to me a few years ago.

"This is a purse made by that same designer as your mother's."

She touched the tan strap, the monogrammed leather. "Yeah, it looks like this. But it's bigger and shaped different."

"Probably a Never Full MM." I laughed at her blank expression. "I'll teach you all about luxury purses, don't worry." We put the LV back. "Which other ones do you like?"

She perused, and we talked about different purses, and then she wandered to my shoes. After a few more minutes of trying to keep her distracted, Mena entered, with a knock on the door.

Her eyes went wide. "Oh, oh my. Quite a collection you have here."

I laughed. "Yeah. I wasn't, um, expecting to need this room, obviously."

Her eyes sharpened. "Will that be an issue?"

I shrugged. "No, we'll figure it out."

She glanced down at Isabela. "Would you be comfortable spending some time with Titus?"

Isabela nodded, and took Mena's hand. A few moments later, Mena returned to my spare room, leaned against the doorway.

"Your relationship with Mr. Bright is new, I take it."

I nodded. "It is."

"This is an awful big stressor to put on a brand-new relationship."

I sighed. "Yeah, it sure is. Unexpected for both of us. But the most innocent one here in all this is Isabela." I held her gaze. "I don't know what you talked about with Titus, but I can assure you, no matter what you think you may know about him, whether from court documents or from public media, it's not anywhere near a full picture of the man he is."

"The picture I have of him is one of a very complicated and complex man." She chose her words with care. "I know the stories in tabloids are often exaggerated if not wholly untrue, but he's still a public figure, and a rock star. I take it until recently he didn't even have a permanent address."

"Did your sources of information on him tell you he wanted to be a part of Isabela's life, and that her mother prevented it?"

She nodded. "That's a matter of court record. I read the transcripts and went through all the files. It didn't appear to me that Ms. Hernandez had much by way of good reason to prevent Mr. Bright from seeing his daughter, and in my opinion, it's a miscarriage of justice that he was prevented from doing so. Simply being famous and a man doesn't mean he's unfit to be a father. He wasn't given a fair chance."

"I'm glad you see that." I regarded her. "Yes, our relationship is new. Yes, he's a rock star. Yes, he's lived the rock star life, and why shouldn't he? If anything, he's a victim in this whole thing. But I can tell you unequivocally, Titus Bright will *be here* for that little girl. He'll do his best to love her, and in my personal experience, that's pretty damn good."

"What about you, Ms. McGillis?"

"Me?" I looked away, then back. "I'm with Titus,

ride or die. And…" I swallowed. "I was once a little girl in need of love and attention myself. So, yeah, I'll do my best for her, too."

She nodded. "Good. Because she's going to have a hard time adjusting. Death of a loved one is traumatic for anyone, but when it's the only parent and the only family you've ever known…well, she'll need a lot of patience."

"Trust me, if anyone can understand that, it's Titus and I."

Another nod. "I think, all things considered, Isabela is fortunate to have you and Titus. I've worked on plenty of other cases far more complicated and unpleasant for everyone."

"I'm sure you have." I looked around the room. "So, what now?"

"Well, there's paperwork to file, and you're going to need time to get this room arranged. Isabela's going to need the rest of her things. Something is going to have to be done with Maria's things, but since she and Titus didn't have a relationship, that's not necessarily something you, or rather he, has to deal with."

"I guess we'd better get started, then."

～

Mena had taken Isabela to pack her things—which, understandably, was predicated to be a very difficult event. It was all so sudden, for everyone.

I was panicking, but on the inside. For Titus, and for Isabela, I was keeping it down, pretending it was all hunky-dory.

Titus saw through it, though.

We were standing in our bedroom, looking at the closet, now stuffed to overflowing since I'd moved some of my stuff to make room for his—and trying to figure out how I was going to fit everything from the extra bedroom into the tiny amount of space available. And by tiny, I mean none at all.

Titus was watching me, and I could feel him thinking.

"What, Titus?" I turned on him, crossing my arms. "I can feel you thinking."

He rolled a shoulder. "I dunno."

I huffed. "Out with it."

"Well, when it was just you, this house was pretty much perfect, right?"

I groaned, picking up the direction he was going. "Titus, come on."

"I'm just saying." A soft kind smile. "And it was enough room for just you and me." A gentle teasing glint in his eyes. "But you have a lot of stuff. And…" a hesitation. "I'm already attracting attention, around here. Paparazzi are beginning to pick up on my movements, that I'm here. Neighbors are coming out to watch whenever my truck is on the street."

"But I love this house." I sounded like I was whining—because I was.

"I know, me too." He held me by the arms. "Just something to think about."

"No, you're right." I met his eyes. "Especially if, someday, you and I want to think about…" I trailed off, weirded out that I was even having the thought.

He just smirked at me. "Think about what?"

I shrugged, a tiny lift of one shoulder. "The future. After things with Isabela are more settled."

"The future in what sense, Laur? Say it. Just…try it on for size. Doesn't mean it's happening any time soon, just because you say the words."

I laughed, self-conscious. "Having kids. There, I fucking said it—happy? If we want to think about having *kids*, or rather *a kid*, someday, in the future, *maybe*—we'd need a bigger house. And yeah, I've noticed the guys with cameras camped out down the street, so privacy would be a concern."

He nodded. "I know this thing with us just jumped from a new relationship to something else entirely, in the space of, like, an hour."

"It went from a new relationship to starting a family at warp speed. We had one night alone in bed together." I rested my forehead against his chest. "It's all happening too fast. I don't know how to do this."

"I know."

"What if I'm not going to be any good at this?"

"At what?"

I laughed bitterly. "You and me—being in a relationship. Being a…shit—a stepmother to Isabela."

"I think we can't think about it as being parents, right off the bat. We just have to all learn how to…be, together. The three of us. It's a lot for all of us. Let's not put any extra pressure on the situation by trying to force some preconceived notions of family on the whole thing. She barely understood that she even had a father, from what I gather. Now, suddenly, her mom is dead and she has a dad and a you, and everything is upside down. It's gonna take her time just to process that Maria is really gone."

I nodded against his shirt. "I wonder if Dr. Hines can recommend a friend. I think Isabela's going to need to talk to someone, and I think the two of us are, as well, to learn how to cope with suddenly being thrust into this position."

"I'm sure she can."

I twisted my head to look up at him. "I'm not ready for this, Titus. But I'll do my best."

A laugh, a soft huff. "Yeah, neither am I. But what choice do we have." Another laugh. "Well, you *do* have a choice."

"No, I don't."

"Laurel."

"Titus."

"You have a choice."

"So do you."

"She's my daughter."

"And I love you."

Silence.

"You're crazy." He wrapped his arms around me. Kissed the top of my head. "But I'm grateful for you."

I looked past his chest and arm at the racks of clothing. "Titus?"

"Hmmm?"

"We should look at houses."

"Good thing we know a good realtor."

I chuckled. "Yeah, good thing."

Another silence.

"Laur?"

"Hmmm?"

"We should probably christen this room. You know. Just for, like, symbolical purposes."

I cackled. "You would think that." I rubbed his chest. "We have to make room for Isabela. It'll take a few weeks even if we found a place tomorrow."

He laughed. "You forget who I am, and the power of a check for the full asking amount." A squeeze of his hands around my waist. "She's going to be going through enough adjustments. I don't want to have her start to get settled here and then move."

"You just bought a house for Jeremy and Bex."

"Laurel. I'm one of the top-earning musicians of all time, babe. And I spend fuckin' shit all. I don't think you get it. I do my best to live like not much has changed since I started playing, because some of the guys I came up with got big ol' heads and started accumulating houses all over the place and garages full of supercars and they trade up wives like they're fuckin' interchangeable, and I do *not* want to be that fuckin' guy. I'm a simple man, babe, and I like to live a simple life."

"Oh, that's rich."

"What? I play music, and until you, that was it. I didn't have much else to live for. Now I got you—and Isabela." A huff. "My point is, I got cash out the ass. I don't spend. I invest, and I save, and I put it all back into my shows. I could buy a fuckin' neighborhood in Bel Air, babe. No shit."

"So you want to just…go buy a house. Bam, just like that."

"Yeah. Tell Mena we need some time to adjust things, go find a place, and hire a company to fill it with furniture. I mean, the shit you got here, are you attached to it, sentimentally?"

I moaned a laugh. "Not really. I bought it all to match the house."

"Right. So we rent this place out as fully furnished. Pack our shit, pick a house, fill it up. We can get it done in a fuckin' weekend."

"You're crazy."

"I am not."

"It takes weeks, months, to choose a house. Longer, to close and all that."

"Again, need I remind you of the deal you yourself worked out, for Jeremy and Bex? How long did that take?"

I blew a raspberry. "Shut up."

"You pick."

"What? Pick what?"

"The house. The furniture. The decorations." He touched my chin. "Blank check, babe. Make us a home."

"You don't care?"

"Not that I don't care, more that I trust your judgment over my own. I've never had a home. Wherever you are is home. I've been a fuckin' vagabond my whole life. What the shit do I know about houses and which couch to fuckin' pick, and which fuckin' knickknack to put on the little fuckin' shelves and shit? I know shit all. I know music. And I know I love you, and I trust your judgment."

I laughed. "I think you maybe should have squeezed one more F-bomb in there, babe," I teased. Something occurred to me, then. "You know, I don't think you need to try to impress Isabela. That's not what she needs."

He held his silence a moment. "I know. Maybe I am trying, a little bit. But, am I wrong? About any of this."

"No," I said with a sigh. "No, you're not. We need more space. And it would be better for Isabela to have stability from the get-go."

"I'll call Mena, see if she can buy us a few days." A sigh. "I don't like it—I really, really don't. But if she comes here and then we move again, I'm just worried it'll mess her up even more. I don't know."

He dialed Mena's cell number from the card she'd given us, and spent a few minutes on the phone with her, explaining his thinking and working out details.

When all was settled, he handed me my phone back. "Let's go buy a house."

CHAPTER FOURTEEN

I EXPECTED LIZZY AT THE HOUSE WE'D PICKED, AND POSSIBLY Teddy. What I didn't expect was everyone.

And by everyone, I mean Braun and Seven as well as the girls.

With a good half dozen box trucks—all the girls had called in favors from every staging company and home goods store they knew, as well as all the little boutiques we collected from across the LA metroplex area.

The home we'd chosen would have shocked me, if the me from six months ago could see me now. I'd assumed I'd never own a place as expensive as the one I grew up in. I'd assumed I'd always be alone, so why would I ever want to spend stupid amounts of money on square footage I'd just be alone in? I'd assumed so many things about myself, about my future, and every single one of them was wrong, it was turning out.

Four bedrooms, five and a half bathrooms. Five thousand square feet on two and a half acres, in Malibu, overlooking the ocean—but well back from any danger of erosion, in our lifetime at least.

Twenty million dollars.

He'd paid cash.

It had required some speedy creative asset juggling on Jeremy's part, apparently, but it had gotten done in what surely was record time—but then, at that financial level, things just worked differently. You got what you wanted, when you wanted it, how you wanted it. The house was vacant, having been a spare West Coast pad for some richer-than-god celeb, so we got keys within forty-eight hours of seeing it. The staging had been moved out this morning, a cleaning crew had spent a whirlwind few hours scrubbing the shit out of it, and now my crew and I were ready to descend like reverse piranhas.

Funny how things came together when you knew the right people and had an unlimited amount of money to throw at a problem.

In the intervening two days since we'd been blind-sided with this whole situation, Titus and I had made sure to spend a couple hours each afternoon with Isabela. The first afternoon, we took her to get ice cream and to play at a park; the poor girl had just sat beside us, eating her cone and looking morose. The second afternoon, we'd just brought her to our now-packed-up house and sat with her, let her watch TV. That had gone better; she was still largely unresponsive, however.

Mena assured us that was completely normal, and to just be there, to let her have space.

Dr. Hines had made several recommendations, including that I continue to meet with her regularly—the other recommendations had been for a therapist for Isabela, as well as a family specialist to help the three of us learn how to build a healthy foundation.

I considered all this as we slid up to the new house in Titus's truck.

It was a lot. But I was lucky—I had all the support I could possibly want or need, and then some.

Titus, driving, glanced at me over Isabela's head—his truck only had the bench, and we'd talked about needing a more family-oriented car but hadn't gotten around to that just yet. We'd been kinda busy, after all, and it did have a lap belt for her.

"You good?" he murmured.

I laughed. "Yeah, I'm good."

To Isabela, then. "Yo, Is. You good?"

She gave him a funny look. "Is?"

"Too soon for nicknames?"

She nodded seriously. "Yes."

A laugh. "Okay, then. Just Isabela." A pause. "So, you ready to see our new house?"

"Why did you get a new house?"

"The other one was too small."

She looked at me. "Is it because you had too much stuff?"

Titus choked on a laugh, and I shot him a glare. "You know what, sweetie? That's exactly the reason. I just had too much stuff, so we figured, we might as well get a new one so we have plenty of room."

A thoughtful pause; we were sitting in the driveway in front of the garage while everyone else waited for us.

"Do I have to go back to my old kindergarten?"

Titus eyed her. "Um, well?"

"Do you want to?" I asked.

She shook her head. "Nuh-uh. Mrs. Waller was mean, and Jenny Alitz was a poop." She glanced at Titus as if to gauge his reaction to her potty mouth language.

"Jenny Alitz was a poop, huh?" he asked, stifling a smirk.

"Yeah. She stole my crayons, and then when I asked for 'em back, she pulled my hair. And *then* when I got mad and pulled hers back, *I* got in trouble."

"That is pretty poopy," he agreed. "Well, this is pretty far from where I gather you lived with, um… where you last lived, so it would probably be best if you started at a new school. But you kinda just started the year, didn't you?"

She shrugged. "I guess. I dunno"

"So you'd be okay with a new school?" Titus asked.

"Yeah. As long as Jenny Alitz isn't there. She used to be my best friend. But then we got into a fight about if Elsa was better than Rapunzel, and I said Elsa was better and she said Rapunzel was better just because Jenny had blond hair that was almost as long as Rapunzel's, but Rapunzel doesn't even have any powers no more 'cause her hair got cut off."

Titus was blinking at me over her head, having not a clue what she was even talking about. I just laughed.

"How about we go in and look around?" I suggested. "We can figure out schools later."

"Okay."

"But for the record?" I nudged her with my elbow. "Elsa is *totally* my favorite."

She smiled at me, and while I could wish earning her acceptance would be that simple, I knew better. It was a start, though.

We all exited the truck, Isabela opting to slide my way; she hesitated at the edge of the seat, since the truck was lifted and on oversized tires with no step. Her eyes met mine, and I knew she was debating whether she felt comfortable enough with me to ask me to lift her down.

I held out my hands to her. "It's a pretty long drop, huh? You think Titus should put a step on here for us short folks?"

Isabela just nodded and extended her arms to me, allowing me to lift her down. I was met with a barrage of hugs from the girls, with awkward glances at Titus, and adoring, sympathetic looks at Isabela.

Kat was the first to approach Isabela. She knelt down in front of the child and gazed at her seriously. "My name is Kat. I know exactly what you're going through," she said, her voice low and serious, as if she was speaking to an adult rather than a child. "I want you to know that there's no wrong way to feel. It's okay to be angry, even at your mom. I know people don't always know how to talk about this stuff, especially with kids. Just know this, honey—you're going to be okay. You won't forget her. No one can replace her, and no one is trying to. Everything is a lot right now, and it's confusing, and it's hard, and you're feeling so much that you don't know what to feel. And that's okay."

Isabela regarded Kat with serious, understanding dark eyes. "Your mommy died, too?"

Kat swallowed hard. "Yeah, she did. I was about your age. There was a car accident and—and I was okay, but my mom wasn't. I didn't have a dad, or anyone."

Isabela glanced up at Titus, beside her, then at me on the other side. "So where did you go?"

"Foster homes."

"What's that?"

A slow breath. "It's like…temporary adoption. Do you know what adoption is?"

A nod of her head. "When a kid doesn't got any mommy or daddy and so a new mommy and daddy take them home and they make a new family."

"Right. Foster parents are like that, but it's not forever, just for a little while."

"I don't think I'd like that very much."

"No, I don't think you would. I didn't, I know that

much. Looking back, I'm grateful I had *somewhere* to go, but—" She stopped herself, pain in her eyes speaking of things a six-year-old didn't need to know about. "Um. Yeah, I'm thankful I had somewhere to live. But you, honey—*you're* super lucky because you have Titus and Laurel. And they *are* forever, and Titus is your real dad. So that's pretty awesome. I know it doesn't feel like it right now, though."

Isabela looked past Kat to the house, and then the group of adults gathered in a cluster behind Kat—Lizzy with Sabrina, who was just past a year old, now, Braun beside her; Autumn with Seven, Teddy, and Zoe. Then, back up to Titus. "Who is everyone? Are they all your sisters or something?"

Titus laughed. "No, they're…well, I guess sort of? They're all Laurel's friends."

"Sisters works," I said, looking around at everyone. "Sisters from different misters, and they're your friends too, buster." I looked down at Isabela. "Look at them as aunts and uncles."

Isabela frowned thoughtfully. "I never had none of those."

Kat booped her on the nose. "Well, honey, we're gonna have a lot of fun." She slung her purse around to rest it on her knee and rummaged in it, coming up with a full-size candy bar. "Let's start by spoiling your dinner."

Isabela looked at Titus and then me, then back to Kat. "I can have the *whole* thing?"

Titus just shrugged. "Go for it, kiddo. Chocolate solves a vast majority of problems, at least temporarily."

"Let's go pick out your room, huh?" I said, smiling my thanks at Kat.

We'd all known Kat had had a difficult childhood, but like most of us regarding our pasts, she'd been pretty sparse with the particulars. I'd known she'd grown up in the foster system, and that some of the places hadn't been great, but I hadn't ever gotten the story of how she'd been orphaned. Judging by the look in the eyes of everyone else, it didn't seem like anyone else had known, either.

We all trooped in, Isabela happily devouring the candy bar and not really paying attention to much except the feet of the person in front of her.

The front door was a massive, arched piece of dark wood with black straps at the hinges, and a black wrought iron handle and lion's head knocker—the exterior of the house was white stucco, the architecture firmly Spanish Mission style. Within, the floors were Spanish mosaic tile, blues and greens and yellows in swirling arabesque patterns. White walls and high white ceilings held up by thick dark beams. There was a study off the entrance and a full library on the opposite side, a wide staircase with dark steps and wrought iron spindles, and a handrail to match the steps; beyond the staircase, a short hallway with a powder room led to the open-plan kitchen and living room. The entire back wall was glass, doors that accordioned open, to each corner creating an indoor-outdoor living space, with the outdoor being a secondary kitchen and dining room under a dark wood pergola wreathed in climbing flowers and ivy, providing shade. Beyond the outdoor living area, a rectangular infinity pool overlooking a magnificent view of the ocean, with the pool surrounded by carpet-like grass woven through with a path of round paver stones leading to a spreading oak tree with a park bench underneath it.

Isabela looked around, taking everything in with wide eyes, now holding on to the empty wrapper. "This is where I'm going to live?"

"We all will," Titus said. "You, Laurel, and me." He knelt in front of her. Held her gaze. "How does that sound?"

"It's so big. And so fancy."

Titus smiled, gentle and caring. "Does it seem like somewhere you could be at home?"

A little shrug. "I guess."

"It's pretty different from where you lived before, huh?"

A slow, shallow, slight nod. "That house where Ms. Mena brought me over, it was like that."

Titus frowned. "You'd think for ten grand a month, she'd have been able to afford something nicer." This was more to himself than to Isabela.

"Mommy told me you sent us a bunch of money every month, but she didn't want to spend it, so she put it all in a account to save it for when I got older." A pause, filled with sadness. "Sometimes, she would tell me she had too much month left at the end of the money, and she'd tell me she needed to borrow from me. She said it was my money, not hers."

Titus sighed, standing up. "I'll have to look into that. But I didn't—"

I squeezed his hand. "Maybe we should talk to Mena about some of this. For right now, let's go up and look at the bedrooms."

Lizzy caught my attention. "So, we have enough stuff for, like, three houses, and I mean that very literally. So you'll have enough to choose from so you can make this place look and feel amazing." She looked around. "Quite a place."

I was feeling very overwhelmed by everything, and thus emotional. "Thank you, Lizzy."

She frowned at me playfully. "Hey now, Ice Queen. Don't go getting all misty-eyed on me."

I shoved at her. "I think the Ice Queen has thawed out. Or started to." I breathed out slowly, shakily. "I'm just so thankful for you guys. I don't know that I could do this without you."

She pulled me into a hug—a rarity for us, since neither of us was typically affectionate with each other. "You don't have to find out. We're here. That little girl is going to get a *lot* of love."

She gestured at Titus, who had taken Isabela by the

hand and was leading her toward the staircase, asking her how she felt about rock music, and had she ever considered playing the drums. It was such an odd, touching sight—the tall, lean, tattooed, pierced rock star dressed in ripped blue jeans, and the slight little girl wearing a pink sundress and blue jelly sandals. Holding hands, her little face tilted way, way up to look at him, her little voice chattering, his deeper one growling answers.

Once they were upstairs, all the girls converged on me.

"How are you holding up?" Teddy asked. "That must have been quite a shock."

I rolled a shoulder. "I don't know that I've really processed it. It's been a whirlwind couple of days." I covered my face with both hands and let out a sigh, allowing myself to really feel the shock of the past couple days, now that I had a moment of safety with my girls. "I can't believe he has a daughter. I can't believe we're moving. I love my house. I planned on living there forever. I was just starting to get used to the idea of being with him. And now this? It…it feels like it's too much."

Zoe and Autumn closed in for a double hug. "It *is* a lot," Zoe said. "But you can do this."

"You can," Autumn agreed. "If I can get married, you can do this."

"Am I, like, her stepmother?" I asked, to no one in particular. "What if I end up being the evil stepmother from Cinderella?"

Lizzy had Sabrina on her hip, the little girl babbling and cooing and chewing on a teething toy; I suddenly had Sabrina in my arms, the adorable little girl grinning at me and whacking me with the toy.

"Hey now," I said, laughing as I warded off giggling blows of the teething toy, "no no, none of that." To Lizzy, then. "Is this where you tell me that if you can get married and have a baby, I can do this?"

Lizzy nodded. "Sure is. But it looks to me like you *are* doing it. Nobody ever said it would be easy, because it won't be. It's a huge, complex, difficult, overwhelming situation. But you're equal to the task, Laur. You have all of us as a support structure. And most importantly, you have that man up there at your side."

Kat hung on me from behind, her cheek against mine. "This is where you say thank you, Teddy."

I cackled. "Thanks, Teddy," I laughed, "you're the best at luring unsuspecting men into falling in love with us crazy-ass bitches."

Teddy gave a cutesy, demure shrug, kicking up one foot with her hands flinging palms-up. "I do what I can."

Autumn shook my sidearm. "Hey, now. I helped."

I wriggled out of the cluster-hug. "Okay, okay, the Ice Queen hasn't thawed out *that* much. Too many hugs."

The rest of the day was spent choosing furniture from the crazy amount of stuff the girls had arranged, having the movers—and the men—bring it in where we wanted. While this was happening, the movers from my house showed up, with our clothes in wardrobe boxes as well as our kitchen and bathroom stuff and the various needful knickknacks. I planned to go back to the house myself later to pack up and transport my purse collection myself—you didn't trust several hundred thousand dollars in vintage luxury purses to anyone but yourself.

Kat had set Isabela up with her phone so she could watch shows while we worked—hours flew by, and then suddenly it was dusk and Seven, Braun, and Titus tromped into the kitchen, each of them carrying an armload of food—there were pizzas, Chinese food, Thai food, Italian, and Mexican, as well as cases of beer and a package of juice boxes for Isabela.

I'd chosen a massive dining room table, simply to fill the space available as it was simply enormous; there were sixteen places, a bench on one side and chairs on the other, with heavy, fancy chairs with thick, padded arms on the ends. With everyone in attendance, over half the seats were filled.

And I had a vision flash into my brain and lodge there, stark, vivid, and real—Isabela running around after a tow-headed little boy, Sabrina following behind, with other children all around, laughing and playing. I saw Teddy, and in a dreamlike way I could tell she was laughing at something said by the man she loved even though I couldn't see his face or features. I saw Lizzy with Braun, Autumn with Seven—and in the dream/vision/whatever it was, she was pregnant...as was Zoe; I saw

Kat, too, holding the hand of a small black-haired little girl who looked just like her. And in the vision, we all sat together at this table, laughing, eating—my mental camera panned around the table, seeing all my friends… my family, my sisters…all of us together, all of us happy.

"Laurel?" Lizzy's voice. "You okay?"

I looked around at everyone, at this table, here and now. "Yeah, I'm good." I looked at Isabela. "Isabela, I would like to formally welcome you to Six Chicks Real Estate family."

Isabela just blinked. "Okay. Thank you?"

Laughter from everyone.

Seven flipped open a box of pizza. "I never got a formal welcome."

Autumn teasingly elbowed him. "You're not a chick."

"Oh. I would still like an official welcome to the extended group, then."

"Hey, if there are official welcomes going out, I think I should get one—I was the first to dip my toe into the office pond, so to speak," Braun said. "It ain't easy being the first."

I gestured at Lizzy. "You're the boss, boss."

Lizzy sighed, laughing. "Fine. Braun, congratulations on being the first. Seven, I know Autumn isn't easy to get along with, so good on you for tackling *that* particular challenge."

Autumn threw a lime wedge from the tray of tacos

at Lizzy. "Hey, I resent that comment. I am the most easygoing and fantastic person there ever was."

Lizzy snorted. "Okay, babe, keep telling yourself that. Titus, you must be a glutton for punishment, falling for Laurel. She's as complicated as she is beautiful. To all three of you, welcome to the club. We're a weird, foul-mouthed, crazy bunch of women, but we're loyal."

"Hear hear," Teddy said. "*You* guys may be foul-mouthed, but *I* happen to be a *lady*."

Kat rolled her eyes. "I'm a lady too. I'm just a lady who likes to say *fuck*."

Isabela huffed. "You shouldn't say that around me, you know. I'm very a-pressionable." Her lip quivered. "Mommy said that word when she was mad. And then she…she told me not say it, and she shouldn't have said it, because I'm a-pressionable."

"*Im*pressionable," Titus murmured around a mouthful of pizza.

"'Kay." She glanced at Kat. "What do you do when you…when you miss her so bad you want to just…" She trailed off, unable to find the right words.

Kat's smile was sad and understanding. "So bad you just want to…not die too, but just…not be anywhere. Not be anyone." She was sitting on the other side of Isabela, while I sat across from her, while Titus was at the head of the table. "What do you do? You just let yourself miss her. It's okay. You can talk to her, in your head. You can talk to any of us about her. You can just go sit somewhere by yourself until you feel better. Because here's the real secret, honey—it'll pass. And that's okay too. It doesn't mean you don't love her, or miss her. But it's okay to let the missing her pass. It's normal and it's okay."

"Now who's the one with hidden depths?" I asked, the question aimed at Kat.

Kat rolled her eyes. "They're not hidden. I just don't use them very often."

"Maybe you should," Teddy said, grinning. "It's hot on Laurel, the whole emotional depth and availability. It's like a whole new Laurel. Just think what you could be like!"

Kat shook her head, snorting. "No. And don't you dare make me the next victim of The Ad." A glare around the table, especially at Teddy. "I mean it, Theodora. I don't want a man. I don't need a man. The only part of a man I need is his—"

"A-*HEM*," Teddy cut in. "Language, Kat. Little ears."

Isabela rolled her eyes. "I know what you were gonna say." She glanced at Kat. "You were gonna say his mouth. For kisses. I caught Mommy kissing someone, once. They didn't have no clothes on, and they were making funny noises. I had a bad dream and wanted a drink of water. Mommy said she was just kissing her friend."

Kat snorted, spluttered. "Yeah, honey. Exactly. The only part of a man I need is his mouth, for kissing."

"Lots, and lots, and lots of kissing," Zoe said, unable

to stop her spluttering laughter. "The kind with no clothes on. And funny noises."

"Okay, that's about enough of *that*," I cut in. "Let's be appropriate."

This, of course, drew even more uproarious laughter from everyone, with Autumn, beside me, grabbing my arm to stop herself from falling over with laughter.

"You...*you* are telling *us* to be appropriate," she guffawed. "Oh god, that's rich."

"What?" I asked, feigning innocence.

"You're really leaning into your new role, ain'tcha?" Zoe said, wiping tears from her eyes. "Let's be appropriate, says the queen of inappropriateness. Aren't you the one who was telling us about...um, special kissing...in challenging and adventurous places?"

I sighed. "That was the old Laurel. Behold—" I gestured at myself, and took Titus's hand. "The new and improved me. Now at least fifty percent more appropriate, in the necessary situations, of course."

"Oh, of course," Autumn said, sighing with the fading gales of laughter. "But really? Only fifty percent?"

I smirked at her. "I can't be totally appropriate *all* the time, can I? I have to stay on brand to some degree, after all."

Dinner wound down, with the vast majority of the food being devoured—largely by the men. Once it was done, Titus got Isabela's attention.

"So." He squeezed her hand gently. "Want to see your room, now that it's all made up?"

She nodded. "Yeah."

"All right, let's go."

I went with them, and found myself trailing behind Titus and Isabela as they ascended the stairs, watching once again as they held hands and chatted on the way up the stairs.

Isabela's room was a little girl wonderland—a white loft bed overflowing with pink bedding and pink pillows and a bookshelf under it, a dresser, a desk, and an open-top chest full of toys—beside the chest was a storage shelf of square boxes filled with more toys, which were the things Isabela had brought with her, along with her clothes.

I hadn't seen this room get done—I'd been overseeing the kitchen. "Wow, where did all these toys come from?"

"Jer and Bex," Titus answered, his voice quiet as we watched Isabela explore the room. "They're all things that Kenzie has grown out of or doesn't play with anymore. We can get her new stuff, obviously, but this gets her going, right?"

I elbowed him. "Why aren't they here?"

"Who? Jer and Bex?"

I nodded. "They should be here. Next time, invite them. They're part of the crew now, too."

He nodded. "They're the closest thing I've had to

family, since Tommy." A tilt of the head. "And I guess since they have so many kids, they'd be a good place to get some advice, huh? When things get challenging."

"And hopefully Isabela will have fun playing with their kids."

Isabela looked around. "It's all for me?"

"Sure is, kiddo," Titus said, pointing at the shelf. "That's all your stuff—what you already had. The stuff in the box there was given to you by some friends of mine. They have daughters around your age, one older by a year or so, and another two younger than you. You'll meet them soon." He pointed at the dresser and the closet. "All your clothes are there, and the shelf under the bed is all your books from your old room."

Isabela noted the huge, overstuffed beanbag chair, so big Titus could have sat on it with room to spare. "Can I sit on that?"

Titus laughed. "Course you can. It's yours, and that's what it's for."

She just stood in the center of the room, staring around. Finally, she looked at us. "I like it."

Titus sat on the beanbag chair, flopping down heavily, and gesturing to her. "Come here, huh?" She sat down on the bean bag, not quite cuddling up to him, but not on the edge either. "I know it's not…your old room. I know it's different." He reached up behind him and grabbed a book at random, glanced at the title. "*Fox in Socks*. Huh. Looks weird." He glanced at Isabela. "You like this one?"

She gave a funny little smirk. "Yeah. But you have to try to read it superfast."

He tilted his head and frowned. "Why, is it a tongue twister book?"

She just snickered. "Yeah. It's funny."

"Oh." He cleared his throat. "Well, good thing I happen to be an expert at tongue twisters."

She blinked at him. "You are?"

He nodded. "Oh, for sure. Whenever I'm ready to go out on stage, I do a bunch of tongue twisters to warm up."

"You go out on stage?"

He hesitated. "Did, um…do you not know who…I mean, what I do for a living?"

She shook her head. "Mommy didn't tell me. Just that you were busy all the time traveling."

"I'm a musician. Um, like, in a rock band." A clearing of his throat. "Although nowadays I'm sort of a solo act."

"Are you famous?"

"Yeah, I am."

"Like, how famous?"

A chuckle. "I mean, there's not, like, a scale of reference. But, I do have my own Wikipedia page."

"I don't know what that means." A puzzled frown. "Are you more famous than Channing Tatum? Mommy says he's the yummiest man who ever was." The frown became more puzzled. "But I never got that. How is he yummy? Did she try to eat him?"

"I mean, Channing Tatum is pretty famous. I don't know about yummy, that's probably more of a question for Laurel. But I guess I'm sort of…on that level, yeah. Most people know who I am."

"I don't."

"Well, you're six. Do you listen to a lot of heavy metal?"

She rolled her eyes. "No, duh. I don't even know what that is." A pause. "Mommy always listens to the radio songs in the car. And she sings along, but she doesn't sing very good and it hurts my ears. She says it doesn't matter because I'm the only one who ever hears, and I can't make fun of her because I'm her kid."

My throat closed—everything about her mom was in present tense.

"Your mom…uh." He cleared his throat. "She sounds like she was pretty special."

Isabela was quiet. "Yeah." A deep, serious look up at Titus, then. "She's really gone? Forever and ever?"

He had to whisper his answer. "Yeah, kiddo. Forever and ever."

A long, long silence. "Can you read the book, now? And you gotta do it fast."

He cleared his throat again. "Uh, okay. Here we go. Never read a book to a kid before, so, you know, cut me some slack." Quieter, then, mumbled, "I also quit school sophomore year, so I don't read very well to begin with. But, here we go. *Fox in Socks*." He cleared his throat one more time. "Uh, okay. Fox, socks, Knox, box." A pause, and a glance at her. "How'm I doing so far? Pretty good, right?"

She gave a little laugh. "You just started, silly. Keep going."

I watched as he read the book, picking up the pace as the rhythm increased, and by the time he got to the Tweetle-beetle battle, he was really into it, trying to go faster and faster until he inevitably stumbled over a wrong syllable.

When he finished the book, Isabela was smiling. "So, what's my grade for my first time? A-plus, right?"

She shrugged. "Maybe a B. You'll have to practice."

"Oh boy. I dunno, that was tricky."

"You said you were good at tongue twisters."

He snorted. "Yeah, short ones. Like, 'Sally sells seashells by the seashore,' and 'red leather yellow leather,' and 'the big black bug bit a big black bear and the big black bear bled black blood.'"

"That one sounds hard."

"Yeah, you try saying it five times fast."

So she did, and stumbled halfway through the first time, and then, just to show off, Titus went through several times, each time faster than the last, never stumbling.

Isabela turned around and searched the shelf, finding

one particular book. She looked at me. "Can you read this one?"

I came and sat down on the giant bean bag chair, Titus's long legs wrapping around my hips. "Sure, sweetie. Let's see." I took the book, and sighed. "*Guess How Much I Love You?*"

Isabela watched with wide, sad eyes as I opened it. "That's Mommy's favorite book to read to me. She would make her voice all soft and nice."

"I'll do my best." I took a deep breath, and began reading, in my softest, quietest voice.

When I'd finished the story, my throat was tight and even Titus was blinking a little faster than normal.

Isabela took the book back from me. "Thank you."

I smiled. "Of course, sweetie."

She just held the book. "Can I…can I be alone, now? I want to think about Mommy."

Titus ruffled her hair. "Sure. We'll be downstairs if you need us."

We paused together at the top of the stairs, and I rested my head against his chest. "What in the hell did we get ourselves into?"

He shook his head. "She's six. How is she handling it so well? Like, she's amazing."

I huffed a laugh of agreement. "Right? I was thinking that, myself." I gazed up at him. "You're really good with her."

He sighed. "Thanks." A long pause. "I wish…" He trailed off.

"What?"

"I dunno, it's hard to say it right. Clearly, Maria was a great mom to her. I always had this resentment, you know? Like, this anger. I felt so wronged. She tricked me into impregnating her, didn't tell me until after she'd had the baby, asked for money, and then refused to let me see my own daughter even one time. How do I reconcile that to someone who so clearly loved and took great care of that little girl in there? What do I do with that?"

"People can have different sides of themselves, I guess, right?" I scratched his jaw. "And people also do change. I don't know. I know you can have your own version of Maria, and your experience with her is your own personal experience. Nothing can change that. But Isabela has her own experience of her mother. The person that you are with me, with her, that's a different kind of person than the rock star who goes out on stage, the one who signs things and poses for pictures with fans and all that. And it's not the same as the rock star legendary for a wild, hard, crazy life. It's all *you* right? I guess what I'm saying is, Maria could do the things to you that she did, and still be a wonderful, loving, attentive mother who worked hard to provide for her child and put aside money for her future rather than spending it on herself. The two don't have to be mutually exclusive."

He nodded. "Yeah, I guess you're right. It's just

tricky to put it together into a single picture of a person, you know? I suppose I shouldn't expect to understand Maria, though—I met her literally one time, but she's had this huge effect on my life ever since. And now? She's changed the entire course of my life."

I tilted my head side to side. "I mean, did she, though? You and I were going to be together, right? She didn't change that. Which means you and I would have lived together—alone, and in a smaller house, maybe, but still together. And whether it was in six weeks or six months, you and I would have had a child together. We still will, if that's what you want with me. But this whole situation with Isabela…it really just accelerated the timeline of how things worked out for us. Now it's sort of a trial by fire. We're together now, sink or swim. That little girl up there is going to need both of us, full time, all the time." I touched his lips with mine, a not-really-kiss, a brush of my mouth on his. "So, really, if you think about it…how much has this altered the course of your life? I would suggest not that much." I chuckled. "Now, if it had happened a year ago, that might be a different conversation."

He laughed. "Is this what being with you is going to be like? You being right all the damn time?"

I nuzzled his throat. "Yeah, pretty much."

"I guess I'm okay with that." He touched my chin. "And just so we're clear and on the same page…yes, Laurel. I do want that with you. A child. Marriage. The whole white picket fence, happily ever after thing. I never thought I did, but then I met you, and suddenly I do."

I wiggled as his hands wrapped around my backside, pulling me closer, tighter against his hard body. "There's no white picket fence, here, buddy. Wrong house if that's what you wanted."

He huffed in amused annoyance. "Smart-ass. You know what I mean."

"Yeah, I do."

"Know somethin' weird?" he asked. "I don't even know where the master bedroom is in this place. My head is still spinning and I don't remember if it's up or down."

I pointed over his shoulder, down the stairs. "That way. Past the kitchen."

He turned, carried me down. "This way?"

"Yup."

To the kitchen. Set me on the island and ran his hands up my jeans-clad thighs. "Not sure how much farther I can go without some sugar."

"Sugar?" I asked, snickering. Reached for the fly of his shorts and undid it, slipped my hands inside, collecting his erection and stroking it. "Is this what you mean?"

He shook his head. "No, I meant this." A slow, deep kiss, his hands sliding up my spine to undo my bra before his fingers delved into my hair. "Fuck, Laurel. Need you so damn bad." A growl. "How can I need more, the more of you I get?"

"Take me to bed, Titus. We can't do this here. As

much as I want to christen this kitchen island right now, we probably should start getting used to doing this stuff behind closed doors."

"Yeah, you're probably right." He glanced over his shoulder at the hallway that led to the laundry room, mudroom, and the master wing. "Through there?"

I rolled my eyes. "Not that many places it could be, honey. So yes. Through there."

"Hey, I've lived in a converted semi the last several years. The whole thing is smaller than the fuckin' garage—shit, one bay of the fuckin' garage. Sue me if I'm not used to a real house yet."

I hooked one arm around his neck to hold on and slid the other between us as he lifted me once more and carried me toward the bedroom. "I'm teasing. I'm just impatient to have you inside me."

"Trust me, I'm just as impatient to be inside you."

We finally reached the door of the master suite and he closed it with a foot while I locked it behind us.

He spun in place, pressing my back to the door. "Now the only problem is that we're both wearing too many clothes."

"You handle the clothing situation, I'll handle *this.*" I caressed his length as he set me to my feet.

He laughed a groan. "I like the way you think, my love."

"You know what I think?" I stepped out of my jeans as he tugged them off, along with my underwear. "I think if we want to have a baby any time soon, we'd better start practicing. I'm nearing forty—it might take a while."

He had his shirt off, his shorts. "Does that mean no condom?"

He had us both naked together, then, and I'd only let go of him long enough to let him peel my shirt and bra off. I clutched his neck with one hand, pulling myself up onto my toes, leaning against him as I guided him to my opening with my other hand.

"That, Titus my love, is *exactly* what that means."

He groaned as I lowered myself to take an inch of him, then two. "Fuck, Laur—I…god. I don't think I can do this standing up." He hooked both hands under my ass and lifted me one more time, staggering with me—not under my weight, but rather under the shaky need to be deeper inside me.

"Then take me to our bed and make love to me, Titus." I wrapped both arms around him and palmed his nape and his jaw and kissed him with all I had as he brought us to our bed. "This time, make it slow. Soft and sweet and slow."

He gently cradled me as he lowered me. Crawled over me, and his arms were the pillow under my head and shoulders, and he nuzzled more kisses against my lips. "Make love." He nudged against me, drifting and bumping against my opening; I gasped as I fed him into me. "Gonna make love to you, Laurel McGillis. Soft… and sweet…and slow."

His forehead met mine, and our lips shuddered together.

"Make love," I whispered, echoing my own words and his. "Make love to me. Make love to me and never stop."

"Never," he whispered back. "Never."

CHAPTER FIFTEEN

I WOKE TO TITUS BEHIND ME.

His arm was a hard strong bar over my belly, his cock soft and nestled against my buttocks. He was snoring. We'd made love last night, soft and slow and sweet, and his voice had whispered *I love you* into my ear as a chant as he plunged into me, as we reached climax together.

This was right.

This was everything. Waking up to Titus in my bed, wrapped around me...it was everything. I needed this.

My eyes watered and my stomach lurched into my chest and I blinked tears of pure overwhelmed understanding...an epiphany. A *knowing*.

This was my forever.

How could I go another day without this? I couldn't. I wouldn't.

I had to do something...for him. So he *knew*,

without a shadow of a doubt, that I was all his, always. What could I do?

How did I show him I needed him, wanted him, that I was totally his? What could I do that I hadn't already done?

I knew, all at once, with absolute clarity.

I wiggled out from under his arm as carefully as I could, so as not to wake him yet. Tiptoed over to my jewelry box, hunted in it for the two items I had in mind. The first I found quickly, a platinum chain of rather thick, heavy links that I'd once found during a showing—it was an obviously masculine necklace, but it was valuable and the previous owner of the house was long since gone, so I'd kept it. Why, I'd never been sure, but I did. And now, I knew why—for this. The second item was harder to find in the rather disorganized jumble of my jewelry. Eventually, I found it, at the very bottom and back of a drawer full of seldom-if-ever worn items.

A ring.

A single karat solitaire diamond, round cut, in a simple gold band. Not much to look at, not very valuable in terms of the weight of gold and diamond. But the age of it, who'd owned it…that was where the value came from. The meaning behind it.

I strung the ring onto the chain, tucked the whole into my palm. Crawled into bed. As I sidled back under the covers and wriggled my butt against Titus, he murmured sleepily, gathered me under his arm again.

Nuzzled his nose against my spine, and I felt his breath on my skin.

But he was awake, then. I felt it in the shift of his breathing. The stir of his muscles. The roll of his shoulders, the tightening of his hand against me, low, just beneath my navel but above my sex. I waited.

"Hi," he whispered.

I twisted in place, already eager. "Hi."

He blinked at me, eyes bright with a sleepy smile. "Been awake long?"

I shook my head. "Mmm-mmm. A minute or two."

He ran his hand over my hip, caressed the outer swell of my buttock, up my spine. "I really, really love this. Waking up with you. Naked, skin to skin. I can say with absolute truth that I have never been happier."

I petted his jaw with one hand, the hand with the ring and necklace in it, keeping the hand closed but for a finger or two, scratching his beard. With the other, I caressed his cock. "Me neither."

He rumbled in his chest as I stroked him to full, throbbing life. "It just got better."

I kissed his chin, his cheekbone. "Why, then, Titus, you should allow me to make it even better yet."

His eyes went half lidded as I fisted his now-hard cock. "God, woman. How could you possibly do that?"

I slid a thigh over him, straddling him without removing my lips from his. "Like this." Took him into me, bare.

He filled me with a single thrust, and I gasped as I split open around him, stretched around him. "Fuck, fuck, fuck, Laurel. If last night was incredible, this is even better. I don't understand how it's possible, but you feel even better every single time I make love to you. How?"

I shook my head, gasping as I rode him slowly, taking my time bringing myself to arousal on him. Grinding his thick shaft against myself, using him to stimulate my clit, taking him for myself, taking my pleasure on him. He just held me, his hands clawing into my ass with the increase of his need, the rise of his pleasure. His clawing fingers raked down my back, dug into my hair, and he demanded a kiss, lips savage on mine even as our joining bodies moved slowly, achingly, delicately.

My lips shook against his as I neared climax. "Titus…" I sat up. Rose up, sank down. One hand pressed flat against his chest for balance. "I love you, Titus."

He held my hips and guided my movements. "I love you, Laurel. So fucking much."

I let the necklace dangle from my fist, the ring dropping to swing in a wobbly circle, the diamond catching the dawn's light. "This was my great-grandmother's— Darlene Oldfield." I had to pause for breath as I moved on him, gasping and moaning as pleasure ripped through me in wave after building wave.

He held my hips and moved with me, meeting my sinking, rolling, rising core with thrusts of his own.

"Laur…" he whispered, voice ragged, broken with ecstasy.

I fell forward, palm planting again on his chest. I had to pause my movements, then, so I could fasten the necklace behind his neck.

"Wear it for me," I whispered, motionless, my eyes on his, my nascent orgasm held off another moment—to be all the more powerful for the denial of it. "Wear it for me, Titus."

"Of course."

"My great-grandfather put it on her finger the day he asked her to marry him, and she wore it every single day until the day she passed." I was weeping, suddenly, but not unexpectedly. "Wear it for me, Titus. Be mine." I choked. "Marry me—I'm asking you to marry me. I'm asking if I can be yours forever."

He was wet-eyed, groaning a masculine version of overwhelmed sobs as he clutched me, pulling me down to kiss me, his thrusts taking over now, surging up into me, filling me and shattering me, smashing me into a climax that shook me to pieces, making me scream out loud with the fracturing intensity of it, my sobs of emotion coalescing with my screams of orgasm.

"Mine," Titus was growling, yanking my hips down to meet his crashing thrusts. "Mine. Mine."

"Yours," I whispered back. "Yours, yours."

He rolled, then, pressed me to the mattress and chased his own climax, then moving hard and fast, taking his release in me, whispering *I love you* as a liturgical chant as a counterpoint against my sobs of his name, my own *I love you* song on my lips. One hand fisted into the pillow beside my face, and the other reached over, to the nightstand drawer. Yanked it open, fumbled for something—found it.

Came back with a black velvet box. "You beat me to it," he murmured, opening the box one-handed, setting it down to pluck out the ring within. "I don't have a hundred-year-old family heirloom, just a plain old four-karat one that I had custom designed."

Still moving. Still thrusting.

I laughed and caught at his ass with both hands, pulling him against me. "Shut up and come first, you dork."

He shook his head, nearly making a lie of it as he shook, lingering at the ragged edge of climax. "Not until you're wearing my ring."

I reached my right hand between us, circled my fingers around him and squeezed, stroked. My left, I held up to him. "Put it on me, then."

He slid the ring onto my finger and kissed my palm, the underside of the gold band. "Now you're mine and I'm yours. We belong together forever, now, my love.

"Forever ever?" I whispered, lips on his, plunging my touch around him to hasten his crash into orgasm.

He laughed at the reference. "Forever ever." His movements went frantic, then, smashing against me with a long low groan. "Laurel, Laurel, god…god…god, my love, my love, my love…"

I let go and wrapped my thighs around him and clung to his neck and bit his earlobe and met him with my own frantic wild thrashing thrusts. "Titus, Titus, yes, my love, yes—give it to me, give it all to me."

He exploded, then, bursting apart within me and filling me with a flood, with wet heat and crashing love, his voice wordless with furious detonation in my ear, love whispered, love made, love joined, love tangled.

We sagged together, rolling to cling side by side, gasping in unison, his hands scouring my back and butt and hair, mine in his beard and trailing down his chest and scratching between his shoulder blades.

"You asked me to marry you," he murmured.

"I did." I found the underside of his chin with my lips. "I had to. I had to…I woke up and I just…I had to know you'd be mine, that we could wake up like this together forever. I just…I had to."

"I'm glad you did."

"You're not mad I preempted your proposal?"

"Hell no. It's hot that you proposed first, while riding me." He held the ring on the necklace in two fingers, kissed the diamond. "I was going to propose over breakfast. I was gonna bring it to you in bed and ply you with a mimosa."

I giggled and wriggled against him. "Hey, just

because the proposal's out of the way doesn't mean you can't still do that."

He huffed a laugh. "I guess I have to put on pants for that, huh?"

"Maybe."

"You should stay naked. In case there's time for round two after we eat."

"There's time for round two right now…"

He hummed thoughtfully. "You might be right."

"Assuming you're able to rise to the occasion this soon."

He groaned as I found him indeed rising to occasion. "You, Laurel McGillis, can get me to *rise* faster than I've ever thought could be possible."

"I have two requests."

He rolled over me. "And those would be what?"

"I don't want to be Laurel McGillis anymore. From this day forward, I want to be Laurel Bright. I want to get married as soon as possible and take your name and be your wife."

"Is that one? That feels like more than one."

"That's one. Take me to the county and make me your wife, and then we can have a party for our friends later. That's one."

He filled me. "Okay. And number two?"

I pulled away from him. "Take me to the shower and bend me over the tub while the water gets hot, and then we take a shower together, and then you feed me."

"Again, that feels like more than one."

"Work with me here. It's one thing, three parts: part one, bend me over the tub. I want you from behind, and I want it hard and fast. Part two, get me a long hot shower. Part three, feed me."

He stood up and brought me with him, and took me to into the bathroom and set me on my feet next to the soaking tub. Turned me around and pushed me forward. I spread my feet apart and braced my hands on the cold porcelain as he filled me from behind.

"Wait!" I said. "Water on first."

He laughed, but pulled away, angling for the shower, twisting the water on, not taking his eyes off me—I stayed as I was, bent forward with my hands on the rim of the tub, breasts swaying heavily under me, ass rounded for him. He resumed his place behind me, feathering a touch over my sex.

"Now, where was I?" He circled his touch over me, soft and quick, bringing me to the shaking edge within seconds before filling me one more time, before driving into me with a slap of hips meeting ass cheeks.

"You were right there," I gasped. "You were about to fuck me really, really good."

"Really really good?" A hard thrust. "Like this?"

"Fuck yes," I gasped. "Just like that."

He ground into me, again and again. "Would it be weird if I asked you to marry me every time we were together?"

I laughed, or tried to around the shaking whimper of orgasm. "I don't know. Would it?"

He wanted to laugh too, but couldn't, too caught up in his own pursuit of climax, pounding into me faster and faster, his grunts wordless and wild.

"Laurel, Laurel, oh god—my love," he snarled. "I'm there already."

"Good," I gasped. "Give it to me. Don't hold out. Just fuck me until you can't fuck anymore."

He surged into me and filled me and exploded into me yet again and I came around him, my climax triggered by his, and we came together, crying out as we shattered together—as we were made whole together, each mended by the other.

"Marry me, Laurel," he whispered, thrusting slowly and gently as our climaxes subsided. "Marry me. Please, please marry me."

"Right now," I answered. "Today. I'm your wife, Titus. I'm your everything, always."

"You mean it? Today. Justice of the peace, today?"

"You, me, and Isabela. Today."

I felt something wet drop onto my back—his tears. I pulled forward, stood up, turned in his arms and kissed his chest, his cheeks, his tears. "What is it, Titus?"

"I just…" He let me kiss his tears away, didn't try to hide them, didn't act ashamed of them. "I've never belonged to anyone. Never…never thought I could have this. Have a life like what we're building. That I could have…a wife. Children. A future." He touched his forehead to mine. "I always thought I'd die like Tommy."

"Not happening. I won't let it."

"Promise?"

I kissed and kissed and kissed him. "Promise. You're mine, and I'm yours, and our future is here, together, with Isabela and the little one I'm hoping you put in me, either last night or this morning."

"Aren't you on birth control?"

I laughed. "Yeah, but a girl can hope this will the one percent chance that it fails."

He cackled, sniffled, and laughed again. "Never hoped for that before."

"I'm going to go off the birth control. It'll take a few months before we have any real chance of conceiving. Unless you'd rather wait."

"No. I want it all. I'm not scared of it. Any of it."

I led him into the shower, and we were wreathed in steam. "Wash me off and feed me, husband."

"Did you know I make killer pancakes?" he asked, running a bar of soap over my breasts.

"I did not. You'll have to show me."

"Don't we need the certificate to be husband and wife?" he asked.

I shrugged. "A technicality. I'm your wife right now because I want to be. The certificate just makes it formal and legal. The real marriage is when you decide that's what you want. And I want, so therefore, I declare myself your wifey."

He laughed, continuing to soap me up, more out of the desire to caress my naked curves than to actually do any cleaning. "Well then, wifey, I guess by that logic that makes me your…what's the husband equivalent of wifey? I don't even know."

"Hubby," I answered.

"Hubby. Huh. Okay. I hereby declare myself to be your hubby. Now and forever."

I took the soap from him and washed his manhood. "Now rinse it off good so I can show you how excited I am to be your wife…with my mouth."

He growled as I dropped to my knees. "Have I ever mentioned how much I love the way you think?"

"You may have, once or twice."

A pause. "Oh, shit, Laurel. Your mouth feels *so* fucking good."

I was totally focused on the enjoyable *job* at hand—or, rather, mouth—and had him thrusting into my mouth and groaning, when—

"Why are you in the shower together?" a small, sleepy, confused voice said. "What are you doing?"

With a shriek, I fell backward to my ass on the wet marble, turned and saw Isabela in the doorway of the bathroom—or, rather, a faint outline of a small figure just barely visible through the swirling fog, which I hoped also helped disguise us, somewhat. "I thought you locked the door last night," I muttered, standing up.

"I thought I did too," he answered. "Hey, uh…we're just…uh…saving water. By, um, taking a shower at the same time."

A pause. "Oh. Okay. Well, I'm hungry."

"Give us a minute, and we'll be right out," he answered. "You like pancakes?"

"Uh-huh."

"Okay, well, let us finish getting clean and then you can help me make pancakes. I'll even show you my secret ingredient."

"Okay." A second later, the bathroom door closed with a click.

When she was gone, I laughed. "Well that was unfortunate timing."

A laugh. "No kidding." A groan as we finished cleaning up. "So I guess that's what being a parent is like, huh? Ill-timed interruptions?"

"I guess so," I muttered. "Now…where was I?"

"Laurel, you don't have to…oh *god*. Well—I guess maybe you do. Fuck, *fuck* yeah, you do."

"Just be quick about finishing," I muttered, picking up where I'd left off.

"With the way your mouth feels, that's easier than I'd like."

When I'd drained him of every last drop and was wiping the last smears of him off my lips, I stood up and we made quick work of washing off. Titus shampooed his hair, rinsed it, and palmed my ass as he tugged me against him for a quick kiss. "Take your time finishing up. I'll get breakfast started."

"You sure? She may have questions."

"What should I say, if she does?" A laugh as his voice went falsetto. "'Why was Laurel on her knees, and what was she doing to your bathing suit area?'"

A shrug and a laugh as I doused my hair under the spray. "I dunno. Maybe just distract her so she doesn't realize you didn't answer the question?"

A nod as he stepped out and grabbed a towel off the rack. "I like that plan—don't answer the question and distract. Hey, just like politics."

I laughed as I began rubbing shampoo into my hair from the ends upward. "Exactly."

He finished drying off and peeked his head back into the shower. "Hey—you're amazing and I'm in love with you. In case that didn't get communicated clearly enough."

I smiled in the direction of his voice without opening my eyes—I was rinsing the shampoo out. "I know, you too, and you too." I laughed at his grunt of annoyance at my nonanswer. "Go make pancakes, Titus. I love you."

CHAPTER SIXTEEN

TITUS, ISABELA, AND I EXITED THE COUNTY COURTHOUSE, Isabela between Titus and me, her hands in ours. Titus and I were legally married before the judge and the court-appointed witness, and I'd begun the process of filing to have my name legally changed to Laurel Bright. We'd decided to wait a few months, in the end, just to finish the process of settling in and getting to know Isabela more.

She was, we discovered, a precocious, adorable, curious, funny little girl with a mischievous streak a country mile wide. She was an early riser, a ravenous eater, and far too insightful for her own good. Or rather, for ours. Every time we turned around, she was up to something else—trying to make her own breakfast and making a godawful mess, or "helping" with the laundry and adding way too much detergent, or bringing a garter snake inside from the backyard and playing with it in her room without telling anyone.

We brought her to therapy once a week. I continued seeing Dr. Hines, but the sessions were reduced from twice a week to twice a month. After Isabela's therapy sessions, we always went to get ice cream together.

Business was good, life was good, being with Titus was better than good. We got to make love every night—and, as the weeks slid by, we discovered the benefits of morning sex over night sex, because keeping track of the whirlwind that was Isabela was a full-time job for both of us and we were usually wiped out by the day's end.

Titus was still doing pop-ups all over the country, but he worked the dates out ahead of time so Isabela and I could attend, and watch him from the side of the stage.

As the weeks slid by faster and faster, I watched Isabela fall in love with Titus every bit as much as I had. She and I were slower to find emotional bonding, but as she learned I wasn't setting out to try to replace her mom, she began to warm up to me, and to accept me.

It was all a slow process, and we didn't rush it.

Thus, it was almost three months after we all moved in together that we made our trip to the courthouse. Isabela was happy to be included, and so we stood together in front of the judge and were married, with Isabela between us, smiling as she looked on from Titus to me to the judge and back.

When it was done and Titus and I were husband and wife, Titus lifted Isabela in his arms—she'd recently begun allowing him to pick her up.

"Hey, Monkey." He'd picked that pet name for her, and she'd run with it, often doing her best monkey impression whenever he said it. "So. Laurel and I are married. You know what that means?"

She shook her head. "Nuh-uh."

"It means Laurel is your stepmother."

She blinked at me for a long moment, which I'd come to learn meant something unexpected was about to come out of her mouth. "Are you gonna make me sleep in the attic with the mices?"

I laughed, and did my best old crone cackle. "Yes, my pretty. To the attic with you, and your little mice too," and I ticked her.

She laughed and crawled around to hang on to Titus's back, out of reach. "No tickling!"

I reached for her, and to my shock, she let me take her and settle her on my belly, holding her in a hug, face to face. "You're *my* little monkey too, Isa-belly." That was *my* nickname for her, and the first time she'd answered to it without correcting me, I'd been overjoyed. I held her gaze, serious, now. "I know I'm not your mom. I'm never going to try to take her place because no one ever can, so just remember that, okay? But I *do* love you. As much as any person can love another person. And I'll just be Laurel to you, okay? But if you ever wanted to call me… any—um. Anything else besides Laurel, you can. Okay?"

Beside me, I heard Titus swallow hard.

Isabela nodded. "Okay." She stayed in my arms, but looked at Titus. "Could I call you Daddy?"

Titus blinked hard, cleared his throat. "Y-yeah, Monkey. You can. I would be honored if you called me Daddy."

"Okay." She patted me on top of my head with a look in her eyes that was far too knowing and aware for her age. "Don't worry, I'll get there with you too." She booped my nose, hard enough that I wrinkled my nose and forehead in surprise. "I love *you* as much as any person can love any person, Laur-la." That was her nickname for me, born out of a slip of the tongue that had stuck.

I was stunned breathless. "You do?"

She smiled. Despite being only six years old, she sometimes seemed wiser than me. "Yup, I do." A thoughtful pause. "I know! I could call you…Mom-la. Like Laur-la, but Mom-la."

"Mom-la," I whispered. I felt a tear drop down my cheek. "I would really like that, Isabela. So, so much."

She frowned at me. Touched the tear, then looked at her wet fingertip. "Why you cryin'? I thought you'd be happy."

"I am. Sometimes adults cry when they're so happy they don't know how else to show it."

"Oh. That's weird. Crying is for sad."

I laughed through tears. "Yeah, I know. Adults are weird."

She looked at us each, then wiggled to get down. "So when do we have the party?"

"Tonight," Titus answered. "Remember when we first moved into the house, how everyone came over? It's gonna be like that, only all we have to do is have fun. There's gonna be an ice cream truck, and tacos, and pizza, and a friend of mine is going to play some cool music, and there's a bouncy castle. The biggest, coolest, most badass bouncy castle Jeremy could find. And trust me, Jeremy can find the coolest stuff."

"Ice cream truck *and* a bouncy castle?" She started to bounce on her tiptoes, as if she could feel the bouncy castle under her feet at that very moment. "Will there be other kids to play with?"

"Jeremy and Bex's kids will all be there," Titus answered.

"Yay! They're so fun. When I had a sleepover at their house, Jeremy made a big fort out of blankets in their living room and we watched Disney movies on their big iPad and we got to sleep in the fort with sleeping bags and everything. Violet wrecked it in the middle of the night, though, and it fell on us and we couldn't see nothing, and Jeremy had to fix it and he said bad words, and Bex got mad at him for saying bad words, but *she* said the same bad words to him." A pause. "Adults are funny." As if that explained the whole thing.

Which, I suppose, it did.

That sleepover had been great for us, too…for

slightly different reasons, though; we'd also taken a turn watching Jeremy and Bex's kids so they could get a night alone, which was something that was rare indeed for them. The next day when they came to pick up the kids, Jeremy had been positively glowing, vibrating with happiness, and I presumed their night had been a success. For us, that many kids had been slightly overwhelming, but with Manny to help, it had gone as smoothly as six kids under the watch of newbie parents could be expected.

"So." Isabela looked from Titus to me. "Now what?"

"Now?" We were at our new family car—a Porsche Panamera, upon the recommendation of Lizzy; Titus was buckling Isabela into her seat, and his nimble fingers made quick work of the five-point harness. "Now, we go to the mall and *buy* you anything you want."

She squealed and kicked her feet. "Shopping! My favorite!"

Titus laughed, pointing at me. "I blame you for that."

I shrugged. "Shopping is my true talent, so I'll take the blame."

"Wait, so *you* guys get married, and *I* get presents?" Isabela asked. "I don't know if that makes any sense, but I *like* it."

"I don't know if it makes any sense either," Titus said, "but I like it too."

When we got to the mall, I quickly discovered that when Titus said *anything,* he really, truly meant anything at all. He ended up having to get Jeremy to swing by the mall with his truck to haul the insane amount of things he'd bought his—*our*—daughter. Dollhouses, doll clothes, doll cars, dolls, clothes for Isabela, more than could be quantified.

On the way home, Isabela was quiet. "Ti—Daddy?"

Titus's face lit up like a neon sign when she corrected herself. "Yeah, Monkey."

"I want to give the stuff I got to someone else."

"What? Why?"

She shrugged, was quiet for a while. "I mean, I want the clothes, and maybe one doll. But…when…when I stayed with Miss Mena, before I came to live with you, after…after Mommy…" She trailed off, unable to say it, or to find the right way to say it.

"Passed away?" Titus suggested.

"Yeah, after that. Miss Mena told me about her job. She said her job was to help kids who didn't have no one to take good care of them. Like me, before I went with you. If I didn't have you and Mom-la, Miss Mena told me I would've had to go stay with other people. And she told me when kids go stay with those other people who aren't their all-the-time parents, I forget the word, that they don't have stuff. Like toys to play with, or nothing. And I got lots of toys to play with already, and I was thinking about how some of those kids don't got anything, and I was thinking maybe we could get Miss Mena to help us find kids to give it to."

"You are a remarkable young lady, Miss Isabela Hernandez," Titus said, sounding choked up. "You truly amaze me. I think that would be a wonderful thing to do."

"I still want to keep the clothes and maybe one of the dollies," she said, sounding hesitant. "But not everything."

"It's absolutely up to you what you keep, honey," Titus said. "We bought all that for you, because we love you. And it's yours do whatever you want with."

"Okay."

Two hours later, we were following Mena down a side street in a not-great part of suburban LA, with Jeremy behind us in the big red truck, the bed of which was full to overflowing toys that Isabela had decided to give away, supplemented with more stuff Jeremy and Bex's kids had decided they didn't need anymore. Not just the bed of the truck, either, but a whole flat-bed trailer of the type used by landscapers—Jeremy had made a few calls and gotten some friends to kick in even more.

Mena immediately had a list of recipients, and we were on our way to the first stop. We pulled up and gathered around the truck and trailer.

"Okay, so this house has two little girls, sisters," Mena said, mainly to Isabela. "They're about your age.

Why don't you pick three things for each girl. Do you know how many that would be?"

Isabela counted to three, and then three more. "Six?"

"Wow, you are *so* smart!" Mena exclaimed. "Good job. This is your plan, so I want you to help me give the toys to them."

Isabela looked equal parts nervous and excited. "What should I say?"

Mena thought a moment. "Tell them…it's extra Christmas."

"I love Christmas!" Isabela said. A frown flitted across her features—probably the realization that the next Christmas would be her first without her mother, but she rallied with admirable swiftness. "Extra Christmas."

Titus lifted her up to the bed of the truck, and she picked out two dolls, two packages of doll clothes, a collection of Little Golden Books, and a big pink Jeep for the dolls.

Titus and I watched as Isabela and Mena carried the items in question up to the front door, and Mena rang the doorbell. A moment passed, and then the door opened, revealing a young Hispanic woman with two small black girls peeking out around her legs, their hair in box braids with colorful beads on the ends. We could hear a word here and there, and then the excited squeals of the girls as they realized what was happening, and that it was really happening.

Isabela came back glowing, chattering. "Daddy,

Mom-la! That's even more fun than getting presents for me. They were so excited!"

Mena watched Isabela chatter excitedly. "Mom-la?" she said to me, in a quiet murmur while Titus crouched and listened to Isabela.

I smiled. "It started when she tried to say my name but it came out 'Laur-la,' and then earlier this morning after Titus and I got married, she asked Titus if she could call him Daddy, and then I think she realized that might've hurt my feelings so she called me Mom-la."

"That's really sweet," Mena said. "She's adjusting remarkably well."

"She really is. She has sad moments, of course. But...I think because Titus immediately was just, like, *so* full of love for her, it made it easier."

Mena nodded. "Best possible outcome for a scenario like that." She nodded at the door of the house, where the foster mother and the two little girls were waving at us. "This? It's amazing. Those little girls have probably never gotten anything like that in their entire lives."

"It was all her idea," I said. "We didn't, like, try to talk her out of it, obviously, but we didn't bring it up— she did, all on her own."

Mena shook her head. "Really amazing."

"She put it all together herself, that there were kids out there like her who had a lot less, and that she suddenly had a lot, and that she could do this for them." I glanced down at Isabela. "I'm a pretty proud Mom-la."

"You should be." Mena sighed, ruffled Isabela's hair. "Well, we have a lot of stops to make before all this stuff is given away. You ready for the next house?"

Isabela nodded, jumping up and down and clapping. "Can we do this all the time?" She looked up at Titus. "You're famous—you probably got a whole lot of money. Couldn't we give stuff away to people all the time? It's so much fun to see them so happy!"

Titus blinked, seeming stunned by the suggestion. "You know, Monkey…you might just have a point, there." He glanced at Jeremy, who watched with a knowing expression on his face. "Jeremy—"

Jeremy held up a hand. "The moment you called me about this, I called a friend who's a lawyer specializing in nonprofit corporations to start drawing up paperwork to set up a 501(c)3. Just need a name and the funding."

"Isabela's Extra Christmas," Titus said. "Pull whatever funding we need." He glanced at Mena. "I don't suppose you have any interest in running a newly founded nonprofit startup, do you?"

Mena bit her lip, grinning. "Wouldn't you know, that's been a lifelong dream of mine?"

I arched an eyebrow. "You're kidding."

She shook her head. "I was a foster kid. I've been trying to work my way up to management so I could someday get a job running a nonprofit, helping kids like me. There's not enough out there designed to help fosters. It's a really hard, thankless job, and they don't get enough support."

Titus held out his hand. "Welcome to Isabela's Extra Christmas. Set it up to make the biggest impact possible on the most amount of people. You'll have more funding than you know what to do with, I promise." He looked at me. "Can you get your crew in on this?"

I was already on the phone. "Way ahead of you, babe." Lizzy answered, then. "Lizzy, hey. Is Braun with you? Good, put me on speaker. Oh, you're with Autumn and Seven, even better! So, we're starting a nonprofit for foster parents and kids. Providing toys, clothes, food, I don't even know—everything you can think of. No, like we just had the idea right now, we're getting it all worked out. But I want to know if you guys are in. Financing, obviously, because we're gonna need funding to get the ball rolling, but just… involvement in general…yeah. Yeah. Good, great, I knew you guys would be in. Okay, cool. I'll put you in contact with our point person, Mena. Yeah, I'm calling Kat next."

I hung up, and grinned. "Well, Lizzy and Braun and Autumn and Seven are in."

Titus laughed. "Between Braun, Seven, and me alone, that's, like, two-and-half billion dollars in financial power behind this."

Mena's eyes bugged out of her head, and she coughed around a shocked laugh. "What, *what*?"

I just laughed. "Two of my best friends are married

to Braun Bennet and Seven St. John. And I'm married to this guy." I jerked a thumb at Titus. "That's a lot of money. And my girls and I are obviously not hurting ourselves. This is gonna be huge, Mena."

She took a deep breath. "Well, this went from zero to sixty in a hurry—toy giveaway inspired a six-year-old, to a fully funded nonprofit." She shook her hands and grinned. "Let's get these toys given away, and we'll tackle the rest as we go. I have cases, still, obviously, so it's gonna take a few months before I can transition to running it full time. Just so we're all on the same page."

I had Kat on the line. "Hey, Kat. You got a minute?"

She paused, and I heard the audio quality shift as she switched it from speaker to headset. "Yeah, what's up, Laur?"

"How would you feel about helping us run a nonprofit we're starting?"

She sighed. "I mean, my schedule is pretty full, you know that. What's it about?"

"Well, we took Isabela shopping to celebrate us getting married this morning, and she decided, after helping us buy out half the mall in clothes and toys, that she wanted to give the toys away to other foster kids."

Her breath caught. "Oh. Um. Yeah. I…yeah."

"That's not the whole story, though," I said. "It sort of just…snowballed, you know? And now, suddenly, we're starting a whole nonprofit corporation, called Isabela's Extra Christmas, and we want you to be part of it. I guess, partly just as one of my best friends, but also I figured because it's something I assumed would be…close to your heart."

"This was all Isabela's idea?"

"It started with giving away toys and Jeremy and Titus sort of…ran with it. But it was her idea to start with, yeah."

"That little girl is…" She swallowed hard. "She's something else."

"Reminds you of someone, doesn't she?"

Kat didn't answer right away. "How can I help?"

"That's up to you, babe. You decide the level of your involvement."

"It's gonna help foster kids?"

"Yeah."

"I…" She sighed, a soft, shuddery sound. "Anything and everything. I'm in, Laur. All the fucking way. If I can help other kids not go through the hell I went through…? I'll do it. I'll do it all."

"I know, honey. That's why I called you." A thought occurred to me. I beckoned to Mena and whispered a request for the address of the next stop, and relayed it to Kat. "Meet us there. You can help us with the toys, to start."

"On the way. I'm close anyway, I was showing a condo downtown."

"Okay." We were in the car, then. "Kat…this is all you. Take this and run with it, okay?"

Kat laughed. "Oh, honey, this is gonna get the full-octane Katja Spears treatment, believe me. I think I've been waiting for this my whole life."

"I know you have, Kat. I'll see you soon." I paused, and then went for it: "Love you, babe."

She inhaled sharply; we'd never said that between us two before. "Love you, too, Laur."

"Was that Auntie Kat?" Isabela asked, after I'd put my phone into my purse. "Is she gonna help us give stuff to people?"

"She sure is," I said. "She was one of those kids who grew up with not-all-the-time parents. Foster parents, they're called."

"I think she needs more hugs. She seems sad, sometimes."

Oh, from the mouths of the young. "Isa-belly, you are exactly right. She needs a lot more hugs. I bet if you gave her all the hugs you can, it would help her be happy more."

A sigh, as if taking on the weight of the world. "Okay, but I'm not sure if I can give her enough hugs. I think you guys might have to help."

I laughed. "Yeah, you're probably right. The problem is, Auntie Kat doesn't always like hugs, especially from adults. She might be more willing to allow herself to be hugged if they came from you." I huffed a sad laugh. "I'm not sure she even understands how badly she just needs a hug, sometimes."

"Can't you just tell her?"

"It's a little more complicated than that, unfortunately."

"Adults are weird."

"We sure are," Titus said. "We make things way more complicated than they need to be a large majority of the time."

❦

Late morning turned to early afternoon, and then finally around four we dropped off the last of the toys. We were supposed to be at home already, getting ready for the party, which was supposed to start at 4:30. We finally trooped inside at 4:15, and nothing was ready.

We hadn't even had time to straighten the house, much less do any other party preparations, but none of that mattered. We collapsed together onto the couch, me in the corner with Titus beside me, and Isabela across both of our laps, her head on Titus's, her feet on me.

Titus squeezed her shoulder. "I'm proud of you, Isabela. You did a really mature and amazing thing today. You inspire me to be a better person, you know that?"

She snuggled closer to his chest. "It was really fun. Watching people get presents and be all excited is almost more fun than getting presents for me."

"Well there is a saying about that you know," Titus said. "'Tis better to give than to receive."

"What's 'tis mean?"

"It is. Kind of like an old contraction we don't really use anymore."

"What's a contraction?"

"Like it's instead of it is, or can't instead of cannot, like that."

"Oh."

"So we just use it's instead of 'tis?"

Titus laughed. "I guess? You're sort of swinging above my pay grade here, babe."

"I don't know what that means, but it sounds not true. You make a lot of money."

Titus laughed even harder. "You're funny, kiddo. I just mean you're asking questions I don't really have solid answers to."

"'Cause you didn't finish school?"

"Right-o."

"Why don't you just finish school now?"

"Because there's no point. There's nothing I want to do with my life that I need a diploma or degrees for. Anything else I need to know, I can teach myself or learn other ways."

"So can I quit school, then?"

"You may not," Titus said. "You still have lots to learn. School is good for you. I shouldn't have quit. I wish, looking back, that I'd had someone make me stay in school. It worked out for me okay, but there were some times that I wished I'd had something to fall back on, you know? Like, I was committed to music, and at a certain point I was locked into it. I had no choice but to make it. You're just a kid, and you have your whole future ahead of you, and by god you're going to get the education I didn't."

"But what if I want to be a rock star like you?"

"I'll support you and help you along the way, honey, but you'll be a rock star with a high school diploma at very least. If you graduate high school and you know without a single doubt that all you want to do with your whole life is to be a touring musician, we can talk about it then. Until then, though, you're going to go to school and get the best grades because you're such a smart young lady."

"I teached myself to read before I was in kindergarten. Mommy didn't believe me, so we went to the library and she picked a book I hadn't read before and I read it to her so she could know I wasn't just saying a book I already knew all the words to."

"Like I said, smarty-pants. And maybe you're gonna be the CEO of a big company. Or the president of the whole country. But you need an education to do that stuff. So you gotta stay in school."

"Can a girl even be president?"

"Sure, of course," Titus answered. "There hasn't been a girl president yet, but there will be, someday. And maybe it'll be you. You can do anything you put your mind to, Isabela. And Mom-la and I will help you get there."

The doorbell rang, then, the first of our friends showing up for a party we weren't in any way ready for.

But as I got up to answer the door, I discovered our friends had brought the party to us. Teddy had managed to get a last-minute catering order put together by some sort of miracle, and Jeremy had the bouncy castle getting put together, and Zoe and Autumn were putting up decorations in the backyard while Braun and Seven hauled in cases of soda and beer and wine…

And just like that, the house was buzzing with friends.

Family, really.

Sabrina was couch surfing, her chunky little knees bouncing as she drooled on herself and chattered, while Violet looked on with the critical stare of an expert.

There was Titus's friend in the backyard too—who turned out to be Elsworth Callahan, lead singer and guitarist of a country-rock crossover band.

The evening was spent dancing and eating, standing around in big circles of conversation and laughter, the big circles breaking off into smaller ones. The younger kids wore themselves out in the pool and on the bouncy castle and were settled asleep into various bedrooms and air mattresses we'd put out for that purpose, until by the time the stars were out only the adults were left awake, except Manny, who'd taken over Titus's PS5 and was shouting at online friends as he killed zombies or something.

We were all around our table, sipping wine and talking.

Lizzy was making eyes at Braun—or rather, they were having an entire nonverbal conversation.

I caught her eyes. "Out with it already, Lizzy. I know you've got something to say."

She cleared her throat. "I dunno. Today is about you and Titus."

I waved a hand. "If we wanted to make the day all about us, we'd have had a more traditional wedding. We're married, and my last name is Bright, now, and we're happy." I sighed, emotion choking me up. "I'm just...I'm glad to have you guys as my...friends isn't a good enough word. Sisters. As my family. And if you have some sort of news to share, I can't think of any better time to share it."

Lizzy blinked rapidly. "Okay, well, um. I guess I can say it, then. Braun and I are expecting another baby. I just found out yesterday. I'm ten weeks."

There was a chorus of squealing and congratulations all around, which quieted as everyone noticed that I was markedly silent.

Kat was restraining a grin. "Laurel?"

I'd had it in my pocket all day. Waiting for the perfect moment. I slid the capped pregnancy test from my back pocket and set it on the table. There, in the middle of the window: PREGNANT.

Stunned silence.

"I, um. I don't know how far along I am since I just took the test this morning, but just going by the math, I'd say ten weeks is about right." I looked to Titus first. "I was going to tell you separately, when we were alone, but we haven't had a single second alone all day, and…"

He shot out of his chair so fast it fell over backward, yanked mine away from the table and lifted me clear off my chair in a single scoop, my legs going around his waist as he spun us in circles, laughing in my ear.

"No, no—it's perfect…absolutely perfect. There's no other way I'd rather find out than like this, with all of our friends." He looked over my shoulder at them around our table, as they watched us with joy on their faces. "With our family."

Lizzy and I hugged—and a very pregnant Autumn joined in.

"Three babies at the same time," I sniffled. "I'm gonna have a baby."

Autumn nosed my cheek. "If you need any advice on being pregnant, just ask," she said. "I'm pretty much an expert by now."

I snorted. "I bet you are."

Lizzy kissed each of my cheeks. "I really hope we give birth at the same time. That would be epic."

"Yeah, except that would leave Teddy, Zoe, and me to run the entire office for two months while you guys are on maternity leave," Kat said.

Teddy waved a hand. "Eh, it'll be fine. We'll handle

it." She jumped up and joined the group hug. "I can't believe two you are pregnant at the exact same time." She sounded choked up too. "I'm so happy for you, Laurel." She squeezed Lizzy's shoulder. "And you. Mama times two!"

All of a sudden, there were nine people all gathered in a giant group hug, clustered around the core of Autumn, Lizzy, and me. It was suffocating, but delirious.

When the group hug finally disbanded, I found myself sitting on Titus's lap.

I met his dark gaze. "You're not mad I didn't tell you separately, first?"

"Mad? Hell no. I'm happy. That's news that should be shared."

"And you're happy that I'm pregnant?"

He pressed me to his chest. "Beyond happy. I can't think of anything that would make me happier."

"We have to tell Isabela tomorrow," I said.

"Yeah." He caressed my hair. "You're gonna be such an amazing mommy." A pause. "Take that back—you already are."

"I never thought I could be, or would be." I met Teddy's eyes. "I guess I just needed a little nudge."

Teddy smiled at me, sighing deeply. But I noticed her eyes went to Zoe, who was watching everything with a reserved, neutral expression. Autumn noticed it, too.

The three of us exchanged glances.

If there was going to be another version of The Ad, we knew who the next victim would be.

Victim—ha. The next lucky recipient of the incredible fortune Autumn, Lizzy, and I had known. How else could you look at it, but as fortune? As the greatest, most improbable kind of luck? I mean, how many times can the same trick work?

Three more times, I hoped.

I wanted to see the rest of my friends find the kind of delirious happiness I knew, to be overflowing with joy, with love, with everything I never thought I wanted, much less could ever really have.

Yet, there I was—on the lap of the man I loved, with a baby growing in my womb, and a lovely, sweet, smart little girl upstairs who called me Mom-la.

What else could I want?

What else could anyone ever want?

THE END

ALSO BY
JASINDA WILDER

Visit me at my website: **www.jasindawilder.com**
Email me: **jasindawilder@gmail.com**

If you enjoyed this book, you can help others enjoy it as well by recommending it to friends and family, or by mentioning it in reading and discussion groups and online forums. You can also review it on the site from which you purchased it. But, whether you recommend it to anyone else or not, thank you *so much* for taking the time to read my book! Your support means the world to me!

My other titles:

Preacher's Son:
Unbound
Unleashed
Unbroken

Delilah's Diary:
A Sexy Journey
La Vita Sexy
A Sexy Surrender

Big Girls Do It:
Boxed Set
Married
On Christmas
Pregnant

Rock Stars Do It:
Harder
Dirty
Forever

From the world of *Big Girls* and *Rock Stars*:
Big Love Abroad

Biker Billionaire:
Wild Ride

The Falling Series:
Falling Into You
Falling Into Us
Falling Under
Falling Away
Falling For Colton

The Ever Trilogy:
Forever & Always
After Forever
Saving Forever

The world of *Wounded:*
Wounded
Captured

The world of *Stripped:*
Stripped
Trashed

The world of *Alpha:*
Alpha
Beta
Omega
Harris: Alpha One Security Book 1
Thresh: Alpha One Security Book 2
Duke Alpha One Security Book 3
Puck: Alpha One Security Book 4
Lear: Alpha One Security Book 5
Anselm: Alpha One Security Book 6

The Houri Legends:
Jack and Djinn
Djinn and Tonic

The Madame X Series:
Madame X
Exposed
Exiled

Dad Bod Contracting:
Hammered
Drilled
Nailed
Screwed

Fifty States of Love:
Pregnant in Pennsylvania
Cowboy in Colorado
Married in Michigan

Goode Girls
For a Goode Time Call…
Not So Goode
Goode to Be Bad
A Real Good Time
Goode Vibrations

Billionaire Baby Club
Lizzie Goes Brains Over Braun
Autumn Rolls a Seven

Standalone titles:
Yours
The Cabin

Non-Fiction titles:
You Can Do It
You Can Do It: Strength
You Can Do It: Fasting

Jack Wilder Titles:
The Missionary

JJ Wilder Titles:
Ark

To be informed of new releases, special offers, and other Jasinda news, sign up for Jasinda's email newsletter.